"I'm not asking ... the mother of my ..."

Hank clamped his mouth shut. "I'm sorry."

"Is that it? A mother for your children?" Katherine had to raise her voice to keep it steady. "Is that what you're after?"

"Katie, don't be ..."

"Don't patronize me, Hank! And don't push me into a corner. I won't be pushed." She whirled to face him. "I won't get lured into something just because you want a replacement mother for your daughters. I'm not applying for the job. Is that clear?"

His face froze in stunned fury. But the biting words that cut through the room next didn't come from Hank.

"Clear enough for me. How about you, Dad? Does that spell it out for you?"

ABOUT THE AUTHOR

Some time ago, Peg Sutherland learned that a friend was infertile and that the experiences she underwent were, unfortunately, fairly typical. "It often destroys marriages and self-confidence," says Peg, "and I wanted to write a book about women in this predicament."

Peg has an innate understanding about another aspect of her heroine, too. "I'm about to become a stepmother," she says, "and that's not always an easy thing to do, especially considering the bad press given to the stereotype!"

Books by Peg Sutherland

HARLEQUIN SUPERROMANCE
398–BEHIND EVERY CLOUD
428–ALONG FOR THE RIDE

Don't miss any of our special offers. Write to us at the following address for information on our newest releases.

Harlequin Reader Service
P.O. Box 1397, Buffalo, NY 14240
Canadian address: P.O. Box 603,
Fort Erie, Ont. L2A 5X3

Abracadabra

PEG SUTHERLAND

Harlequin Books

TORONTO • NEW YORK • LONDON
AMSTERDAM • PARIS • SYDNEY • HAMBURG
STOCKHOLM • ATHENS • TOKYO • MILAN

Published October 1991

ISBN 0-373-70473-9

ABRACADABRA

For CJL,
who helped me understand
what it truly means to learn
you will be childless,
but not by choice.

PROLOGUE

April 21, 1985

SEEING THE PITY in her best friend's eyes was what finally made something snap inside Katherine Barnett.

She had been free for months. Free of the icy sweat that broke out on her forehead and palms whenever she was around her brothers' children. The erratic heartbeat whenever someone mentioned a baby. The almost uncontrollable urge to run rather than walk down a grocery store aisle of disposable diapers or bottle formula.

Anxiety attacks, her doctor had called them.

Just plain crazy, Jerry had said when he'd walked out for good after that episode on Christmas morning at her folks' ranch.

Katherine didn't blame Jerry, not exactly. He'd been through a lot, too. And even though his leaving hurt—almost as much as everything else that had led up to the end of their marriage—it had numbed her to the extent that all her other emotions receded.

Until the day she bought the gift for Sita.

Forcing herself to enter the baby department at the Houston store had taken all the courage Katherine possessed. Five times she had ridden the escalator up and down, each time unable to force her feet in the right direction.

I can't, protested the part of her that remembered only too clearly the doctor's words. *I can't go look at those things. I can't buy baby things for someone else, as if it doesn't matter.*

You have to, countered the part of her that remained loyal to old friends, the part of her that wanted to conquer the disappointment in her heart. The part of her that wanted to prove something to Jerry. *You have to get on with your life.*

Getting on with her life had hurt beyond her wildest imagination. Walking past displays of bassinets and tiny, doll-sized clothes and crib mobiles that played soft, tinkling melodies had been an exercise in masochism. The part of her that would never be filled had hurt with its emptiness.

"If this is a gift, you can have it wrapped at customer service," the silver-haired salesclerk had told her with a cheerful smile. "No charge."

Even the salesclerk had seen that Katherine couldn't possibly be buying the gift for herself, for her own baby. Even in a day when miracles abounded, when fertility drugs could give triplets to barren women and someone like Sita could know months ahead of time that the tiny life growing inside her was to be a girl—even in a day of such miracles, there were no miracles for Katherine Barnett. That required a magic beyond the powers of modern medicine.

After stashing away her credit card with shaking hands, Katherine had escaped to the women's lounge on the third floor of the store. She had huddled in a stall, crying silently, shoulders heaving, using up the rest of the roll of paper to dry her tears. Then, exhausted but once again enshrouded by the numbness that had become her best protection, she had taken the gift to customer service for wrapping.

Until now, though, the baby shower had been, well, not a snap, exactly, but better than she had hoped. Maybe she really had immunized herself against the hurt.

The first pangs of emptiness floated in on a cloud of pink. Pink paper, dotted with teddy bears and rattles and bouquets of balloons. Pink booties nestled in crinkling pink tissue. Downy pink blankets and cuddly pink sleepers.

She tried to harden herself against it. Things felt a little odd, as if she were hiding in someone else's skin. The walls of the small, square room—as familiar as Katherine's own apartment but twice as welcoming and homey—closed in on her ever so slightly. The friendly warmth became a trifle suffocating, the family coziness almost threatening. The voices were louder, too loud; the smiles too big. The faces of women she had known for years seemed surrealistically distorted.

Beads of cold perspiration dotted Katherine's overheated face. Her eyes skimmed the surface of the merrymaking, looking for somewhere safe to focus. They landed on Sita. Her mouth turned metallic, dry, at Sita's undisguised happiness. With a sadness born of futility, Katherine suddenly knew that life would be easier if she never again set eyes on Luisita Melindez.

No! her heart protested as she stared down at the hand that had started to shake. How could she possibly feel that way about the woman who had been her best friend since high school? The woman who had shared her wistful, homesick secrets their first year of college? The woman with whom she had shared her first cramped apartment, with its red wallpaper and mildewed refrigerator? The woman who had stood by her side, cheeks wet with tears, when Katherine had whispered "I do"?

Katherine's heart raced as she fought against the irrational urge to escape from Sita. Because now Sita was embarking on something they could never share. Sita was pregnant.

It's unlikely you and your husband will ever have a child.

The doctor's words crept into the empty corners of Katherine's heart, as hushed and solemn and unintentionally taunting as they had been eighteen months earlier. She tried to push the memory away. She had to get through this evening.

She smiled weakly at Sita as her friend reached for the big box with the multicolored bow, the one Katherine had brought. Her sparkling black eyes shifted in Katherine's direction and she smiled her understanding.

The shaking had traveled up Katherine's right arm and down the left, had moved to her other hand. The runaway pace of her heart twisted her insides—the useless insides that would never allow her to be a mother. *Smile,* she ordered herself. *For Sita. Do it for Sita.*

She smiled back reassuringly, and Sita turned her attention to the package, tearing into it at the urging of the sixteen other women in the room.

A round of "ooohs" signaled that the wrapping paper had been duly demolished and the box opened. Katherine didn't look as Sita pulled out the bright quilted rainbow for the wall in the new baby's room.

"A rainbow!" Sita's voice was thick with emotion. Rainbows had become the hallmark of their friendship, a reminder of the day after a rainstorm they had argued over a dark-eyed member of the university tennis team and had ended up swearing that no man would ever come between them again. Sitting under a tree on campus, fanning notebooks to move the thick summer air, they had giggled and made lists of all the reasons neither of them ever wanted to date the tennis player again.

And they had spotted the rainbow. They had taken it as a sign that nothing would ever again come between them. Katherine had meant the quilted rainbow as her promise that the new life growing inside Sita wouldn't come between them, either. But now, in the midst of her pain, Katherine didn't know if she could keep that promise.

"Katie, that's really special," Sita said huskily. She ran her fingers lovingly over the pastel satin.

Katherine looked across the room into her friend's eyes, praying she could overcome the crazy, panicky urge to bolt. She wouldn't let this rule her. She wouldn't let this ruin her friendship with Sita the way it had ruined her marriage.

Sita's dark eyes were filled with love. And something else.

Pity.

It was a look Katherine recognized. She'd seen it first in the eyes of the balding doctor who had encouraged her through years of testing and waiting and probing and prodding and praying. Then, in her mother's eyes, and her brothers' and their wives'.

But it hurt more coming from Sita. It hurt as sharply as the contempt in Jerry's eyes when he had finally taken off his wedding ring and walked out the front door.

"I'll find myself a real woman next time," he had said, hatefully, bitterly. "Sterility is one thing, but now you've let it make you crazy, too."

It hadn't helped to reassure herself that Jerry had suffered as much as she had during their three-year struggle to become parents. It hadn't helped to remind herself that her panic attacks had only escalated every time Jerry reacted with anger instead of understanding. Just as it didn't help now to reassure herself that Sita didn't mean to feel sorry for her. She wondered how many other women in the room knew, how many pitied her, too.

"I'm glad you like it," she answered, forcing the words past a throat that had closed up, blocking almost all the air to her lungs. If she didn't get out of here soon, she would suffocate. Fighting down the compulsion to jump up, to run away, Katherine smiled a frozen smile.

As soon as the gifts were open and the group of chattering women moved toward the refreshments, Katherine slipped down the narrow hall of Sita's rented duplex to get her purse. She avoided looking at herself in the mirror, knowing from experience that she would seem drawn and pale, that her blouse would be clinging damply to her clammy skin.

When she reached the front door, she could see Sita easing in her direction, trying to move away from the friends who reached out to detain her.

Her knees weak, Katherine hurried out the front door and vowed she would never set herself up for pity again. She didn't need children, she told herself as she jerked the car away from the curb. If she didn't need them, how could she be incomplete without them? And if she weren't half a woman, who could pity her?

The trembling stopped. The perspiration began to dry. Her heart slowed to a normal rate.

Only the emptiness remained.

CHAPTER ONE

October, 1991

CIGAR SMOKE SWIRLED, sweet and heavy.

Poker chips clicked on naked wood.

Card slapped against card.

A fourteen-year-old girl with a silver dragon in one ear and four neon beads in the other slouched in the doorway, glaring.

Friday-night poker and motherless children just don't mix. Hank Weisbecker knew that. He had learned it the hard way, the first Friday night of every month for the past two years. *So I'm a glutton for punishment,* Hank told himself as the fifth card skidded across the table, coming to a silent halt just under his knotty, calloused fingers.

Heather glared at him from the doorway leading from the cramped living room into the cramped dining room, jammed now with four oversized male bodies. The dragon quivered malevolently in her ear. She propped her hands on her hips—Hank had decided the gesture must be passed down through the female genes—and opened her mouth to speak.

Jessie Ruiz, cigar dangling from the corner of his mouth, beat her to it. "Pot's light. Who didn't ante?"

Rolling her eyes in exaggerated frustration, Heather whirled and stalked toward her bedroom.

Tossing in the chip that entitled him to play the round, Hank lifted his cards and fanned them for a look. Two ladies. He could draw to the queens and maybe end the streak of lousy hands that had come his way tonight. If the hand didn't pan out, he would fold and try to reason with Heather—a possibility that seemed as unlikely as drawing an inside straight. Fourteen-year-olds, he was learning, don't reason.

Roy Getzfred, his pale eyes puppy dog bright with excitement, opened with a bid by throwing two chips into the center of the table.

"How many cards?" Jessie's swarthy face was still and expressionless as he looked around the table to see who wanted replacement cards for this round of five-card stud.

"Gimme three," Hank said, wondering if Stu Mahaffey's cards were as good as his suddenly fidgety hands indicated. When Stu had good cards, it was all he could do to keep his hands still. Stu either tapped on the table with the fingernails he chewed back to the nub, or tugged on the sleeve of whichever gray T-shirt he happened to be wearing at the moment or tore the cellophane off another cigar, even if he already had one burning out in the ashtray at his elbow.

That's what Stu did now. More cigars were offered on the altar of Friday night poker with the guys than were ever smoked. They simply went out the next morning with the rest of the trash—crushed beer cans, corn chip crumbs, plastic tubs scraped clean of onion dip.

A small hand on his arm distracted Hank as the new cards were dealt. "Yo, Daddy?"

One at a time, Hank stuffed the three new cards into his hand. "What, Scooter?" A ten. No help. Then a queen. The pile of multicolored chips in the center of the table suddenly looked friendlier. Like family.

"Daaaddy?" The high voice demanded Hank's attention.

He looked down into the round, freckled face at his elbow, edgily flicking the corner of the card he hadn't yet seen. "What is it, sweetheart?"

"Can I stay up and watch MTV?" The brown eyes were hopeful, the smile endearing in spite of—or maybe because of—the missing front teeth.

"Tammi, I told you it's bedtime." Hank noticed Stu swiftly downing a fistful of salted peanuts. No doubt about it, Stu had a hand worth betting on. Or one worth bluffing on. "You don't need to be watching that junk anyway."

Hank peeked under the corner of the third new card, still facedown on the table in front of him. The queen of hearts. Oh, did she look sweet. The pot definitely had his name written all over it. The night was looking up.

Tammi slithered under his arm and wiggled into his lap, almost upsetting the can at his elbow in the process. "But, Daddy, tonight's..."

"Shh," he said softly, listening as Stu upped the ante. Hank struggled not to grin. Nothing Stu had could possibly top four ladies. "Wait just a minute, Scooter."

Tammi squirmed in his lap, her tiny elbow jabbing him in the ribs and her dark brown ponytail swishing in his face. "But, Daddy, tonight's the night they show the new video by Dirty Rotten Kidz for the first time. Can I stay up and watch it? It's s'posed to be way cool. Please, Daddy?" Now the voice wheedled.

Hank matched Stu's bid and upped it. Just a little. Not enough to alarm him. Just enough to send Stu back to his stack of chips one more time. Just enough to sweeten the pot a little more before Hank raked it in.

"Dad?" Heather reappeared in the doorway. Hank didn't have to look up to catch the challenging edge in her tone. "I'm leaving now."

Hank jerked to attention. "What do you mean, you're leaving now?"

Heather sighed deeply, impatiently. "Oh, right. May I go out?" The words were heavy with insolence.

"Not looking like that," he snapped, seriously doubting if any of the other guys around the table had daughters who looked like an advertisement for trouble. *Wanted: Belligerent fourteen-year-old with five earrings and studded leather watch.*

Stu, he noticed, had turned his attention away from his bid and toward the teenager, who had slapped her hands against her thighs in loud disgust. Hank tapped his cards on the table to recapture Stu's attention. "You're up, Stu."

"I am not going out looking like some kind of nerd, if that's what you want me to do." Heather stood in the door, waiting for her challenge to take effect. "I'll lock myself in my room and never come out before I'll dress the way *you* want me to."

"Fine." *Why does Heather always pick times like this to raise a stink?* he wondered.

"Daddy?" Tammi tossed her ponytail in his face again. "Are you using the magic cards?"

"No, Scooter." He watched impatiently, wondering how long Stu would ponder the bet in front of him.

Tammi pointed at the cards in his hand. "Then how come they gave you all the queens? You've got all four. Shouldn't you share? You always tell me to...."

Hank tossed his close-to-perfect hand onto the table in disgust. The other three men hooted loudly. Stu folded his cards.

"Don't believe I'll see your bid, old pal," Stu said with a wicked grin. "Think I'll save my money for the next hand."

Stifling a curse, Hank raked in the pot that wasn't nearly as large as it could have been. Kids and poker didn't mix.

Kids don't mix with much of anything, he thought as he pushed back from the table and deposited Tammi's featherweight frame on the floor. *Kids don't mix with dating or football on TV. And they don't,* he thought, *mix with Hank Weisbecker, either.* Not anymore. As much as he wanted to, Hank just wasn't cut out to fly solo when it came to parenting.

"I'm out this hand," he said, steering Tammi toward the door where Heather still stood, hands on hips and ready for battle. They stood face to face for a moment, and Hank was suddenly struck by how much Heather had grown. Already taller than her mother had been, she reached just past his shoulders.

The realization was like a blow to his midsection. Doris would have been proud. After all the times she'd railed about the injustice of being barely over the five-foot mark, she would have grinned that broad, elfish smile as their daughter slowly inched upward—like her father. *Too much like her father in too many ways,* Hank thought.

"In the living room," he ordered gruffly. If Doris were around, he probably wouldn't be facing a sullen teenager who seemed determined to grab trouble by the throat and a timid eight-year-old with an addiction to racy rock videos.

Heather crossed her arms and stared into space. Tammi, unaware that her curiosity had spoiled one of the best poker hands her dad had ever been dealt, curled up in the corner of the couch with the tiny Pekinese who had taken up residence in the Weisbecker condo a couple of weeks earlier.

Hank opened his mouth to deal with the two females in his life and realized he had no more notion what to say now than he'd had the last time he had tried to talk to a woman he'd met at the neighborhood church. He'd wanted to wine and dine her, but he'd drawn a blank as he sat across from her at a candlelit table in a fancy uptown restaurant, with a bottle of wine he hadn't liked and couldn't afford sitting between them. And no inspiration guided him now, either. Just a few months ago, before Heather's fourteenth birthday, he'd thought he had things under control. No more.

Heather jumped into the silence. "It's Friday night. I don't see why I can't go to the mall. Some kids are going to a movie. Meagan's mom is picking me up in five minutes. I won't be home late."

Why does she always sound like she's the one giving the orders? Hank wondered, feeling his control slip away. Half the time these days, he was an unreasonable bear with her. The next moment he was an inexcusable softie. It seemed he couldn't decide how to act. Tonight, he was determined to hang tough.

"How late?"

Heather glanced toward the dining room, where the noise of a disputed poker hand had escalated into good-natured ribbing. "After *they're* gone."

"You be back by eleven." His toughness fizzled away as he fought the guilt that nagged him every time it was his turn to host the game. The foursome was made up of guys he worked with, other family men. Their language was strictly PG-13 and they never drank enough beer to get rowdy. They were just hardworking men who enjoyed a little relaxation at the end of the work week.

The problem was, when the group came to Hank's, it wasn't always relaxing. Stu's spacious split-level afforded plenty of room for kids' toys and a deck of cards to coexist peacefully. When they met at Jessie's, his teenaged sons barely made an appearance before buzzing out for dates and his wife was glad to escape for a night out with her friends. Roy was a bachelor, with nobody at home to be inconvenienced. But here, in the three-bedroom condo that barely seemed big enough for everyone to breathe without invading someone else's space, poker with the guys became the script for a bad TV sitcom.

"The movie's not over till eleven-twenty," Heather stated with all the contempt she could muster for a father she clearly considered out of touch with reality. Then she held out a hand. "I need money."

Debating the wisdom of starting another battle, Hank fished a wrinkled bill out of his jeans. He watched as Heather stuffed the money into her fashionably ripped jeans and turned toward the door. Did all fathers experience such helplessness, he wondered. Or was that the private hell of single fathers of teenage girls?

Before the door closed behind her, Heather turned back and looked him squarely in the eye. "And I'm not cleaning up after *them* in the morning, either."

The door slammed behind her, leaving him to swallow the unpleasantness of her final, belligerent words. Raking a hand through the sun-bleached wisps of hair slipping over his forehead, Hank turned back to the couch for round two with Tammi. But the youngster was asleep, the fluffy dog clutched to her chest, her lips

barely parted. Hank wondered when they stopped
sleeping that way, looking so defenseless, so vulnerable.

Right after they punch five holes in their ears, he decided as he picked up the sleeping child and headed
down the narrow hall toward her bedroom, the Pekinese scampering at his heels. It was hard to imagine
Tammi turning into another Heather in a few short
years.

But then, it would have been hard to imagine Heather
sprouting dragons and neon from her ears five years
ago. Five years ago, when they had moved into this
condo in the heart of one of Omaha's popular old
neighborhoods, Hank and Doris had felt the world was
just beginning to open up for them. A few years in the
condo, Doris had said, while his career took off, and
they would be able to buy the house of their dreams.
Invest in college funds. Take two-week vacations. Buy
a station wagon and fence in the yard.

They'd had it all mapped out, Hank thought as he
tucked Tammi into her narrow bed. But their plans had
been missing one important detail—Doris wouldn't be
around to enjoy it. Doris wouldn't make it home from
work one night when her car skidded off a bridge in an
ice storm.

And without Doris, none of it was coming true. Here
they sat, two years after her death, trying to scrape by
on Hank's income. Trying to make a life with only
Hank to run the show. Now, missing out on the bigger
house, the college funds, the station wagon seemed like
small potatoes. How important could they be when
Hank couldn't even figure out how to raise the girls?

Doris had always known. She'd always known how
to smile and make everything all right. She'd always

known how to make him feel like he was the one who'd worked out the problems. She'd always known how to handle the girls.

Hank never seemed to know.

Heaving a weary sigh, Hank leaned forward to kiss Tammi's cheek. Before he turned to leave, the dog—what had its tag said? Baxter?—whimpered softly from the floor. Hank answered the pleading look by lifting the dog onto the bed, where it curled up in the crook of Tammi's knee.

A familiar ache—an ache of loneliness and helplessness and love tinged with fear—nosed its way into Hank's heart as he clicked on the Roger Rabbit nightlight and backed out of the room.

Thank goodness for the poker game. Too many nights, when that ache started to spill its poison into his soul, Hank had no distraction. Thank goodness for a cold can of beer and a deck of cards and the haze of cigar smoke.

"Hey, Daddy, we've taken a vote and decided you should bring back your poker consultant." Stu leaned back from the table as far as possible to make room for his barrel chest, which was gradually shifting to become a middle-aged belly. Like the others in the room, he worked outside, at physical labor. But for Stu, the physical labor wasn't staying the effects of middle age. "We think she's right. If you get the good cards, you should share."

The others laughed and Hank couldn't resist a chuckle at his own expense. They were good guys. His best friends, in spite of the fact that he was crew chief and they all answered to him when they traveled Omaha's streets, maintaining the trees and greenery in the city's parks and along its roadways. Over pruners and lifts and bundles of pine needles, he was the boss. Over a poker table, he was just one of the guys.

"Little Miss Bigmouth is asleep for the night, wise guy," Hank retorted with a grin. "So you're on your own. And I warn you, I'm out for blood."

"Your problem is you're not getting enough recreation, if you know what I mean," Stu said. The men around the table laughed, knowing Stu's theory that there was nothing steady sex wouldn't cure.

"Just deal the cards," Hank ordered.

"Maybe he's right," Jessie said, studying the cards being dealt in his direction. "A little R and R never hurt anybody."

Roy, whose favorite R and R was pumping iron to keep his neck the same girth as most people's thighs, suddenly grew more interested in the conversation than in the cards in his fist. "Know what I read? Or maybe I saw it on 'Oprah.' I can't remember. It was one day last week, and I remember it was the day after we cleaned up Hummel Park because—"

"The point, Roy," Stu prompted. "Get to the point."

"Right. Know where they say is the best place to meet women?" Roy paused for dramatic effect, then continued in disappointment when he saw his buddies were more interested in the size of the pot riding on the current hand than in his news flash from the singles scene. "In the grocery store. Can you beat that? In the grocery store."

"Makes sense," Stu mumbled, then upped the ante. "Who shops for groceries? Women. My wife does all the shopping."

"So who'd wanna meet your wife anyway?" Jessie said quietly. When the second-generation Mexican-American took a jibe at one of his co-workers, it was usually at Stu, his best pal. "Even Hank's not that desperate. Say, Hank, how about I fix you up with Elaine's niece, Vickie? She'll be coming to stay with us in a couple of weeks."

Roy crowed as his two pair topped the cards in Stu's hand. "Elaine's niece? That'd be cradle robbing, wouldn't it?"

"Naw," Jessie said. "She's Elaine's older sister's girl. Real smart. Good-looking, too. Tall and blond. A cheerleader at the university her last two years."

The cards he was shuffling stilled in Roy's hands. "I'm buying if Hank's not in the market."

Jessie ignored his baby-faced co-worker. "How about it, Hank? I'm not kidding. She's a looker."

Hank feigned intense interest in the cards in his hand. "Maybe. Sometime."

"That settles it," Roy interjected. "She's mine."

"Back off, Roy Boy. You don't think I'd let you loose on my niece, do you?"

Roy looked wounded and launched into a diatribe on his gentlemanly ways with women. Hank didn't catch the lively exchange between the two men as he recalled his last disastrous date. He'd actually liked the woman. And she had liked him. When she'd invited him in for a drink after the movie, Hank had been certain he was on the right track with a woman for the first time in two years. Nancy. Petite and soft-spoken. A lot like Doris. Until she'd lured him to the couch with a couple of stiff martinis and jumped him.

All Hank had been able to think of was all the noise about safe sex. Nancy had seemed distinctly unconcerned. And Hank had found himself suddenly and disconcertingly unable to take advantage of the sexual revolution. He'd heard it happened to all men sooner or later, but that hadn't eased the humiliation. Hank hadn't been able to face her again. He squirmed in his chair just thinking about it.

"So whaddya say, Hank? Lemme give you her number and you can get in touch. I'll tell her to expect to hear from you. How about it?"

Absently, Hank folded his hand while Jessie raked in the pot. "Maybe. I'll let you know, Jess."

KATHERINE BARNETT dashed down the stairs two at a time, sneakers tied together and draped around her neck. Revived and relaxed from the yoga routine that kept her thirty-one-year-old muscles taut, she paused to pinch a brown frond off the spider plant hanging in front of the round window on the landing.

"You did good," she assured the green-and-white plant, bushy with new shoots in spite of the rigors of the recent move from one state to another.

All the plants had survived the move in fair shape, she mused as she finished her sprint down the stairs. Even Fibber and Molly had had a fairly uneventful trip, although nothing was ever completely uneventful where the two cranky parakeets were concerned.

The only casualty of the move had been Baxter, who had scampered out the back door during the hubbub of hauling in boxes. Katherine's throat constricted once again as she thought of the tiny, pug-nosed animal who had been her companion for six years.

Fibber chirped querulously as Katherine passed the living room on her way to the kitchen. She took two steps toward the cage and Molly fluttered her wings in vigorous demand.

"You want out?" Katherine queried the green birds. "To explore?" She was reaching to slide open the cage and let them have the run of the house for a while when the knocker on the back door sounded.

"Oops," she said, preparing herself for the screech of protest when she failed to let them out. "We've got company. Maybe later."

Katherine took a quick look around the spacious rooms of the old house, and her chest swelled with pride. Hers. All hers. From the cut glass mirrors over the carved mantels in living room and dining room to the steamy little gabled attic that she would one day finish as her reading room, it was hers.

Right now, it still had that incomplete look that said all the knickknacks hadn't been unpacked and most of the curtains were still folded in their wrappers. But Katherine Barnett was a homeowner.

The door knocker sounded a second time, and Katherine shot through the dining room and into the airy kitchen. Penny Gray's thin, impatient face peered through the circle of glass in the door.

"You cannot go to the grocery store dressed like that!" Penny declared as she dashed into the room.

"And why not?" Katherine looked down at her faded jeans and roomy sweatshirt.

Penny sprawled in a ladder-back chair, her long, slim legs clad in funky animal-print cotton slacks. The matching top was cinched at her tiny waist with a wide metallic belt.

"Don't you want to look…" Penny waved her hand, as if she hoped to pluck the right word out of thin air. "Sexy? Devastating? Or at least cute?"

Katherine's nose wrinkled. "Look at this body. Devastating? Face it, friend, I'm just not the type. And I gave up trying years ago. Besides, it's just the grocery store."

"No, it's not. The Corner Market is . . . well, it's just the best place in the neighborhood to meet people," Penny said.

"The grocery store?"

"The Corner Market is not just a grocery store. Trust me. Have I ever steered you wrong?"

Katherine grinned. Granted, she had known her new next-door neighbor less than three months, but Penny had a proven track record for good advice. They had met when Katherine was assigned to photograph the revitalized neighborhood for an issue of *Midwesterner* magazine. As a real estate agent who worked out of her home in the neighborhood, Penny had seemed like the perfect contact to help locate model homes to shoot.

Penny had indeed been a big help with the assignment, and during the week they worked together Katherine fell in love with the neighborhood. When she returned to Iowa, she'd asked Penny to keep her eyes open for a house. They'd both been pleasantly surprised when the house next door to Penny's came on the market. And during the two-month process of making offers and applying for loans and agonizing over Federal Housing Administration appraisals, Katherine and Penny had become pretty good friends.

But even the prospect of becoming better friends with her new neighbor didn't convince Katherine she should worry about dressing up for the grocery store.

"My new neighbors will just have to take me the way they find me." Katherine untied the tennis shoes draped around her neck and dropped them to the floor. "I grew up in the kind of town where you had to get yourself gussied up to go to the drug store. I don't have to impress anybody anymore. At least, not with my looks."

"Gussied up?" Penny rolled her eyes. "I knew I should never have sold this place to a Texan."

Katherine felt a twinge of guilt. Texas. She should phone her folks. She'd been here almost two weeks and she still hadn't called. She shook off the guilt and smiled as she stepped into her shoes and bent to tie them. "So, shall we go? Or will you be too mortified to be seen with me?"

Penny unfolded her long, thin body and waved her new neighbor toward the door. "Nah. I'll just tell them you were raised in a barn. In Texas. They'll understand."

In less than ten minutes, they had walked through the neighborhood and were pushing their carts through the store. Katherine had to admit, they didn't have grocery stores like this in Sylvester. Or even in Des Moines, where she had spent the past five years. Muted classical music lilted gently through the store, which was softly lit and decorated with plants and baskets hanging from the ceiling. Freshly brewed coffee was dispensed for free in one corner, and in another, samples of some of the more exotic offerings of the Corner Market were available for munching.

Within five minutes of entering the store, Penny had spotted at least half a dozen of their neighbors and had waved them over to introduce them to Katherine. By the time they meandered from the coffeepot back toward the fresh vegetables, Katherine's head was swimming with the names and faces of new people. All interesting. All friendly. All, like her, unattached and unencumbered.

The more Katherine saw of her new neighborhood, the more enchanted she grew with it.

"I'm going to head over to the deli while you graze for veggies," Penny said, wrinkling her nose at the bins of fresh produce. "I don't go for anything that healthy."

"You don't have to," Katherine said, scrutinizing Penny's slender frame. "You look like you never gain an ounce. Me, I have three wardrobes—small, medium and time-to-hit-the-panic-button."

"Justice at last." Penny veered off with her cart. "Makes up for being nicknamed Beanpole in high school."

As she filled a bag with white grapes, Katherine had the disconcerting feeling that she was being watched. She glanced around, only to see a man to her right quickly look away. She smiled to herself and went back to choosing grapes. When she heard someone clearing his throat near her elbow, she wasn't surprised to look up into a pair of hesitant eyes.

"How...um, that is...what do you do with this stuff?"

From his outstretched hand, which held a container of tofu, Katherine looked up into his eyes—eyes with pale blue irises rimmed in darker blue, like summer sky ringed with midnight. Fine, sun-splashed hair drooped softly over a high, broad forehead. A friendly, vulnerable face with a dimpled chin and a little-boy smile was made more endearing by the crinkles framing the blue-on-blue eyes.

His body was slim, but almost instantly she noticed the well-defined shoulders that lead to forearms corded with muscle and dusted with thick, blond hair. He worked hard. The strength in his arms showed that. And outdoors—the deep tan on his arms and face

showed that. Tan and blond, like an over-thirty beach
bum dropped into the middle of downtown Omaha.

And he wasn't very smooth at picking up women. His
limp line showed that.

Katherine liked all of it. The hardworking
outdoorsiness and the not-so-smooth pickup. She
smiled, hoping she looked friendly but not overtly inviting.

"I don't do anything with it," she admitted.

"Oh. Well..."

It clearly wasn't an answer he had expected. He'd
been hoping a half hour with Julia Child would lead up
to an evening with Dr. Ruth, she supposed. And now he
didn't know what to say. His eyes were confused, even
a little shy, perhaps. If this was part of his routine,
Katherine thought as she hid a smile, it was certainly
effective. Maybe he was smoother than she thought.

"It's a meat substitute." She decided to take him at
face value. What if he really was a shy lumberjack? A
timid construction worker? The strong, silent type? The
muscles in his arms worked as he twisted the package in
his hand to look at it uncertainly. "Chinese cooks do all
kinds of things with it. But I'm not a big fan."

He nodded, then looked up with a mischievous glint
in his eyes. "Then I guess you wouldn't come to dinner
if it's on the menu."

She shook her head. Shy perhaps, but not completely tongue-tied. Also good. "No. But you might
try..." She looked around the bins. "You might try
avocado. Or artichoke hearts. Fresh mushrooms are always a big draw. I've known plenty of women who fall
for a nice, fat mushroom."

"Raw or sautéed?" His soft voice was touched with an irony that said he didn't take himself too seriously. Katherine liked that, too.

She laughed. "You phony. Feigning innocence of fresh produce, when all the time you knew the two best ways to serve mushrooms."

His eyes gleamed impishly. "No. Truly. I'm seriously considering tofu soufflé for dinner tonight. With a fruity but subtle wine. Sure you won't join me?"

She couldn't help chuckling at his send-up of a wine snob. "I'm sure."

"Then what do I do next?"

"What do you mean?"

"Well, my buddies said the best place to meet a woman is in the grocery store. But if she won't take you up on tofu soufflé, what's a guy to do? Try another woman? Move on to the freshbaked bread? Become a monk?"

Katherine folded her arms across her chest, fighting a grin. Could he tease and be sincere at the same time? she wondered.

"Maybe a whole new line," he ventured with a boyish grin. He shifted from one foot to the other, tapping his forehead and pretending to think. "How's this? What's your sign? No, wait. That's outdated. Maybe this. Live around here? No, that's no good, either— you're obviously not from around here."

She raised an eyebrow. "Oh?"

"Not with that drawl. A foreign import, maybe. But a native? Not a chance."

"As a matter of fact, I am from around here. Around the block, in fact. The pink Victorian. The one with the turret." She couldn't resist egging him on just a little. Just enough to make sure he didn't stop nibbling at the bait. Even the way he dressed made her like him. Coming from Texas, she instinctively trusted a man in faded jeans, a plaid flannel shirt and scuffed snakeskin boots. He couldn't be all bad if he didn't have on topsiders and khaki pleats, could he? "I've got an idea."

"What's that?"

She looked around as if to make sure they weren't being watched, then leaned closer. He smelled of soap and spicy shaving cream—nothing exotic. *There's too much to like about this man,* she warned herself. She lowered her voice to a whisper. "Next week. Aisle two. Canned beets. Same time. I'll bring the can opener."

"But..."

She backed away and dropped her bag of grapes into her cart, not taking her eyes off him. Slim in the hips, too. And tall enough. Not too tall. Just about right. And right now he looked...bemused. More than a little intrigued.

"Happy cooking," she called out as she pushed her cart in search of Penny.

Pickups weren't Katherine's style. But if Penny was right, and crossing paths with your neighbors was almost unavoidable, she would be seeing the Hesitant Gourmet again.

And she wouldn't mind that at all.

HANK ABSENTLY TOSSED the plastic package of tofu from one hand to the other, his eyes drawn to the petite figure retreating with her grocery cart. He grinned, then plopped the unappetizing food back into the display bin.

Back to business, he told himself, looking around for grapes and tomatoes and the few fresh vegetables he knew how to cook that his girls would also eat. Mrs.

Whitesides couldn't sit on her porch all day watching
Tammi play in the park, so he'd better finish up.

He didn't have time to remain distracted by a little
sprite in sweatshirt and jeans. Saturday was errand day
at the Weisbecker home. After grocery shopping, there
was vacuuming to do and a car to wash and a run to the
hardware store for a washer to repair the leaky faucet.
And an overflowing laundry basket.

Hank sighed as he grabbed fruit juices and milk out
of the dairy section. Being Mr. Mom didn't leave time
for playing pickup artist at the grocery store. Which was
just as well, he mused. He hadn't exactly swept her off
her feet.

She had grinned, though. Like a pixie. With her
fringy bangs and that short, bouncy ponytail, she had
looked just like a pixie.

Like Doris.

The realization stopped Hank dead in his tracks.
Damn it, he thought, piling cans of soup into the cart.
*That's it, isn't it? That's why you walked right up to her
as bold as brass and tried to start a conversation. Because she reminded you of Doris.*

She wasn't dark like Doris, but she was short and slim
and sort of like a . . . well, like a pixie. Not all dolled up
and made up and carefully turned out. Just sort of
fresh.

Like Doris.

Frowning at himself in disgust, Hank looked at the
contents of his cart and tried to decide if his purchases
would get him through another week of breakfast,
lunch and dinner. He always seemed to hit Thursday
with nothing left but potatoes and half a bowl of cereal
crumbs.

To hell with it, he thought, knowing Mrs. Whitesides must surely be getting impatient. He headed for
the checkout.

AS THEY FINISHED IN THE checkout line and picked up
their plastic bags for the walk home, Penny pumped
Katherine for more information on the mystery man
with the ineptly charming pickup line.

"What did he look like? Tall, dark and handsome,
did you say?"

"No. Tall, maybe, but blond and...pleasant looking."

"Pleasant looking? That sounds like something
you'd say about your Aunt Tilly."

Katherine chuckled, turning her face up to catch a
faint autumn breeze. "Nice arms. Strong."

"Oooh. Strong arms. The better to crush you to his
chest with, my dear."

"If you're going to turn into a matchmaker, let me
know now so I can plan my defense," Katherine teased.

They turned off the sidewalk, which was flanked by
houses of every era since the late 1800s. There were
several Victorian mansions like the one Katherine had
bought, painted in bright pastels and frilled with white
gingerbread trim. Sturdy Cape Cods, compact bunga-
lows and copycat antebellums with wide porches and
graceful columns blended with a few newly constructed town homes built in the style of East Coast row
houses.

It was a fabricated neighborhood, a fairyland built by
a group of developers whose idea was to bring back an
old neighborhood near town. Some of the houses had
been moved in. Others, faithful imitations, had been
built next door to the real thing. All of it had been

carefully landscaped, dotted with merchants and snapped up by upwardly mobile young professionals.

That's why Katherine had fallen in love with the neighborhood. It had been picture-book perfect, an enchanted village where the real world couldn't possibly intrude. Within months, she had bought the house and set in motion her plans to move from Des Moines, where the magazine was based. As a photographer, she was always on assignment throughout the Midwest anyway. Where she lived didn't matter, as long as she could attend occasional planning meetings. And Omaha was only a few hours away.

The brick pathway from the sidewalk led along one edge of a park, where benches were tucked away in alcoves of shrubs, and fountains and wading pools burbled companionably. On Saturday afternoon, the park was well populated but not crowded. A young couple tossed a Frisbee. A woman galloped through with a schnauzer on a leash, passing a couple holding hands and someone playing with a smaller dog.

Suddenly Katherine's eyes widened. Not just *a* dog. *Her* dog! Baxter! The case of the disappearing Pekinese was about to be solved.

Katherine's heart leaped excitedly. Baxter was back! Right there, playing with someone. A child.

The sight of the child gave her a jolt, and when Katherine approached the giggling little girl, she found she couldn't speak for a moment. She took a deep breath as the child looked up. She was fine limbed and olive skinned, and her open face was punctuated with dark eyes, thick lashes.

Katherine felt as if she were staring into a mirror—a mirror of what had been. And what might have been.

A mirror that revealed herself as a child and a mirror into a childhood that would never be.

"Hi!"

The young voice was sunshine bright, the smile so cheerful it hurt Katherine's heart. When she opened her mouth to speak, she was surprised to find herself short of breath. She spoke quickly, to get the words out before her breath floated away. "Hi, sweetheart. Looks like you've found my lost Pekinese."

The little girl's open expression was replaced by a look of confusion. She hugged the dog to her narrow chest. "He's mine."

A little girl. Little girls had always hurt more than little boys. All those pink dresses. And patent leather shoes. Pigtails and ribbons. This one looked just the way Katherine had always imagined...

A metallic taste coating Katherine's mouth distracted her. *Oh, no. Not again. Not now. Not after all this time.* She squeezed her eyes shut for a moment, but it only increased her awareness of her heartbeat, which was faster—just a little faster, but still accelerating.

She opened her eyes and looked down at the child. She could barely form a coherent thought. What was she supposed to say now? "He's a sweet dog, isn't he? He ran away two weeks ago. I'm..." Was that a quiver in her voice? "I'm glad you've taken care of him."

"He's mine now," the little girl said softly, dropping her cheek against Baxter's soft fur.

"Oh. Well..." Katherine's knees were beginning to shake. She tried to slow her breathing as she let her grocery bags settle onto the grass. She knelt in front of the child, mostly because she wasn't sure she could stand any longer. *Not now,* she coached herself, trying in vain to remember a yoga technique she could use to regain control, to calm herself. Her mind was a blank. All she knew was the trembling and an undeniable pull toward the little girl. As if they were somehow linked.

Wishful thinking, she chastised herself. "Sweetheart, I . . . uh . . ."

"I'm not your sweetheart. And he's not your dog. He's mine now."

The little girl's voice had grown stubborn, but Katherine barely heard it. Other voices were beginning to surface now. Voices she hadn't heard in years. She pushed them away, frightened at their reappearance. "But I've had Baxter for a long time. It hurts to lose someone you love. You can understand that, can't you?"

Katherine was looking over the little girl's shoulder, to avoid looking into her big, dark eyes, so she didn't see the sheen of moisture welling there. She didn't see the trembling chin.

When the little girl burst into tears, Katherine's instincts told her to turn and run, because her impulse was to do something she knew she wasn't brave enough to handle.

What she wanted to do was take the child in her arms and comfort her.

CHAPTER TWO

As SHE WATCHED the little girl cry, Katherine's arms ached as they hadn't ached in years.

"You keep him," she said, struggling for breath, her words barely audible. "It's okay. You keep him."

Penny's voice, confused and uncertain, broke in. "Katherine, that's not right. Isn't this the dog you told me about? The one you've had for years? You can't just give him away. That's not—"

"It's okay." Her head was light, spinning and floating out of control. She tried the deep, controlled breathing she used in yoga, but found she could only manage rapid, shallow breaths. *Not this. Please, not this.* "I . . . I just need to get home."

"Are you all right? You look—"

"Fine. I'm fine."

But she wasn't. Her body was in the grip of demons she couldn't control. And she was losing herself in the little girl's eyes. Those dark eyes, swimming in tears, drowning in hurt. Katherine reminded herself forcefully that this little girl didn't need her comfort. Somewhere she had a mother who could do that job. The thought made it easier for Katherine to take control of her trembling limbs and stand. She was vaguely aware that someone else had joined them.

"What's wrong here?"

The deep voice commanded Katherine's attention. Fighting to keep her rapid breathing from lapsing into full-fledged hyperventilation, she looked up into another pair of eyes. Familiar eyes the color of a summer sky. Worried eyes that no longer held a hint of teasing interest.

The sudden appearance of the man from the Corner Market gave Katherine a momentary reprieve, a brief chance to regain control. Breath came back to her in a welcome rush. But her brain still refused to supply her with the words she needed to explain what was happening. If only she could run. Forget the little girl. Forget the tear-filled eyes. Forget the empty ache in her arms. Forget. Again.

Finally able to focus on the center of her forehead, as she had learned to do in yoga, and clearing her mind as nearly as possible, Katherine only half listened as Penny explained the situation. When she felt her breathing begin to slow, Katherine met his eyes in flickering glances. Perhaps she only imagined that they grew warm with understanding.

She looked away as he squatted in front of the little girl to explain it to her. Rubbing her temple, Katherine shifted her eyes to the young couple tossing the Frisbee and laughing. She tried to imagine herself as the Frisbee, soaring through the crisp fall air. Her head whirled. She wondered what it would be like to faint, right here in the park, with her frozen yogurt melting in her bag. She had fainted once before but couldn't, right this moment, recall when or where.

"Scooter, remember when you found the dog? I said then it belonged to someone else." The man's voice was soft as he tried to soothe the child's wounded feelings. "Remember how we tried to call the telephone number on the tag—the number in Iowa—and found out the phone had been disconnected?''

"So then he belonged to me," the girl said, a defiant jut to her lower lip.

"No, you just looked after him for a while. Now we know who he really belongs to, so we have to give him back."

"But I don't want to give him back."

He sighed deeply. "Tammi, I want you to think for a minute how you would feel if we brought this doggie home from the pet store and you named him and made a bed for him and then he disappeared. Wouldn't you be happy if someone found him? And wouldn't you want them to give him back to you if they knew he belonged to you?''

The little girl stared at the ground, sniffling to dry her tears. After a long moment, she nodded silently, then walked over to stand in front of Katherine. Katherine forced herself to look at the child, who held out the long-haired, tail-wagging animal. Fresh tears spilled over the rims of her dark little-girl eyes.

"It's okay," Katherine protested. She just wanted to escape, before she went completely to pieces. "It doesn't matter..."

"Yes, it does," the child's father said, firmly but gently.

Wondering if she would ever again regain the precious control that had disappeared in a matter of seconds, Katherine reached for the dog being held in her direction. The little fingers that brushed hers were as soft as Baxter's fur, even more delicately made than the limbs of the tiny animal now in Katherine's hands. The touch of those small fingers made fresh wounds on top of old scars.

She mumbled a quick "thank you," avoiding the eyes that had been so appealing in the soft lighting of the Corner Market. Retrieving her plastic bags, Katherine slipped an unfamiliar vinyl leash over her wrist and set the dog on the ground. Baxter danced at her feet, wiggling in happy recognition.

Every step she took toward the haven of her new home left the child one step farther away and brought Katherine closer to regaining control. But the subsiding of her hammering heart and quivering limbs left her feeling weak and fragile.

"Katherine, what's wrong with you?" Penny asked as they mounted the steps to Katherine's back door. "You look like you don't feel well."

"I'm fine." She set her bags on the porch and fumbled for her keys. Baxter bounded around the tile floor as the door opened, yipping at her heels and tangling his stubby legs in the leash that trailed behind him.

I am fine now, she told herself, reaching back to the porch for her grocery bags. *I'm fine. The voices are gone. The panic is gone.* But when would it come back? Now that she had relived the old nightmare, would she once again find herself at the mercy of physical reactions she couldn't control? Would she once again become the emotional basket case she'd been before her divorce?

Katherine ignored the fearful pang in her heart as she rifled through the cabinets for a can of dog food.

Penny set her own bags on the rustic kitchen table and cleared her throat loudly. "Baloney! Something's wrong with you. Back at the park, you certainly weren't acting like the Katherine Barnett I know."

Katherine leaned over to place a small bowl of dog food on the floor in front of Baxter. While he ate, she unhooked the leash.

"You're right." She forced a cheerful normalcy into her voice. She knew she could do it successfully; she had done it many times before. "It did upset me to see Baxter. I had decided I'd probably never seen him again, and it just threw me, I guess."

She *had* missed him. That wasn't a fabrication. All her pets were special to her. Fibber and Molly. Rascal, the gerbil who dashed along his treadmill in her studio. Even the plants she nurtured so lovingly had become living individuals to her. But solemn-eyed, pug-nosed, rusty-colored Baxter was her weakness. He was always ready with unconditional love when she felt low.

But she was having a hard time blaming her attachment to the Pekinese for what had happened in the park. *You didn't just overreact,* she chastised herself. *You had a panic attack. Face it—you lost it.*

Looking Penny straight in the eye, Katherine called forth her best laugh and an award-winning false heartiness. "Besides, I guess I'm just not very good with children."

The words grated like chalk on a blackboard. But they did the job. Penny smiled and stretched out in the ladder-back chair to watch her neighbor put away groceries.

"Who is?" Penny asked wryly, pulling a cigarette out of the pack in her roomy pocket. "I thought Kevin and I had a great relationship after his dad and I split. We got along great. But now that he's away at college, Kevin's like a stranger."

As usual when Penny mentioned her son, Katherine fell silent. She opened the refrigerator, wishing her mind didn't always go blank when people talked about their children. Wishing she could make pleasant small talk.

Penny looked at the cigarette in her hand, then tore it into three small pieces and dropped them into her pants pocket. "I'm trying to quit. I figure forty is a good age to start making changes in your life, right?"

Katherine nodded as she put her fresh vegetables away.

"Say, was that the guy you met in the grocery store?" Penny asked. "I could tell by the way he looked at you that you'd met. That was him, wasn't it—the little girl's father?"

"Umm, yes. That was him." Katherine's face was tight as she folded up the plastic bags and stuffed them into the cupboard under the sink. Her mind raced rapidly, searching for a conversational detour. But Penny didn't slow down long enough.

"I've met him before. At a neighborhood association meeting. Hank something. I was told he didn't have a wife, though. Must be a weekend father."

"That must be it." She hoped Penny didn't notice the weak flutter in her voice. A weekend father. The Hesitant Gourmet moved swiftly into the off-limits category.

"He doesn't know how lucky he is, not having to sweat it seven days a week," Penny continued, suddenly breaking out in a wicked grin. "Besides, having kids makes it too easy for people to pin an age on you. Now that Kevin's away, I can con people into thinking I'm thirty-five again." She laughed. "As long as they don't look too close and the Retin-A keeps working."

As Katherine methodically, leadenly, put away the small stock of groceries, she prayed for a reprieve. She still felt weak, and her brain was too muddled for coherent conversation. *Please go home now,* she pleaded silently, while Penny launched into a description of the old residential hotel building just five blocks away that was being renovated into condos. *Just leave now, so I can pull myself together.*

But when Penny finally decided to take her own groceries home, Katherine quickly learned that the silence wasn't so blessed after all. Even the radio, tuned loudly to an oldies station, couldn't cover the sounds in her head. Sounds she hadn't heard for years.

It isn't likely that you and your husband will ever have a child. Those words had stopped hurting years ago, she told herself, clutching Baxter as closely to her chest as the child had almost an hour earlier.

It's you who'll never have a child, babe. Not me.

The disintegration of her four-year marriage to Jerry didn't cause many sleepless nights anymore, either. She tried, when she thought of him at all, to remember the good times, before his youthful enthusiasm had soured so completely, had turned into bitterness as he increasingly sought to blame her for their inability to produce a child.

Adoption is the best answer for you and your husband. It was an answer that hadn't suited Jerry. It was a solution that threatened his all-important definition of masculinity.

And in the end, after her faith in her own womanhood had been completely eroded by disappointment, impersonal prodding, pitying glances and Jerry's ruthless taunting, Katherine didn't have the heart for adoption, either. Adoption wouldn't have made her marriage better. It wouldn't have restored her lost confidence or restored the feeling of completeness she had lost.

This test may hold the answer for you and your husband. But it hadn't. Three years of testing had turned up nothing but futility and despair. Pinning her hopes on new techniques to encourage conception and running from one specialist to another had taken its toll. The tests were almost worse than the infertility, leaving her feeling demeaned and dehumanized, less of a woman.

To hell with these tests! This is your problem, not mine! That's how Jerry had seen it. Always her problem, never his. A problem of uncertainty that left her hoping every month and raging against fate when those hopes were dashed. A problem that had turned into anxiety attacks, triggered by nothing and anything. Anxiety attacks that Jerry—her once sympathetic Jerry—simply couldn't tolerate. Anxiety attacks that Katherine had learned, slowly and determinedly, to control through relaxation techniques and yoga.

Until today.

I'll find myself a real woman next time. And she supposed he had. As for herself, Katherine had found a new way to fill her life with meaning. She had gone back to college, learning photography in the basement of the administration building from the mush-mouthed Texan who shot publicity stills for the university's public relations office. The photography had captured her fancy more surely than the English lit and chemistry in her curriculum. After college, photography had become her life.

Katherine dropped into the rocker in her new living room. Today, her protective facade had fallen away when the young girl had started crying right in front of her eyes. The tears had awakened a fearful anguish in Katherine.

An anguish she would give anything to squelch once again. One she *had* to squelch, because she refused to give in to the anxiety attacks that had ruled her life for months before her divorce. She was whole now. She wouldn't let anything change that.

Not even a pair of dark, little-girl eyes. Or the teasing blue ones that were part of the package.

WHAT HAD STARTED as a pleasant Saturday trek to the grocery store certainly wasn't ending up that way.

Tammi's face was solemn. She had never had a pet before. In fact, Hank had given only grudging permission for her to bring the lost dog home. Permission that had been granted simply because the combination of wistfulness in Tammi's face and the hunger in the dog's eyes had been impossible for a softie like Hank to refuse.

And now it was causing Tammi pain. The pain of loss. The kind of pain she already knew far too well for an eight-year-old. Hank decided to give it one more try.

"Hey, kiddo?" When she looked up at him, her dark eyes reproachful, he stopped to drop the grocery bags on the sidewalk and squat beside her. "What's this behind your ear, kiddo?"

Reaching over, he produced a shiny quarter and flicked it in front of her face. Her expression changed to one of disappointed resignation.

"Oh, Daddy."

Now Hank felt like crying, too. He could remember when one of his silly tricks had been sufficient to banish the tears of both his daughters, magically turning tears into sunny smiles and silly giggles. Nothing seemed to work anymore.

He slipped the quarter into her jeans pocket. "Does that mean I can't make your frown disappear anymore? No more 'Abracadabra, presto-chango' and I'll find a smiling face in its place?"

Obligingly, Tammi conjured up a weak smile.

Hank's heart twisted at the young face that looked so familiar. He didn't need pictures to remember Doris as long as Tammi was around. Dark and impish, she was a pint-sized version of her mother.

"You've got to believe in the magic before it can work, isn't that right, Mr. Cadabra?" Hank made a fist, then worked his thumb to create the illusion of a mouth, a ventriloquism trick that had always delighted Tammi.

"Right, Mr. Prestidigitator." Hank kept his lips still as he affected a high voice and moved his thumb to keep up with the words.

Hank shrugged and tilted Tammi's chin up. "See? You've gotta believe."

"Do you believe in magic, Daddy?"

Where, he wondered, did an eight-year-old learn skepticism? From TV? From her teenaged sister? Or from the harsh lessons life had already taught her firsthand?

"Sure," he said as convincingly as possible. He straightened the white bow clipped over her ear to hold the hair out of her eyes. "I believe in magic."

Now it was Tammi's turn to shrug, her eyes turning even more somber. "Did Mommy believe in magic?"

Hank gnawed the inside of his lower lip. Had Doris believed in magic? She had believed in him. Sometimes that had seemed like magic. "She sure did, Scooter."

"Then why didn't you use magic to bring her back?"

The wind rushed out of Hank's lungs. He thought he had dealt with the kids' reaction to Doris's death two years ago. He had explained the accident so carefully, so straightforwardly; had told them, fighting his own tears, that their mommy wouldn't be coming home. That she had gone to heaven. He had held them while they cried. He had answered their questions and done all he knew to reassure them.

Obviously, it hadn't been enough. He was convinced that Heather's sudden leap into a difficult adolescence during the past two months was tied to Doris's death. And now Tammi was challenging him to explain the unexplainable.

"Because..." He groped for the right words. Nothing he could think of sounded adequate. "Because my magic isn't that strong, sweetheart."

She nodded, her expression clearly saying that his answer didn't surprise her in the least.

They finished the walk home in silence.

When Hank unlocked the condo, the sound of rock music assaulted their ears. At least, Hank assumed they still called it rock. It sounded nothing like the music he had grown up calling rock and bore no resemblance whatsoever to the country rock he now preferred.

Tammi flopped into a chair in the living room, staring straight ahead, her face sullen. After he dropped off the bags of groceries on the kitchen counter, Hank headed for Heather's bedroom.

Another confrontation, he thought as he pounded on the door. *The cap to the perfect afternoon.* He pounded as loudly as he dared without risking serious damage to the bedroom door and still received no answer. He turned the knob. "Heather?"

She was sprawled on the bed, eyes closed, a *People* magazine lying open but abandoned on her chest. One leg was bent at the knee, the other crossed over it and bouncing to the beat.

"Heather?" He walked over to the power button and punched it, filling the house with unaccustomed silence.

Heather bolted upright, instant anger flushing her fair, slim face. "What are you doing? You can't just bust in here like—"

"How else am I supposed to get your attention?" he demanded, reminding himself one beat too late that answering her indignation with his own was the most direct route to an argument. He tried to soften his tone. "I pounded on the door and you couldn't even hear me over the music."

"It wasn't that loud," she protested, slamming the magazine onto the unmade bed.

Hank noticed the sheets, still rumpled at 2:00 p.m., and the miniskirt that was so short he had forbidden her to wear it to school. He decided to refrain from mentioning either.

"Yes, it was," he insisted, trying hard to keep his tone even. "We heard it as soon as we got off the elevator."

Heather rolled her eyes. "I'll use the earphones, then."

"Why don't you clean up this room first." Hank could have bitten his tongue. He hadn't meant to bring up the bedroom. Yet. He never meant to be so hard on her. He remembered what it was like being a teenager. He hadn't been an angel, either, he recalled—as his mother never failed to remind him. Two wrecked cars. A suspension from school. And there was the time he'd called collect to the farm outside McCook from Lincoln, more than two hundred miles away, at three in the morning, after he'd run out of money and gas at about the same time.

He'd always sworn to be one of those calm, rational parents who could sit down and hash things out with his kids. What a joke!

"What's wrong with my room?" Heather crossed her arms stubbornly and lay back on the bed, dismissing him.

"This week-old pizza box, for one thing. All these clothes that ought to be in the washing machine, for another." Her closed expression, the one that told him she had tuned him out completely, turned his righteous indignation up a notch. "Don't you care that—"

"All right!" Her impatient voice interrupted him. "I'll clean it up. I'll turn down the music. Just don't yell at me anymore. Okay?"

Playing the big bad dad wasn't working today. It wasn't even worth pointing out that Heather was the only one raising her voice. Deciding to give her a little space, Hank backed out of the room and closed the door.

HEATHER HATED HIM. That's all there was to it. She hated him. And he hated her, too. She stared at the ceiling, willing her tears of frustration to be transformed into anger. These days, all he ever did was yell at her. And lately, Heather realized peevishly, she couldn't tell which made her madder—when her dad tried to boss her around or when he acted like she'd suddenly turned into a grown-up on her fourteenth birthday.

When he did that, it felt just like he was ignoring her. Like she didn't even exist. He probably wouldn't even notice if she walked out the door in this miniskirt. The only time he ever noticed was when something she did messed up his peace and quiet. He was too busy with Tammi. His precious Tammi.

Heather looked at the Mickey Mouse watch with the studded leather band on her arm. Two-twenty. Blakely and Kristie would be here in ten minutes. He didn't even seem to notice her two new friends, although she was sure he would fuss about them, too, if he once looked up long enough to really see them.

He didn't seem to see them any more than he ever seemed to see her.

She was glad of that. Blakely and Kristie were more fun than any of the dorky little kids who had been her friends for so many years. They were more like her. Grown-up. Not still into kid stuff. Meagan, who until this summer had been her best friend, still liked roller skating and Putt-Putt. Heather smirked into the mirror over her dresser as she quickly added more eye makeup.

Roller skates and Putt-Putt! Thank goodness she'd left all that behind. Heather reached into the back of her desk drawer and pulled out a fistful of dollar bills, wondering if it would be enough to see her through a Saturday afternoon and evening. The other kids always seemed to have more money than her. If she didn't have to watch Tammi after school every day, she could get an afternoon job and have money of her own to spend.

If only. If only. It was all just wishful thinking, anyway. Nothing ever worked out right anymore.

When she heard the doorbell, she slipped her feet into the laceless high-tops at the foot of her bed and hurried down the hall. As she passed through the living room, she heard Tammi sniffling from the kitchen. Soaping Dad up for a big hug and kiss, Heather told herself cynically.

"Got it," she called out as the doorbell rang again. But it was too late. Hank had already come through the door, a blubbering Tammi hiked up on his hip. Heather opened the door but motioned for Blakely and Kristie to stay out in the hallway.

"It's for me, Dad," she said breezily, turning the latch on the door so it would lock behind her as she left. "We're going to run to the mall, okay?"

She stood in the doorway, wondering if he would even come over to see who she was leaving with. He would realize right away that Kristie was at least six-teen, and he probably wouldn't like her running around with someone so much older. And if he saw Blakely, with her neon sunglasses and the butterfly transfer on her bare shoulder, he would have a conniption. She almost hoped he would. But he was too worried about Tammi's tears to even notice that she was leaving. The little brat sniveled about everything, Heather thought with disgust.

"The mall?" Hank patted the younger girl's cheek. "What time will you be home?"

"By dinner," she promised, knowing she had no intention of coming home before bedtime.

HANK GLANCED TOWARD the closing door, then returned his attention to the youngster dampening his shirt with her inconsolable tears. Had that been Meagan at the door? He hadn't been able to tell. He hadn't seen the girl in months; probably wouldn't recognize her if he did. They changed so quickly once they reached adolescence.

"Now, Scooter," he said as he headed back to the kitchen. He wondered when Tammi had grown so heavy. "You've got to forget about Baxter."

"I can't," she sobbed, wiggling out of his arms to huddle in one of the vinyl kitchen chairs.

"You will." He opened the cabinet doors to put the canned goods away.

"No, I won't," she vowed. Something in her voice captured his attention, and he turned back to look into her stubbornly convinced eyes. "I'll never forget Baxter. Just 'cause he's gone doesn't mean I'll forget."

Hank sighed and turned back to four cans of dinosaur pasta in cheese sauce that the shelves seemed too crowded to hold. He shoved things around, looking for a way to wedge the cans onto the shelf.

"Maybe we could get another dog." He winced as he said it, knowing he was looking for the easy way out. There never seemed time to clean up after three people, much less a dog. Why, he wondered suddenly, couldn't Heather help more? Had she even straightened her room before she left the house? He doubted it. Maybe he was too soft on her; maybe that was the problem. He had to try being consistently tough. Maybe.

"I don't want another dog. I want Baxter."

His hands suddenly hit upon the perfect solution to all his problems. Or, at least, some of his more immediate problems—like a pouting daughter and overcrowded shelves. Six cans of dog food. He took them off the shelves and replaced them with the dinosaurs, which he was sure were only edible by digestive systems younger than ten years old.

"I've got an idea," he said, sitting down at the table beside her and setting the dog food between them. "How would you like to take the nice lady the rest of our poochie food?"

"She wasn't a nice lady," Tammi said, the disbelief in her red-rimmed eyes demonstrating that she thought his words indicated a definite lack of allegiance.

Hank didn't happen to agree, but he suspected he and Tammi were judging on different merits. The woman's sense of humor in fending off his come-on at the Corner Market had made him smile; so had her round little backside and her teasing, hazel eyes. He didn't know her name yet, but she had made a point of letting him know where she lived. Hank knew exactly where she meant; the house with the turrets was hard to miss.

His experience with women might be a little on the rusty side, but Hank knew enough to recognize interest in a woman's eyes when he saw it.

"I have a hunch that if we take her the rest of our dog food and get to know her better, she'll be happy for you to visit Baxter anytime." He tweaked the upturned nose she had inherited from her mother. "How about it? We'll go right after church tomorrow."

Tammi glanced up, a glimmer of hope brightening the skepticism in her eyes. "You really think I could visit Baxter sometimes?"

"Of course," he said, holding up his hand Mr. Cadabra-style. "What do you think?"

"No doubt about it," his fist answered in a high-pitched voice. "She'll be crazy about the kid."

Tammi giggled at the silly voice coming from behind her dad's motionless lips. Heaving a relieved sigh, Hank grabbed a grocery bag, and the two of them filled it with dog food and the chew toy they had bought just the day before.

She'll be crazy about us, he told himself as he headed to gather up the clothes that needed washing. And maybe the guys were right. Maybe a little female companionship was just what he needed.

CHAPTER THREE

HER SANDY BROWN HAIR still damp from the shower, Katherine filled a copper teakettle with water and put it on to boil.

Afternoon tea, she thought with satisfaction. The perfect way to end a morning of dusty unpacking and start a lazy Sunday afternoon.

Three photo assignments had kept her out of town most of the time since moving in, so there still were plenty of unpacked boxes. But Katherine had had her fill of unpacking for one day. Instead, after tea, she planned on a half-hour of yoga exercises, which always left her feeling strong.

Filling a strainer with oolong tea leaves and clipping it onto the edge of her grandmother's china teapot, Katherine made a mental list of things to do the rest of the day. Yoga, then watering the plants, and a walk with Baxter and her camera. The park would be a good place to begin.

Recollections of her encounter in the park gnawed at her peace of mind, and with it a restless uneasiness at the vivid image of smiling blue eyes. Katherine willed her mind back to her plans.

A relaxing day to enjoy her new neighborhood was in order, because tomorrow she loaded up her VW and hit the road for four days. Her assignment said Kansas—some football-coach-turned-author who would be profiled in the next issue of *Midwesterner*. That meant four days of dressing out of her canvas bag and eating out of paper bags.

Almost as if reading her mind, Fibber squawked a high-pitched protest from the living room.

Katherine grinned. "I know, I know," she called out to the pint-sized protestor. His wings flapped vigorously at the sound of her voice. "I'll miss you, too, you old grouch."

As she peered into a still unorganized cabinet for sugar, she caught sight of Penny through the kitchen window. Her neighbor was awkwardly wrapping insulation around an outdoor water pipe in preparation for the Nebraska winter that would soon grip them in a fury of ice and wind.

At last putting her hands on the decorative tin can that held sugar cubes, Katherine stuck her head out the back door.

"It's teatime, neighbor. How about a break?"

Penny waved and looked at her watch. "I've got an appointment in an hour and a half," she called out.

"There's time. Come on over."

Within ten minutes, Katherine had laid the coffee table in the living room with a teatime spread that did justice to the Victorian flavor of the house.

"The Queen Mum would be proud," Penny said, crossing her long legs at the ankle and letting them stretch across the dark, rich colors of the oriental rug.

"Did you say you're showing a house this afternoon?" Katherine poured hot tea from the teapot, dotted with tiny yellow roses, into gilt-edged matching cups.

"Two. But first, I have a kid coming in about a job."

"A job? What kind of job?"

"I'm trying to find a high school kid to do some work after school, maybe on weekends." Penny reached for another cookie. "Things are so hectic that I'm spending too much time on busywork and not enough time on selling. Trust me, the commission on opening mail and making photocopies doesn't make the car payment."

"Good for you. I'd love to have a gofer. Maybe after I get a little of the work on this house behind me, I'll..." The trill of the doorbell interrupted her. "Who could that be?"

"Probably new neighbors bringing casseroles and sinful desserts as a welcoming gesture," Penny said. "Everything you've heard about Southern hospitality goes double for Nebraska."

"So I'm finding out." Katherine groaned as she stood. "I've just finished off one casserole and have half a strawberry-rhubarb pie that I don't need tempting me in the freezer, thanks to open-armed new neighbors."

It was new neighbors. One of them tall and blond and well muscled in a gray crewneck sweater and jeans, the other shorter. Much shorter. She held a plastic bag in both hands.

Katherine's smile froze on her face. It had taken most of the evening before—and a half hour of yoga on the tail of a three-hour frenzy of productivity—to push aside her heartsick memories. True, she had a new darkroom as a result, and a workroom and studio in what had once been a first floor parlor. But now, with her equilibrium safely restored, here was another harsh reminder.

Get a grip on yourself, she told herself firmly, monitoring her physical reactions. So far, so good. *It's only a child. Don't let it throw you again.*

"We came 'cause I'm sorry about being sad yesterday," the little girl piped up in what sounded like a carefully rehearsed speech. "And to bring you some doggie food. We already had it at home. In the kitchen."

"Well, thank you." The words came slowly as Katherine fought to hold on to the control that had begun to feel tenuous. She realized she had waited half a beat too long to step back and invite them in.

"We wanted to welcome you to the neighborhood properly, too," the deeper voice said. "You've just moved in, haven't you?"

Katherine nodded and looked up into the friendly eyes that had seemed so playful at the Corner Market the afternoon before. He nudged the little girl to remind her to hand over the bag of cans.

"Not tofu, I hope," Katherine said, taking the bag but averting her eyes from the little girl. She sounded a little breathless, even to herself. *Maybe,* she thought, *if I can just concentrate on him, I can keep my mind off his little girl. That's it. Just concentrate on him.*

"Not tofu." He grinned, extending a hand. "I'm Hank Weisbecker. And this is my little girl, Tammi."

His hand was hard, the palm layered with calluses that had weathered to leather toughness. The grip was firm, the grasp of a man accustomed to the uncompromising handshakes of other men with calloused palms. Almost as soon as he had taken her hand in his, the grip slackened, as if the softness and size of her palm had startled him.

"Katherine Barnett," she said, her voice once again unsteady. But this time, it was due to the waves of awareness that tripped up her spine with his touch. "Thanks for the welcome."

While he and Penny greeted each other and tried to remember when they'd met, Katherine offered him tea. He looked inclined to accept, until he laid eyes on the china teacups with their delicately curled finger-holds. He shook his head, then perched awkwardly on the edge of a narrow, straight-backed Victorian chair.

"Are you sure?" she asked, making certain she caught his eyes with a teasing glance. "It goes well with tofu soufflé, you know."

Some of his nervousness evaporated at her teasing. His blue-on-blue eyes crinkled at the corners when he grinned. "Maybe you'll come after all, and bring the tea."

Tammi, standing shyly beside her father's chair, spoke before Katherine could respond. "Where's Baxter?"

"I believe he's right over there, under the table." Mustering a smile, Katherine pointed to the long, narrow library table resting along the wall opposite the bay window. *She is awfully cute,* Katherine thought as Tammi settled down on the oriental rug to play with the dog. Her hand jerked, clattering her teacup against the saucer. Carefully, she set them on the serving table.

"Listen, I'd better run." Penny jumped up with typical abruptness. "I've got this girl coming soon, and after that, two houses to show. Wish me luck."

Penny's departure caused Katherine a moment of fluttering unease. Now what would she talk about? As soon as she'd seen Hank at the door, she had realized that the anxiety hovering at the back of her mind had been partly disappointment, an illogical regret that he might have noticed the symptoms of her anxiety attack. That she might not see him a third time. But now that he was here... Goodness, she'd never been very good at this small talk business.

It's not like he's here to...well...you know, she told herself. *He's simply being neighborly.*

She reached for her tea again and remembered Penny's admonition about wearing old jeans and sweatshirts. This was the second time he'd caught her wearing old Levi's and a frayed cotton shirt. But no matter how she dressed, she reminded herself, she was hardly a model for alluring femininity.

His eyes, when she glanced up, looked something more than neighborly, and, momentarily disconcerted, she was grateful when he asked about her work, which led to the story of her discovery of the neighborhood.

"A photographer? For *Midwesterner* magazine?" Hank's look was appreciative, perhaps even a little envious. "That's got to be a lot more exciting than dancing around with a sixteen-foot pruner all day."

"A sixteen-foot pruner?" Her pulse did a little dance of its own. She had been right. A genuine outdoorsy type, not some boring desk jockey. Katherine had never lost her country girl's preference for a man who worked with his hands. "That sounds interesting. What do you do?"

He shrugged and, as if reading Katherine's mind, stared down at his hands. "Trim trees. Plant shrubs. Try to defeat Nebraska's image as a flat, boring plain."

Remembering the T-shirts she had seen emblazoned with telephone poles and the words Nebraska State Tree, Katherine grinned. "That's a tall order."

"That's me. Tell me it's impossible and I'll have you a strategy worked out by morning."

His blue eyes glittered with a mischief gone so quickly she might have imagined it. Was he flirting again? Issuing a subtle challenge? Katherine found it hard to tell. As his eyes wandered around the room, she recalled the touch of his hand, tough and tender. It reminded her how seldom she found a man who met all her criteria. Most, she told herself, were like Hank. One or two little things kept them from being just what she was interested in. Tammi's giggle from the other side of the room reminded her that, in Hank's case, the one little thing was not so little at all.

"But I have to talk about topping trees and thinning out flower beds all week," Hank said. "I'd rather talk about photography."

Photography was her great love. But it always surprised Katherine to find that some people attached a sort of romantic mystique to it. "I like it. But I'm sure that tripods and 100-millimeter lenses get as tiresome as pruners sometimes."

"How'd you get into it?"

"In college, down in Texas. My work-study job was in the photo lab."

A look of understanding slowly came into his eyes. "Aha. Texas." He grinned, propping one booted foot on a knee. Although he was slender, he looked incongruously large perched on the Victorian chair. "I knew you weren't from around here."

There he went again with that teasing in his voice, the teasing that caused a little rush to course through Katherine's bloodstream. "That's right. I believe you accused me of drawling once before, Mr. Weisbecker?"

"Ah b'lieve the way y'all speak does give you away, ma'am."

Hank's pitiful attempt to mimic a Texas accent caught her by surprise; she laughed. Such attempts to poke fun could be irritating, but Hank's good-naturedly pleasant face told her that he only teased about what he liked.

"You'd make a terrible cowboy, Hank. Remind me to find someone else to take along to the next roundup."

"Don't let this city-boy disguise fool you, Katie. I'm right off a Nebraska farm, myself."

The nickname prickled through her. Katie. No one called her Katie. Not anymore. Only her family, and they weren't as close as they'd been when she was growing up. She never thought of her nickname or farms without a nudge of guilt over the present gulf between herself and her family. She didn't like to think about farms. And she didn't want to be reminded of the old Katie.

"But I see you managed to escape, too," she said, smiling into his friendly face. She discovered that it wasn't even hard to smile when she looked at him. It wasn't his fault that he conjured up ghosts. It wasn't his fault he was a weekend daddy, either.

"Yeah, I guess so." His smile turned wistful. "I always thought I'd never want to see another cornfield in my life. Now, I love to go back for harvest. Nothing like an ear of corn thirty minutes out of the field."

She could almost taste the sweet corn. Her smile deepened. "Or coming home with more berries in your belly than in your bucket." The sudden recollection and her enthusiastic telling of it surprised her.

"Or listening to the sound of the countryside at night. Cows in the distance."

"And crickets." She was infected with the magic memories his eyes and voice evoked.

"And barn doors creaking."

"And the front-porch swing. The chains always popped." She remembered crawling up in her father's lap and listening to his stories as she drowsed off to sleep.

"Porch swings. Beat the heck out of drive-in movies, didn't they?"

Their eyes met. Katherine's soft laugh died, a wisp of breath that was almost a sigh. His eyes refused to let hers go and she found that, for just a moment, she was content to remain a prisoner of his gaze.

"Grandma has a porch swing," Tammi chimed in from across the room.

Katherine started as the young voice broke the spell Hank had been weaving around her.

"She sure does, Scooter," Hank said, turning to the little girl. Katherine saw a vulnerability, almost a hurt, which he quickly covered with a tender smile. "The same one I used to sit in when I was your age."

When he looked back at Katherine, a hint of embarrassment at their sentimental meandering skittered around the edges of his eyes. "I sound like an old fogy, wishing for the good old days."

"A couple of old fogies," Katherine concurred, forcing a grin.

"Sometimes I think maybe that's just what I am." He looked thoughtful for a moment, and every vestige of nostalgia disappeared from his eyes.

Katherine was sorry the moment of shared recollections was over. Reflected in Hank's eyes, her memories had been good ones.

"Say, what was the hardest thing you ever had to take a picture of?"

A child, she wanted to say, but didn't. Instead, she allowed herself the tiniest of glows as she warmed to his genuine interest.

"A funeral," she said, mentioning the name of a prominent young artist whose life and death had been chronicled in the magazine. "Finding a way to show the impact without being schmaltzy wasn't easy. Funerals aren't...well, they aren't the kind of social event people identify with easily."

Hank looked away, letting his eyes flit to Tammi, who had pulled the shoestring out of her high-top to waggle over Baxter's head.

"I'm sure that wasn't easy," he said at last.

The truth of her words struck Katherine as it dawned on her that the subject wasn't one Hank wanted to be reminded of, either. Everything he did seemed to reinforce her initial impression of him—a shy, sensitive type, more accustomed to working with his hands than making polite chitchat.

"What about you? What's the hardest thing you've ever had to do on your job?"

Hank laughed softly. "Trim tree limbs away from a live electrical wire in a thirty-mile-an-hour wind, maybe—in the middle of January."

Although he had relayed the words in a self-deprecating manner that said his work paled in comparison to hers, Katherine groaned appreciatively, already envisioning the scene as a series of photos. Hank, she speculated, would make the perfect subject. His face was expressive, his form rugged and his muscles sufficiently toned to appeal to the senses without making him look like a model chosen for his biceps. And the situation he described had the kind of inherent drama that could translate well into photos.

"Not very exciting, I'm afraid," Hank said apologetically.

"Actually, I was just thinking what a terrific series of photos your work might make."

"You were?" He looked surprised. Maybe even pleased, although he tried to hide it. "You're kidding, right?"

"No, I'm not." She leaned forward, elbows on her knees. "I'm talking with the University Press right now about a book on America at work. Farmers. Cattlemen. Bricklayers. Laborers of all types. You might fit in beautifully if we get the project off the ground."

"Well, I...that sounds interesting." Now she was sure. He was definitely pleased. She suspected he received little positive reinforcement for the work he did in a day when most people gave more respect to those who held upwardly mobile office jobs.

"Good." She wondered, fleetingly, about asking him to dinner soon. Once she'd unpacked the good china and found the good lace tablecloth she could do it up right—preferably some weeknight when his little girl was safely ensconced with her mother.

In the midst of her budding fantasy, other unbidden visions intruded. Weekend jaunts to the zoo with Tammi in tow. Sunday picnics at the park, with Tammi refusing to eat the potato salad. Tammi's weekends with her father could all too easily become Saturdays with Dad and his friend.

No, even a casual relationship with a man like Hank wasn't safe. Casual relationships didn't always stay that way just because that's what one intended, she told herself. And she knew her heart couldn't survive falling in love with someone who might someday expect her to take his daughter into her heart as well. She couldn't

bear the notion of opening the door to the uncertainty
of anxiety attacks and the certainty of wishing for the
daughter of her own she would never have.

An invitation to dinner probably wasn't a very good
idea after all. Confirmed bachelors or older, single-
again men whose children had already reached adult-
hood were much better bets. Not as plentiful, perhaps,
but much safer, once you found them.

"I guess we'd better be going," Hank said, without
making a move to leave. She stifled the polite urge to
protest. "Maybe...I'd like to...I mean, I hope we can
get together sometime. Maybe I could show you around
the area. Help you feel a little more at home."

Once again, Hank's bashful sincerity tugged at
Katherine. She struggled with the funny tenderness he
brought to bloom in her breast. But as he stood up,
looking down at her hopefully, expectantly, she knew
she had to toughen her own resolve to stay away from
him. He and his daughter appeared to be close, and
Katherine Barnett was the worst possible candidate for
the third point of that particular triangle.

She toyed with the best way to politely but firmly let
him know she wasn't interested. Nothing sounded right.
What didn't sound rude sounded too ambiguous, and
she certainly didn't want him showing up on her door-
step with his little girl every weekend.

The notion chilled her. "I'm really not...I don't go
out much right now, Hank."

The minute the words were spoken, the teasing light
went out of his eyes. What Katherine saw there now was
all the proof she needed that his shy sensitivity was no
put-on. Hank Weisbecker was no lover boy on the
make; her words had knocked the wind out of him.

Hank's tanned face darkened and his shoulders squared. Katherine wanted to recall her words, to snatch them out of the air between them. Instead, she watched in tongue-tied silence as he called Tammi to his side.

"Well, thank you for letting us drop in." He was stiffly polite. "We hope you'll enjoy the neighborhood."

Their eyes locked. Katherine fought to keep hers from pleading with him to forgive her for something he couldn't possibly understand. She ignored the fact that his were begging her to *let* him understand.

"Yeah," Tammi said, jolting them both with her childishly jubilant voice. "Thanks for letting me play with Baxter. Maybe I'll come back sometime."

Stunned, Katherine looked down at the shining young face. The hopeful smile tugged at her heart. She was tempted to give her blessings to the suggestion. Instead, she thanked them for coming and held the door open for them to leave.

As she cleared the tea tray, Katherine tried to excuse herself. Her words might have hurt, but at least they wouldn't linger. At least they wouldn't still be with him a decade later, poisoning his life.

THE AUTUMN CHILL was welcome. Unlike the dry, blistering heat of a Nebraska summer or the frigid bluster of a Nebraska winter, autumn made the outdoors a pleasure.

After Hank's crew finished a morning of pruning shrubs in one of the city's parks, they walked two blocks to a corner diner during the lunch hour. Then, instead of holing up in the dingy atmosphere of the café, they took their sandwiches and drinks back to the park.

"Man, this is great!" Jessie Ruiz held his dark face up to the breeze as he bit into a liverwurst sandwich. "I got so tired of sweat pouring off my face this summer."

"You won't think it's so great when you're stomping through snow in another month," Roy snorted.

Stu took a long swallow of his soda pop. "Yeah. You'll be wishing for something warm to snuggle up against then."

That was all it took to launch another conversation about women. Or, more particularly, about sex. Hank leaned back against an oak tree and tuned the men out. Sex or sports. Lunchtime conversation seemed to center around one of the two subjects eighty percent of the time.

Sports was fine, especially this time of year when the University of Nebraska Cornhuskers were racking up another record-breaking football season. But sex was something Hank didn't care to dwell on.

Sex. What a disaster. Even getting up his nerve to talk to women was hard enough. And then, when he did, everything seemed to go south on him. Like the last woman he'd dated, when she'd made him so nervous with her heavy-handed come-on.

And now, when he'd finally convinced himself that particular disaster wouldn't repeat itself, and a nice, interesting woman had come along, look what happened. Although she got this strange, almost scared look in her eyes sometimes, Katherine Barnett had been plenty friendly. Until he had said something about getting together. She'd been all smiles when she thought he might be a good guinea pig for this hotshot photo book on cowhands and dirt farmers, but socialize with him? She'd put the quietus on that in a New York minute.

"Yo, earth to Weisbecker. Come in, Weisbecker." Stu snapped his fingers in Hank's direction. "What planet are you on today?"

"You talking to me?"

Stu rolled his eyes. "'Were you talking to me?' Jessie just spent ten minutes giving you a song and dance about his niece, and you weren't even listening."

Hank shrugged as he poured another cup of coffee from his thermos. "Sorry."

"So, are you gonna take Jess up on his once-in-a-lifetime offer, or what?" At Hank's blank expression, Stu shook his head. "The man is on Mars today. The niece, Weisbecker. Jessie says she'll be in town this week. Looking for a job. How about it? Don't you want to show her a little Omaha hospitality?"

The heavy innuendo in Stu's final word drew a snicker from Roy. "Is that what you call it, Stu? Hospitality?"

Jessie silenced them with a stony glare. "Hey, this is my niece, okay? Pretend you aren't perverts." He turned back to Hank with a question on his face.

"I don't know, Jessie." Did he really want to set himself up again? Hank thought of the china teacups and the lace curtains in Katherine Barnett's house, thought of her easy dismissal. His heart cringed.

"You'll like her, Hank. And I know she'll like you."

It would be nice, Hank thought, to know that a woman liked him. A woman who maybe grew up on a farm, the way he had. And he could use a break from Heather's smart mouth; even Tammi's need for constant attention was too much for him to handle sometimes.

Doing something for himself might be just the ticket.

Once again, Katherine's face sprang to mind. The way her glossy brown hair swirled around her face—that was nice. The way they had seemed to be in the same place and the same time, far away from Omaha, for a few short minutes the day before. That had been nice, too. But the way he'd felt when she said she didn't date much—that hadn't been nice.

"Where'd you say your niece is from, Jessie?"

"Stromsburg."

The small farm town, settled mostly by Swedish immigrants, was in central Nebraska, not far from the Platte River. Lots of hardy blonds with big, open smiles, if he recalled high school football games.

"She's not *too* young, is she?"

WHISTLING A CHIP-KICKING Willie Nelson tune under his breath, Hank studied the knot of his tie in the mirror over his dresser. It was too fat. Kind of lumpy and off-center. Doris wouldn't have let him out of the house that way. Making a face at his reflection, he yanked it out to start over.

When he had the strip of red-and-blue silk in his hand, he paused to look at it, then trekked back to the closet for the yellow one with the little design in it and held them both up to his tweed blazer for the fifth time in the last half hour.

They both looked fine to him. Which was a good thing: they were the only ties he owned. The need for ties didn't come up very often, a fact for which he was grateful every time he spent an evening trussed up in one.

Vickie Andersen, he figured, deserved a tie. She was in the city now, looking for a job. Hoping, Jessie had said, to get away from her job as a cashier in Stromsburg. Hank thought it would be nice to show her the kind of time you couldn't have in Stromsburg. A nice dinner—one of the big, juicy prime ribs Omaha was famous for—in a place with candlelight and waiters in white shirts instead of waitresses who popped their gum. And afterward, that quiet little bar with the piano. Women seemed to like that. They didn't play much Willie Nelson or Merle Haggard, but it seemed to make a woman feel special. And that would be a nice thing to do for Vickie.

If he was very, very lucky, Vickie would turn out to be a nice young woman who enjoyed an evening of country music and draft beer. And the next time they went out, he could leave the tie in the closet.

You're getting ahead of yourself, pardner, Hank warned his reflection.

He reknotted the tie. It was better. Not perfect, but better. He looked down at his dress shoes to see if they needed a quick shine. His toes felt as uncomfortable as his neck. Hank looked longingly at the well-worn boots peeking from under the rocking chair in the corner.

If he'd been going out with Katherine Barnett tonight, he probably wouldn't be bothering with dress shoes and ties and piano bars, he thought suddenly. She looked like the beer-and-blue jeans type. Down-to-earth. Not someone you had to worry about impressing. She had seemed quite at home in a pair of old jeans, wearing no makeup.

Then again, he hadn't done such a good job of reading her. He'd thought her interest was written all over that heart-shaped face. And look where that had gotten him: egg on his own.

The phone rang as Hank filled his pants' pocket, reminding him of one of the few advantages of having a teenager in the house. You never had to bother answering the phone. Wouldn't stand a chance of getting there first if you did.

To hell with Katherine Barnett, he told himself. He was seeing Vickie Andersen. A nice, simple farm girl. That was the ticket, all right.

"Dad. Telephone." Heather, her voice accusatory, clearly begrudged him the time he would tie up the line.

Sometimes Hank felt like an alien had invaded his daughter's body.

The voice on the other end of the telephone line wasn't familiar.

"Mr. Weisbecker? This is Suzanne. The baby-sitter."

Uh-oh. A phone call from the baby-sitter thirty minutes before she was due was never good news. Hank stuck a finger beneath his collar and tugged.

"I came home from school this afternoon with the flu and I don't think I ought to come over and give it to Tammi," Suzanne said contritely. Hank listened for a scratchy throat, a stuffy nose. She sounded healthy. She'd probably recuperate at a party tonight. Teenagers!

What now? he thought, as he thanked her for calling and wished her a speedy recovery. Although he'd been reluctant about agreeing to this date at first, he now had himself convinced that a date with Vickie Andersen would make for a very pleasant evening. He had her firmly fixed in his mind—tall and big boned, with corn silk blond hair just below her shoulders, blue eyes, no makeup, a simple skirt and blouse. He liked her already. He didn't want to disappoint her. Or himself.

Walking back through the living room, where Tammi sat cross-legged in front of the television, Hank bemoaned once again the rotten trick fate had played on him. He had been perfectly content as a family man, husband and father. Nothing had been of less interest to him than dating. And now, fifteen years after Doris had slipped a wedding ring on his finger, dating was far more complicated than it had been at nineteen. Baby-sitters and safe sex and who called whom were all a part of the mix now. It was too complicated to be fun anymore. Still, he didn't want to disappoint Vickie.

He walked back toward Heather's room, where the door was, as always, firmly closed. He hesitated. Then knocked.

Heather didn't answer, but just as he was ready to knock again, the door swung open. Heather leaned against the doorjamb.

"Well?"

Hank wondered if one of those books on living with teenagers would give him any clues about how to negotiate a truce with Heather. Maybe he would give it a try. Heather's insolence showed no signs of slacking. This could go on for years.

The thought made him want to run away from home.

"I wondered if there's any possibility of your making some changes in your plans tonight?" He knew before the words were even out that they were an invitation to exchange cross fire. "Maybe Meagan could come over here to study?"

"No way!" Heather's face was instantly sullen. "You knew I had plans tonight. I thought you had a baby-sitter."

"She canceled. If Meagan could come over here, you could keep an eye on Tammi and..."

"Daaad. Get real. You know what Tammi's like. The little twerp won't leave us alone for a minute. We'd never get any studying done."

"She'll be in bed an hour from now," Hank said. "I'll pay you for the baby-sitting."

She looked at him speculatively. Why was he doing this? he wondered. Why didn't he just tell her to stay home because he was the boss and that was that?

Hank sighed. Because he didn't do things that way. Heather had made her plans first and it wouldn't be fair for him to pull rank on her. That was no way to win her respect.

But how, he wondered, *did* he win her respect?

"How much?" Her eyes narrowed as he told her what he would pay. "No way! I can't have any fun on that kind of money."

Hank looked at his watch, knowing he had to make a decision right away. Damn! "Just this one night, Heather. I don't ask often."

A sly look came into Heather's eyes. "Hot date to-night, Dad?"

"Don't start, Heather." Despite the stern warning in his voice, Hank felt himself turning red. He had told himself for the past two years that a conversation about the facts of life was overdue for Heather, but he just hadn't been able to manage it. And these days, he suspected, he couldn't tell her much she didn't already know. With movies and TV and magazines and other kids, teenagers seemed to know it all today.

Hell, eight-year-old Tammi probably knew as much as he had known when he and Doris first met.

"Is she young?" Heather persisted mercilessly. "Think she'll put out?"

More blood rushed to Hank's face, this time in anger. "Can the garbage, Heather. Will you ask Meagan about coming over here or not?"

Heather tossed her head, sending the silver dragon in her ear dancing. "Not."

She turned and grabbed her house key and a fistful of bills from her dresser, crammed them into her jeans and shoved past him toward the front door. "I'm outta here."

"Hold your horses, young lady." Lord, he hated it when he lapsed into sounding like a parent. Life played cruel tricks sometimes. "I thought you were going to study."

She didn't turn back, just slouched in the hallway. "That's right."

"Where are your schoolbooks?"

Heather exhaled with a disgusted sigh. "In my locker. At school."

"How do you expect to study without them?"

"I'll manage, okay? Can I go now?"

"No, you may not." He walked around to face her. God, that stubborn jaw haunted him. He was certain she looked very much as he had when defying his own parents at her age. And where had it gotten him? No college, a hurry-up marriage with a baby six months later, a job with no prestige. He'd be damned if he would let the stubbornness Heather had inherited from him doom her to a life of few choices.

"I only agreed to let you go out tonight because you said you were going to Meagan's to study. Are you?"

"What difference does it make?"

"A big difference. Your grades are in the toilet, young lady. If you aren't planning to study tonight, that's what you should be doing. Maybe you need to change your plans after all."

"There's nothing wrong with my grades," she said belligerently. "I'm not flunking anything."

"You're too smart for the kind of grades you made on your last report card."

"I'm not smart," she said, her voice rising in anger. "I'm not some kind of study dweeb, okay? And I'm not going to stay here and pretend to cook the books just so you can go out and paw some female."

Stunned by her words, he stood stock-still while she dashed past him toward the door. Seconds ticked by before the realization penetrated that she was leaving.

"Don't you go out that door, young lady!"

She paused at the door, while Tammi turned wide eyes away from the TV set to take in the live drama playing out behind her.

"Try to stop me," Heather threatened, staring at him with venom in her eyes. "I don't have to waste my life looking after my bratty sister. And I don't have to take orders from you just so you can go out and fool around."

"You'll do whatever I tell you."

"I hate it here! I hate both of you!" Heather yanked the door open. "I wish I could go live with Grandma and Grandpa! Then I could get away from both of you!"

The door slammed behind her, rattling the framed pen-and-ink drawings of the two girls that hung on the narrow wall in the entryway.

Before Hank could start after Heather, Tammi dashed past him toward her room, sobbing heartbrokenly.

Helplessness rooted Hank to his spot in the middle of the sculptured carpet. He couldn't win. It just wasn't possible.

He thought with mild regret of Vickie Andersen, knowing he had excuses to make and not looking forward to making one more female miserable or angry or worse tonight. But, all in all, it was just as well. With the noises the old station wagon was making, he shouldn't be spending money on prime rib and wine tonight anyway. And he shouldn't be setting himself up for disappointment, either. What woman in her right mind would want to hook up with a man whose two daughters made daily life a battleground?

Hank gave his tie a yank. At least one good thing would come out of all this, he told himself as he shoved the tie into his pants pocket and searched through his wallet for the scrap of paper with Vickie's phone number. At least he wouldn't have to wear a blasted necktie all night.

CHAPTER FOUR

KATHERINE FINGERED the edges of a sensible cotton shirt as she added it to the neatly folded stack on the bed. That was her life, she thought as she packed for another week on the road. Sensible and well-ordered.

"Don't you get sick of all this travel?" Penny's long leg, shimmering in red, washable silk, was draped over the arm of an antique rocker. She was painstakingly peeling the paper away from each cigarette in a brand-new pack, one by one, and spilling the freed tobacco into an oriental-print pouch. "You were gone all week last week, too."

"I've always liked being on the road."

"Don't you get lonely?"

Katherine didn't take the time to reflect on the response that came to mind. She carried her loneliness with her, whether she was on the road or here at home. She smiled as she transferred neat stacks of clothes into her canvas bag.

"Of course not. I'm with people all day." She didn't glance up but noticed that Penny did. "What in the world are you doing to those cigarettes? In fact, what are you even doing with cigarettes? I thought you'd quit."

"Quitting. Not quit. Quitting. Big diff." Penny looked up from the growing pile of paper in her lap. "Anyway, I can't seem to stop buying the damn things.

I figure one habit at a time is enough to tackle. So I'm just working on not smoking them for right now. I'll worry about not buying them later."

Katherine laughed at her new friend's logic. "Makes sense. And in the meantime, you just..."

"Tear them up. Only now I'm saving the tobacco. Whenever I want a smoke, I ask myself which I'd rather smell like—the twenty-dollar-an-ounce stuff my son got me for Christmas last year or this stuff." She took an experimental whiff from the pouch and wrinkled her nose. "So far, it's working. Anyway, so you don't get lonely, huh? Haven't you ever wanted to start a family?"

Penny, Katherine reflected, was just like her clothes— uninhibited. She deflected the question with a quick smile. "I don't think I'm the family type."

"No? Not in the market for an adoring hubby and a couple of cute little rug-rats?"

Katherine's laugh was smooth and on cue. She congratulated herself and stuffed a pair of low-heeled dress shoes into the side pockets of her bag. "Nope. I love my job. Why in the world would I want to trade it in for diapers and teething rings?"

Why, indeed? For at least the tenth time during the past week, a pair of blue eyes floated in front of her face, their soft teasing turning to confusion and embarrassment. Why? they seemed to ask. Why?

"Haven't you ever been married?"

Swinging her packed bag off the bed and onto the floor, Katherine peered at her new friend, who was now toying with a book of matches she'd taken out of the patch pocket on the front of her flowing silk shirt. "What is this? The Spanish Inquisition?"

Penny grinned. "Something like that. Listen, you know everything about me. I just turned forty. I crave nicotine more than sex. I have a kid who's quickly driving me to a bottle of hair color—I found three more gray ones last week. Three! In one week. You know my greatest fantasy is having silicone implants. So, you owe me. The only thing shameful I know about you is that you grew up in Texas."

"That's only considered shameful if you grew up in Nebraska," Katherine countered, plopping down on the bed.

Penny suddenly sat up straight, planting both her suede tapestry shoes on the polished wood floor in front of her. "That's it! Why else would a Texan move to Nebraska? You're hiding from something, aren't you? A sordid episode in your life? I love it! Come on, fess up. You can trust Aunt Penny with your secrets."

Apprehension jolted through Katherine, until she reminded herself that Penny was just being her usual goofy self. She curled her legs up yoga-style and drew in a calming breath. "I'm caught. Even Texas wasn't big enough for me and my ex."

"I knew it. What did the snake do to you?"

Mustering her finely honed talent for sidestepping, Katherine said, "Jerry really wasn't the bad guy in the story. We were just . . . headed in different directions."

Penny looked dissatisfied and ready to launch into another question, so Katherine decided to beat her to it. "Didn't I hear something about a festival in the neighborhood next weekend?"

"If you didn't, I haven't done a very good job." Penny's narrowed eyes told Katherine the swift change in the conversation hadn't gone unnoticed. "I've been working with the neighborhood association on public-

ity for the Shakespeare Festival this year. That reminds
me, you're going to the next association meeting. You
have to get involved."

Only a few months into their friendship, Katherine
already recognized the futility of bucking that tone of
voice. She chuckled. "Is that an invitation?"

"No, it's a direct order. The association is full of
great people and we've done a lot for the neighborhood—tree plantings on Arbor Day, and we got a
drainage problem at the park fixed."

"And the Shakespeare Festival?"

"And the Shakespeare Festival," Penny affirmed.
"This is our third year for the festival. It's great. Everybody turns out and drinks hot cider and gossips—or
flirts, as the case may be—then settles down to watch
the theater students from Creighton University do
Shakespeare. We've got *Macbeth* this Saturday. Want
me to drop by and we'll walk over together?"

"Sure."

"But I promise, if you run into the hunk of your
dreams, I'll vanish into the night."

"I am not going to run into the hunk of my dreams."

"Don't be so sure. I saw him myself yesterday."

"Saw who?" The tips of Katherine's toes tingled; had
she really been sitting with bended knees for that long?
She shifted positions.

"Hank."

Now her fingers tingled, too. Her stern tone of voice
was as much for her own benefit as for Penny's. "Hank
is *not* the hunk of my dreams."

Penny smiled smugly. "Um-hmm. Don't be too sure.
I saw the way you two looked at each other. You can't
fool Aunt Penny."

"You are *not* my Aunt Penny. And Hank Weisbecker isn't the man of my dreams. He couldn't be. He's got..."

"He's got what? Blue eyes? Blond hair?" Penny let escape an exaggerated sigh. "Brawny arms?"

Katherine could envision Hank's attributes only too well. But he also had something far more significant than all his assets. He had an eight-year-old sidekick. "He's got... a receding hairline."

Penny snorted. "He does not. He has a high forehead. There's a difference, toots. Trust me."

"No, you trust me. I am not in the market for the hunk of my dreams. And if I were, it wouldn't be Hank."

PENNY WAVED as the Pekinese on the leash led her down the front steps. "Now don't worry about Baxter," she called back to Katherine from the softly lit sidewalk. "We're getting along great."

"Oh, I don't worry about him," Katherine said from the door. "I just worry it's too much trouble for you. Especially coming over to feed the birds, too."

"It's good for me. Some days that's the only break I take. Hazard of working at home, you know. I have to find an office grunt before somebody accuses me of being a workaholic." She grinned down at the dog, whose short legs scampered along the sidewalk. "Besides, Baxter is saving me from myself. Whenever I think it won't matter if just this once I smell like an ashtray, I walk Baxter instead."

After Katherine closed the door behind her, with the promise that she would be back in town by late Thursday afternoon, Penny walked along the short stretch of sidewalk between their houses. She wasn't fibbing about

Baxter. She enjoyed the company. And the distraction. This no-smoking business was for the birds.

The night was cool and crisp. Fall was no longer simply a promise. The red-and-white striped duster reaching almost to Penny's ankles felt good huddled around her narrow shoulders. She decided to take a quick walk around the block before going in for the night.

Katherine's a strange one, she thought. Clever and successful and cute in a way that always made Penny forget her new friend was over thirty, Katherine was interesting to be around.

But there was something else. Something Penny couldn't put her finger on. She'd only been half kidding when she'd accused Katherine of having something to hide. In spite of her girl-next-door face, Katherine Barnett didn't give of herself as openly as she appeared to.

There was one other thing, too. She never talked about family or friends. And nothing in her home reflected family. Her walls were lined with photos—most of them her own work—but none of them were of family. No mom or dad, brothers or sisters or nieces or nephews. No old home place. No childhood revisited, frozen in fuzzy shades of gray. It was almost as if Katherine existed in a vacuum. As if her life started and ended with her job.

And her pets, Penny reminded herself as Baxter yipped. She looked down at the pug-nosed dog, who was looking intently through the dark, his little body quivering. Penny followed the dog's gaze.

A group of teenagers was gathered on the next corner, lounging around the hood of a car. Penny realized now that they were loud and seemed more than a little out of control.

Although she didn't know them by name, Penny knew who they were. Dressed in fashionably shredded clothes and wearing hairstyles that defied gravity, they were trouble. Sons and daughters of some of the well-heeled professionals who'd settled in the neighborhood, they frequently destroyed the peaceful quiet of the streets with squealing tires and loud music, and they always gave Penny the anxious feeling that she should cross the street to avoid them in the dark.

Penny didn't know if they were serious trouble—drugs and drinking—or just rebellious trouble—outrageous clothes and insolent manners. But she didn't intend to find out tonight. She gave Baxter's leash a gentle tug and turned back in the direction of her house. The dog didn't move. He gave a low whine and sniffed in the direction of the young people.

Leaning over to pick up the dog, Penny kept her eye on the group. It was then she spotted what had captured the dog's attention: standing in the midst of the group was a girl with long, silky blond hair, a girl with a distinctive high forehead. Penny recognized her instantly and knew why Baxter was whimpering.

The girl was Hank Weisbecker's older daughter. She remembered now seeing Hank and the girl together at a block party last spring. But tonight she looked nothing like the timid adolescent who had trailed along with Hank and Tammi a few months ago. This girl was all brash smiles and arrogant posturing. Her skintight miniskirt and knit sweater were intended to reveal the angular curves that were just beginning to mark her metamorphosis from little girl to young woman. She was fighting hard to capture the spotlight in the group of older kids, that much Penny understood.

Dismay gnawed at Penny's stomach as one of the older boys put a possessive arm around the girl's waist. *How long will it be before Hank has real problems on his hands?* she wondered.

She turned and hurried home, suddenly shivering in the October breeze.

KATHERINE FOLLOWED the intoxicating aroma of mulled apple cider to a pushcart along the brick path near the entrance to the park. Penny had already disappeared, having run into a friend who was interested in a condo in the newly renovated hotel a few blocks away. Pleading insatiable greed and protesting that Shakespeare would understand if he were alive today, Penny had hurried away from the festival to give her friend a tour of the condo.

Cupping the warm cider in the curve of her palms, Katherine closed her eyes and dipped her nose near the scented surface. Cinnamon and warmth curled around her face. She smiled.

"Makes you forget you're in the middle of a big city, doesn't it?"

Without opening her eyes, Katherine knew the voice. Soft. Gentle. As intoxicatingly warm as the brew she held in her hands. She'd thought about Hank too much in the past few weeks to have forgotten his voice. Or his eyes. Or the touch of his work-roughened hand.

Her smile deepened. "It is a little reminiscent of home and hearth and the good old days," she admitted, remembering their earlier lapse into nostalgia. "Mulled cider. Autumn evenings. My favorites. We didn't get much autumn in Texas."

She turned toward his voice. She was unprepared for the shiver that welcomed his presence. She took a sip of her cider to hide the pleasure that rippled through her as she took him in. His soft blond hair fluttering in the breeze, ruffling over his forehead, leading her eyes to his. His blue-as-the-sky eyes crinkled at the edges as he gave her a grin that was as welcoming as the sudden swell of excitement in her heart.

The hunk of her dreams? Curse Penny's big mouth for putting dumb ideas in her head.

"My favorites, too. Reminds me of Halloween," he said, his eyes on hers as he sipped his own cider. "There was one old lady in town, she always invited kids inside for hot cider. With a sackful of candy to lug around the neighborhood on a cold night, that cider break was the high point of the evening."

"I thought you lived in the country?"

"We did. But we always went into town to trick-or-treat with our cousins. In those days, five or six blocks in McCook were good for a whole grocery sack full of penny candy."

"You had a great childhood, didn't you?"

His forehead creased in a frown. "Yeah. I was lucky." The crease disappeared. He was smiling again. "Walk with me?"

How could she say no? How could she have said no to him before, when he offered to show her around the neighborhood? She had wondered more than once during the past weeks if she hadn't been too hasty in rejecting his offer of friendship. Now she was sure of it.

"Unless..." He hesitated, his eyes taking on a guarded look. "Unless you're not walking around much these days."

Katherine winced. "I'm sorry, Hank. I . . . I didn't mean to be unkind." Or did she? She tried to remind herself of all the valid reasons she'd wanted to discourage Hank.

Hank looked down at her, his eyes assessing. He shrugged, then took her elbow to guide her in the direction of a fountain just as the lights were turned on for the evening. "Maybe I was moving too fast."

How could she let him take the blame? She searched for an excuse to explain her abrupt dismissal but could think of none before he spoke again.

"How do you like Omaha?"

She smiled apologetically. "I have to admit, I've been working so much I haven't had much chance to get out and about."

She paused to give him an opening. Saw him almost speak, then clamp his jaw shut. He wasn't going to take another chance. She couldn't say that she blamed him. It was up to her now to make the next overture. She, too, kept silent.

"Job keeps you pretty busy?"

She shrugged. "You know how it is." She didn't want to talk about her job. "Are you a Shakespeare fan?"

"I'd say I'm more a fan of the outdoors. Nothing wrong with old Bill, but I guess I'm just not very high-brow."

There was nothing lowbrow, however, about his softly modulated voice or the way he expressed himself. Hank was a man's man, that much was obvious. But he had just enough smooth edges. She smiled. "I have to admit, an outdoor stage in a park makes the Bard a lot more palatable than he ever was between the pages of a literature book in school."

"Being in the park, waiting for the sun to go down...that makes a lot of things...appealing." He reached for her empty cider cup as they passed a trash barrel. Their fingers didn't brush; Katherine was disappointed.

"Ah, but we're missing a porch swing." She knew her words were flirtatious the moment they were out and wondered what had prompted them. She remembered his comparison of porch swings and drive-in movies, with the undeniable connotation. In the language of their day, drive-in movies were for making out. She was grateful for the lowering sun and lengthening shadows. *Are you sure you know what you're doing?* she asked herself.

"You underestimate me," he said, taking the tips of her fingers in his hand and leading her to a quiet edge of the park, where the shadows were already deeper than anywhere else. A large wool blanket was spread on the grass, one of scores that dotted the dusky park as the neighborhood settled down to watch the play scheduled to begin soon.

But as she stood beside the dark blue patch of wool, the idea of settling onto the blanket with Hank seemed a clear-cut act of intimacy. One she wasn't sure she was equipped to handle.

He knelt on the blanket and, with a gentle tug on her fingers, urged her to join him. "Want to watch from here? Unless you're not watching much Shakespeare these days." A faint smile took the sting out of his words.

"You're not going to let me live that down, are you?"

His smile deepened, and even in the half light from the disappearing sun she could see the mischief in his eyes.

"No. A little guilt couldn't hurt the cause, could it?"

"What cause is that?" The words came out on uncertain breath.

His grip tightened on her hand and the mischief grew more pronounced in his eyes.

"Maybe I'd be smarter not to say."

Her soft laughter reached out to him in the night and, for the first time, she allowed her hand to curl around his. *You shouldn't do this,* she told herself.

It was the fantasy of leaning against his chest, feeling him warm against her back, having those strong fingers circle surely and deftly around her waist that caused Katherine to hesitate. Then, asking herself if she hadn't spent too much of the past six years hesitating, letting life pass her by, Katherine nodded. She dropped to her knees. Her face was on a level with his. She looked directly into his eyes. The straightforward attraction she saw there stirred a response in her.

She wondered if she still remembered how to signal a man that she wanted to be kissed. And made up her mind to practice that signal tonight. Until she got it right.

CHAPTER FIVE

THE WITCHES WERE stirring up toil and trouble on-stage and prognosticating dire things to come. Katherine was leaning back on one elbow, submerging herself in the hovering darkness and a tenuous contentment. She felt Hank's warmth at her side. They didn't touch, but she felt the connection.

Suddenly, a compact bundle of energy hurled itself onto the blanket, piercing the quiet contentment that surrounded her.

"Yo, Daddy, look at the witches! Way cool!"

Katherine shot to an erect position while Hank shushed the little girl with a good-natured stage whisper. "And they're going to come after you if you make any more noise. People are trying to hear the play, Scooter."

Tammi giggled. Her eyes landed on Katherine just as another figure sidled up to the blanket and sat on the front corner. Tammi turned to the teenaged girl, who hugged her knees fiercely. "Heather, look, it's Baxter's mother. Wow, this is radical."

Hank, doing his best to keep everyone's voices low, introduced Katherine to the teen. Heather. His other daughter.

The words crashed through Katherine's consciousness. Her ears rang with the words. Tammi. Heather. His daughters. Two of them. One of them young and bouncy and full of her father's mischief. The other half grown, tightly contained and determinedly aloof.

Without being aware of it, Katherine inched closer to her own edge of the blanket. The trees skirting the perimeter of the park began to sway as she studied the lithe, budding girl just a few feet away, nonchalantly peering around the blond ponytail that bounced over one ear. The young eyes were narrowed in distrustful speculation; the young mouth was straight and grim.

His daughter.

A warm young body snuggled against Katherine, clearly never questioning that the woman who shared her father's blanket would snuggle right back.

Tammi did her best to keep her voice low as she spoke. "How's Baxter?"

Katherine swallowed hard. "What?"

"Baxter. Does he miss me? I miss him."

"Baxter? Yes. Yes, he does miss you." Katherine knew what was expected of her but felt uncertain she could comply with convention. Hesitantly, she placed an arm around the shoulders nudged against her ribs. They felt unbelievably narrow. Frail and fragile and in need of protection.

Tammi nodded, her head bobbing against Katherine's breast. "I thought he might. Maybe I'll come see him soon."

"Shh!" The warning hiss came from Heather.

Tammi stuck her tongue out at her sister and lowered her voice. "Don'cha think I should? Come see him soon?"

Hank leaned close. His shoulder brushed against Katherine's arm as he whispered in his younger daughter's ear. "Don'cha think you should can the conversation for now?"

"Can I have some popcorn?" came the unconcerned reply.

"Later."

Tammi sat still for a few moments, sighing impatiently and leaning more heavily against Katherine. The young body smelled of bubble gum and baby shampoo. Katherine closed her eyes against a pain that was almost sweet in its intensity. Breath fluttered in the back of her throat, in a panic to escape. Katherine realized she had ceased to breathe. She exhaled as her hand, of its own will, closed around a tiny elbow.

An agonizing cramp seized her abdomen. She swallowed the gasp that came with the pain and turned her attention to the play. If she could concentrate on the play, forget the child beside her...

Pain gripped her again. She clutched the blanket with her free hand and ground her teeth together to keep the gasp from escaping.

It was happening again.

For one erratic moment, before the next cramp squeezed her middle, Katherine considered jumping up and running for home as fast as her rapidly weakening legs would carry her. By the time the cramp had come and gone, she had convinced herself that she wasn't ready to subject herself to that kind of embarrassment, either.

Get a grip, she told herself. *Breathe deeply. Slowly. Let your thoughts drift off to the tops of the trees. Go with the stars.*

Her back straightened. She crossed her legs in one of the classic yoga positions. She forced herself to pull away from what was happening on the blanket, to focus within her body. She imagined herself floating toward the sky, peaceful and calm and in control. There was no child beside her. Tammi belonged in someone else's life. Tammi didn't touch her life.

Gradually, the pain subsided.

HEATHER IGNORED the applause thundering through the park as the actors left the stage for intermission. Stretching her long legs out in front of her, she sneaked another sideways glance at the trio in the middle of the blanket as she plotted her getaway. A casual trip to the popcorn stand and she was out of here.

The woman acted funny. Kind of stiff and careful. Heather thought of the way she felt sometimes when she had to be with a bunch of her dad's aunts and uncles that she didn't really know. She always felt as if something were expected of her, but she didn't know what, and whatever she did probably wouldn't make them happy anyway. The woman looked as if she felt that way now.

But that didn't make sense. Grown-ups never felt that way. And who was there to worry about? Not Tammi, who was crawling all over this woman like she'd already been adopted into the family. Not her dad. She'd seen the look in his eyes when he said her name. Mushy. Like in the movies, when the guys were ready to jump someone's bones.

Heather tugged at a frayed thread at the knee of her jeans. She supposed that meant he'd be pulling some all-nighters soon. Blakely's mom did that a lot. Got all crazy over some guy and stayed out with him till morning. She'd asked Blakely once if she didn't get scared staying home all night alone. Blakely had just laughed. If her dad started doing that, Heather would just have to make up her mind not to be scared, too.

That wasn't going to be easy. Seemed like she'd been nothing but scared for a long time now. Ever since Mom... But it was worse now. Like all of a sudden she didn't know where she belonged and nobody would tell her. Like it was a big secret and everybody but her knew.

Mom would've told her.

She peered around at the woman, who was smiling stiffly at something Tammi was saying. Her lips looked ready to break.

Heather jumped up. "Gonna get some popcorn." She wheeled to go, but not before Tammi jumped up and started demanding popcorn, too. Under her breath, Heather muttered one of the words her dad had just forbidden her to use on pain of eternal grounding.

"Heather, why don't you take Tammi with you?" Her dad's words were less question than command. Heather recognized the tone and chafed against it.

"Dad..." She turned back, planning a protest. Nothing valid came to her. "I don't want her tagging along. What if I run into somebody I know?"

Tammi looked crestfallen. Heather told herself there was no reason to feel guilty. The little twerp was just doing it to get her way.

Hank pulled some money out of his pocket and held it up to her. "Take your sister. Now."

She glared at him. Then she turned and walked as fast as she could toward the popcorn stands. Let Tammi keep up if she could.

Why, she wondered as she stormed through the crowd, did he always make a big production out of stuff like this? He didn't seem to care, or even notice, that she had a whole new crowd of friends or that she stayed out later than anyone else in the ninth grade. Mom would've noticed. Mom would've had a fit. Mom would've told her she wasn't old enough to stop taking orders until she started paying her own way. But Dad . . . sometimes it almost seemed like he was as confused about stuff as she was.

Heather remembered the day she'd started her period. She'd heard so many kids at school talking about it that she'd been almost excited, waiting for it to happen. Like she would be a woman when it finally happened. But then it had happened and it hadn't been exciting at all.

"Dad, is this what it's supposed to be like?" she'd asked that afternoon about six months earlier. "It's not . . . I'm not sick or anything, am I? This is really the way it's supposed to be?"

He'd looked like he didn't quite know what to say as he handed her the sack from the drug store. He hadn't looked her in the eye. Heather had wondered if she was disappointing him. Maybe this really wasn't the way things were supposed to be.

"Sure, Heather." He almost never called her Heather. He'd always called her something goofy before that—Punkin or Doodlebug or something silly. Since that day, he'd only called her Heather. "Sure, this is just part of . . . growing up. That's all. Don't worry about it." He'd given her a stiff sideways hug, pulling her shoulder awkwardly against his side, then let her go quickly. Then he hadn't looked her in the eyes for days.

She still wondered, sometimes, if she'd done something wrong. Everything would've been better, she knew, if her mom had been around. She could've told her what was really supposed to happen. Another woman would know that.

The rigid features on the face of the woman her father had met shifted into focus. Somehow, she couldn't imagine that face helping her figure any of this out, either.

She felt a tug on her sweatshirt and looked down at Tammi. The little pest grinned a gap-toothed smile. Heather reached down and mussed her sister's hair, then looked around, hoping no one had seen.

"Can I have a drink, too, Heather?" The little girl shook her head to get the tousled hair out of her eyes. Her big, dark eyes were bright with a look Heather recognized. It was the one usually reserved for MTV heroes.

Uncomfortable contemplating what that look might mean from the shrimpy little sister she spent so much time putting down, Heather shrugged and gave Tammi a tug on the ear. "Sure, kid. Let's get in line."

HANK FIDGETED with the zipper on his windbreaker and studied Katherine's profile. He noticed the slight upward tilt to her nose, a strong chin, full lips accentuated by just enough overbite to make for interesting imperfection. Her soft brown hair, which he'd only seen in a ponytail until now, bounced around her shoulders and was topped by a gold knit beret. Probably lamb's wool. It looked almost as soft as her hair.

"You're awfully quiet." He hoped the kids would be gone through the entire intermission. Then he felt guilty for the thought. He turned to look over his shoulder, knowing they were safe in the neighborhood crowd and telling himself a mother would be worried anyway.

Looking disinclined to speak, Katherine nodded. She held her spine straight and she didn't turn in his direction.

"Sorry if the kids made it kind of tough to concentrate on the play." He tried slipping an inch or two closer without calling attention to the movement. Damn! He'd felt all kinds of fire between them earlier, but now...well, what did he expect? "Tammi's kind of a talker."

"No. Don't be silly." She turned to him with a bright smile. In the darkness he couldn't really tell, but something about the smile looked brittle. Or was it something about the way her voice sounded.

"You don't have any children, do you?" Hank suddenly realized how very little he knew about Katherine Barnett. She'd just moved into a huge house. She could have children who were staying with their father until the school term ended. Or she could share custody. Maybe it was only a trial separation. They could patch things up. No wonder...

"No. No children."

Hank was so panicked and preoccupied by the scenarios suddenly popping into his mind that it was a moment before her words sank in. But no children, he realized, didn't mean there wasn't someone. Someone waiting to move over from...where had that silly dog's tag said? Des Moines?

"You're not...engaged or anything, are you?"

The clipped laugh was definitely brittle. She had flattened a hand over her abdomen and seemed to press protectively. "No, Hank. Not engaged, either. Would you like my social security number? Dental records?"

He leaned over and took her chin in his hand and turned her face toward him. He was glad he had. He'd been ready to return her bristly words with a few of his own. But the insecure look in her eyes stopped him.

"Is there some reason you're a little touchy about this?" He smiled gently. "Or do I just aggravate you without even trying? I know I'm good at that. Ask Heather."

Her eyes were contrite. Hank dropped his hand to her shoulder, his gaze drawn to the lower lip caught between her teeth.

"I'm sorry, Hank. Again. It isn't you at all."

She hesitated and he wondered how out of line it would be if he smothered her apology with a kiss. He looked over his shoulder again. No kids in sight.

"I guess I still don't find it easy to talk about my divorce."

"Everybody's doing it," he quipped, hoping to change the serious mood that had settled over her. "Think how hopelessly out of the demographic mainstream you'd be if you were still married."

She laughed lightly and looked into his eyes with gratitude. "You're right."

"Besides," he whispered, leaning closer and wondering if he would actually be bold enough to steal the kiss he could almost taste. Cinnamon and softness. "I'm one of your more monogamous types and I'd have to leave right now if there were any chance this was adultery."

Her laugh was a husky breath from somewhere low in her chest. She seemed to teeter on the verge of leaning closer. He lowered his head.

"Yo, Daddy...oops!" Popcorn showered into his lap. "Daddy, we brought you and...what's your name again?"

Katherine's back snapped to attention. "Katherine. It's Katherine," she said, her voice both surprised and husky.

Tammi stumbled onto the blanket and plopped down between them. "We brought you and Katherine some popcorn. Butter flavored. It's real good. And I got a drink. But you can have a sip if you want it."

Despite his momentary frustration at the abrupt end to the romantic mood he'd been trying to foster, Hank couldn't help but smile at his blithely chattering daughter. He looked over at the corner of the blanket, where Heather had curled up with her own bag of popcorn. He reached over and gave her a pat on the shoulder.

"Thanks, Heather."

"Sure. No prob."

Heather kept her eyes trained on the stage, but her tone was less openly hostile than usual. He wondered fleetingly if Katherine knew anything about teenage girls. She must, he reasoned. She'd been one herself. Maybe if he got to know her, she could tell him about all the secret demons that were making Heather hell to live with right now. And he did want to get to know her—but not simply for the sake of having his own personal child psychologist.

By the time the play ended, Tammi was curled in a heap, head in his lap, sleeping. Heather stared up at the stars, either bored or preoccupied. Hank had tried, once, to slip his hand closer to Katherine, hoping to make contact. She had moved just as slightly herself— in the other direction—and he had worked hard to convince himself it was because she hadn't noticed his overture.

Katherine stood while Hank roused Tammi from her sleep.

"Why don't you let us walk you home?" Hank looked up at Katherine as Tammi rubbed her eyes and yawned.

Heather grunted impatiently.

"Oh, no," Katherine protested. "That's not necessary. You need to get your... little one... home to bed. I'll be fine."

He thought she sounded a little too eager to use the excuse. He stood, pulling Tammi slowly to her feet. When he and Tammi moved off the blanket, Heather yanked it from the ground and balled it up, hugging it to her chest.

Ignoring his older daughter's less-than-subtle hints that she was ready for this little scene to end, Hank tried to think of another opening. "Well, if you're sure. It's really no problem. Tammi'll be awake by the time we go a block and—"

"No." Katherine started backing away. "Really. I'm fine. I'll...uh...it was nice to meet you, Heather."

The stilted words hung in the darkness for too long before Heather answered. "Yeah. You, too."

Hank wondered for the moment about the feasibility of giving a fourteen-year-old a whack on the backside. Too noisy, he decided. Besides, she'd probably get the better of him. When he looked again in Katherine's direction, she had backed off several yards and was about to turn away from them.

"I'll see you later?" It should have been a statement, he realized. But he knew instinctively that he had reasons for turning it into a question.

Katherine paused for a moment and looked ready to speak. Then she raised her hand in a silent wave, turned and was gone.

And he'd been so sure this time. Hadn't she moved that extra inch closer to signal that she was as ready for a kiss as he had been? She had, hadn't she? That hadn't been his imagination, had it? Maybe he'd been lucky to be interrupted by a lapful of popcorn. Maybe it had saved him from humiliating himself.

"Well, you certainly swept her off her feet," Heather purred as Hank watched the petite figure retreating in the opposite direction.

Hank gave a self-deprecating smile his best shot and put his hand on Tammi's shoulder to propel her out of the park. "Yeah, I guess I did, didn't I? A regular Prince Charming, that's me."

"She's pretty." Tammi's words trailed off into another yawn.

"You're right, Scooter. She is."

"Not *that* pretty," Heather protested.

"Yes, she is." Tammi's sleepy voice was petulant. "And she's got a nice dog, too."

"Big deal," Heather snapped. "What does that prove?"

"Does she have any little girls, Daddy?"

"Nope."

The girls were silent for a moment. Hank hoped the opening forays had died without escalating into warfare.

Tammi skipped a couple of steps ahead, then turned back and faced them while she continued to skip backward. "Maybe she needs some little girls, then. Do you suppose, Daddy?"

Heather groaned, and Hank barely caught himself before he did likewise. "That's kind of hard to say, Scooter."

"I'll bet she does. And we need a mommy. Do you think she could be our mommy?"

"Scooter, I don't think—"

Heather's sharp voice interrupted him. "We don't need a new mother. And if we did, it wouldn't be her."

"Now, wait a minute," Hank said as they entered their building. "Aren't you a little out of line?"

"She's not the type," Heather said flippantly. "Too snooty. Anybody could tell she doesn't like kids."

Hank started to disagree, then wondered if maybe his daughter was more perceptive than he had been. Katherine hadn't exactly been enthusiastic about interacting with either of the girls. Not even Tammi, whose effervescence could ensnare anybody's heart. He held the elevator open.

"But that's okay, Dad. She'll probably be good for a couple of overnighters and—"

"That's enough of that." Hank stopped himself just before calling her "young lady" in that supercilious "I'm the daddy and you're the kid" tone he'd always hated at her age. Why was it the only things he seemed to remember from his own mother's actions were the ones that hadn't worked?

"What's an overnighter, Daddy?" Tammi pushed the button for their floor as they stepped onto the elevator.

Heather snickered; Hank glared. "Never mind, Scooter."

"I know what that means. That means you'll tell me when I'm old enough to understand. Right?"

"It's just the truth, Dad," Heather prodded. "I understand. Even men your age need a little—"

"If you don't close your mouth right now," he said with quiet threat, "I'll see to it that your life isn't fit to live for the next month."

"Does that mean you'll spank her, Daddy?" Tammi was incredulous. "You never spank us, Daddy. You wouldn't really spank her, would you?"

Seeing the smugness in Heather's eyes as they exited the elevator, Hank knew he'd lost again.

By the time Tammi was tucked in for the night and Heather was attached to her stereo by a pair of headphones, the magic of the evening had vanished. Rummaging through the refrigerator for a stray can of beer, Hank found only a small carton of fruit juice in a flavor only a youngster could love. He pulled it out, along with a jar of olives, and wandered out to the living room. He tuned the TV to one of the bad science fiction movies that had been his adolescent passion and settled down into the sagging cushion of an armchair.

Images of that evening kept intruding on the grainy black-and-white fantasy flickering on the eighteen-inch screen. Moonlight glistening off golden brown hair. Eyes that had teased, then sobered, then grew veiled and impenetrable. Katherine. Her essence wasn't in the soft, uncomplicated fragrance that floated off her skin and hair or even in the gentle drawl hovering around the edges of her voice. It wasn't even in her smile. No, the essence of Katherine was in her eyes. Those changing, haunting eyes so full of secrets.

He wanted what was behind them.

Hank peeled the small plastic straw off the side of the juice carton and took a short sip. Making a face, he popped a couple of olives into his mouth to kill the syrupy flavor.

Whatever was behind those eyes, Hank had a hunch it wasn't for him to find. That was one message Katherine Barnett was projecting loud and clear. At least, most of the time.

As the couple on TV engaged in a sterile, 1950s screen kiss, Hank was reminded of the long seconds when his lips had hesitated so close to hers. The message in her eyes hadn't been equivocal then. It had been clear and strong and the perfect match for the message his own body had been sending him.

Damn women to hell and back, he thought, swallowing most of the juice in a long, irritated swallow. *Why can't they give it to you straight? What's the point in all this damned game-playing?*

"Well, I'll be damned if I'm going to stroke her ego by chasing after her," he muttered under his breath as he stabbed another olive.

He made up his mind to concentrate on the movie. The aliens had now captured the only man with the knowledge to stop their plan to rule the earth. The woman was sobbing uncontrollably. She would be absolutely no use in stalling the steady onslaught of the aliens or in helping to free the slickly good-looking scientist who held the key to survival for the human race. In a 1954 sci-fi flick, that much was a foregone conclusion. She would cry prettily, but somebody else would have to save the day.

Finishing off the last of the juice and olives, Hank took the two empty containers back into the kitchen and dropped them into the overflowing trash can. He admonished himself once again that he was going to have to do something about his housekeeping skills. As a housedad, he was as useless as the little airhead on TV.

How, he asked himself, *can you expect Heather to learn any better with you for an example?*

By the time he had emptied the trash and settled back down in front of the TV, the airhead blond was sneaking onto the alien spaceship, pencil-thin skirt and all, carrying the ray gun her scientist sweetheart had been unable to perfect. Within five minutes they were watching the spaceship retreat into the sky as she explained how she had figured out the snag that had been stumping him, assembled the ray gun and made her way out to the spaceship.

Damn women! Hank thought in irritation as he pointed the remote control at the set and started looking for another suitably mindless movie. *Just when you think you've got them figured out, they throw a curve at you.*

He found a country music concert on public television, but the music didn't hold his interest. His attention kept straying to the telephone. *Maybe,* he thought, *you aren't so smart after all. Maybe you haven't got it all figured out. Maybe you're not so hot at reading signals. And maybe if you don't call this Katherine Barnett, you'll never get any peace.*

Hank tried to convince himself that wasn't why he stood up and crossed the room. He told himself he was actually on his way to the kitchen to forage for another, more satisfying snack. But he stopped by the telephone. He stared at it. He reached out and put his hand on the receiver.

What are you waiting for? he asked himself irritably. *Some kind of divine message? Pick up the damned phone and get it over with.*

He called directory assistance for the new listing. There were three K. Barnetts. He was glad he knew her address. He listened as the phone rang, surprised to discover that the pounding of his heart was louder in his ears than the trill of her phone.

Her voice, answering on the fourth ring, was reserved and controlled. He could see her again, sitting cross-legged and straight-backed on the blanket, Tammi curled against her side.

"But hark, what light through yonder window breaks?" he said as he leaned against the door frame. "It is the east, and Katherine is the sun."

She laughed softly. "Wrong play. How about 'Double, double, toil and trouble'?"

"No, no," he protested. "Not nearly romantic enough."

Silence. No response from the inscrutable Ms. Barnett. He remembered the guarded look in her eyes. He wanted, for a moment, to hang up the phone and forget it. Did he really need this kind of grief? As he contemplated hanging up, he also remembered the cinnamon-and-apple kiss that had been his for the taking.

I'm not going to miss it again, he vowed.

"After all," he started, "you'd hardly expect me to woo you into agreeing to a night of moonlight and roses with 'Out, out, damned spot,' would you?"

The split second of silence told him she was still reticent. "No, I suppose not."

"Well, how about it? Up for a little moonlight and roses? Or candlelight and wine? Fluorescents and beer? I'm easy. Whatever sounds good to you." Why was he always so nervous about this stuff that he ended up babbling on like a fool? "What I'm trying to say is, I'd like to take you out next week. Maybe Friday. How about it?"

He didn't need the witches of *Macbeth* to interpret the long silence that followed. Before she even spoke, Hank felt himself turning red.

"I'm flattered that you ask, Hank. But I'm going to be out of town. I travel a lot. Business, you know."

Hank didn't even bother to try to convince her that he could wait until she was back in town. After awkward pleasantries, they hung up. Hank stared at the phone. Damn women!

Reaching into his pocket, Hank pulled out a scrap of paper and picked up the telephone again. He dialed. The voice that answered was young and a little timid. Something about the voice fueled the frustration in him, but he tried to hide it when he spoke.

"Vickie. This is Hank Weisbecker. I was wondering if you'd give me a chance to make it up to you for that date I had to break a few weeks ago."

Her eager acceptance didn't do nearly as much to soothe Hank's bruised ego as he'd hoped it would.

CHAPTER SIX

KATHERINE POINTED the lens at the heavy, jewel-encrusted garment and adjusted the f-stop on the camera to accommodate the low lighting in the gallery.

"Might know you'd get a shot of that."

Clenching her teeth at the sardonic voice near her shoulder, Katherine pretended she hadn't heard.

"I said—"

"I heard you, Kent." She shifted positions for a different angle on the ancient Egyptian chastity belt, part of a priceless exhibit from the pyramid of a young princess of the Nile. The exhibit was now in Memphis, but the magazine had sent Katherine and Kent Oranski to preview the exhibit before its Kansas City showing.

Under other circumstances, Katherine would have enjoyed the chance to visit Memphis. But she was going to have to speak to her editor about his choice of traveling companions. Kent was a great writer, but his idea of a successful business trip was a story that could be written between conquests. In all other ways, Kent was a tolerable colleague. He was simply ruled by his testosterone level. This week, Kent seemed to be producing record-breaking amounts of the hormone.

"Is that your secret, Katherine the Cold?"

She lowered the camera and looked up into his grinning face. He seemed so oblivious to how obnoxious his come-ons were that it was almost impossible to stay angry with him. He was like a puppy who hadn't yet learned that it was unacceptable to leave puddles on the living room carpet.

"That's it, isn't it?" His expression changed to teasing concern as he draped an arm over her shoulder. "You're the victim of a cruel plan to keep you pure until your knight errant shows up and..."

She shrugged out from under his arm and moved beyond his reach, already focusing her attention on the display of beauty secrets used centuries earlier by the Egyptian princess.

"Kent," she said firmly, interrupting his prattle while switching lenses on her camera. "I am not a damsel in distress. And you are most certainly not my knight errant. So rattle your saber elsewhere and let me finish my job."

Kent laughed. "That's quite a tower you're in, Katherine. Doesn't it ever get lonely up there?"

She clicked off a series of shots. She hadn't realized, when she'd taken up photography, how wonderful the camera could be to hide behind.

Or had she?

Her voice was cool and even as she looked past Kent in search of a better angle from which to photograph the jewelry case. "Find yourself another tower to rush, Oranski. I'm not in need of rescue."

He shrugged and reached over to tweak her nose. "That's what you say."

"And if I were..."

Kent held up his hands and backed away. "I know, I know. If you were, I wouldn't be first on the list when you cast the role of Prince Charming."

Katherine smiled. "And they say the only things you can remember are telephone numbers and certain vital statistics."

"See? I've been much maligned. Now, if you want to get to know the real—"

"I *do* know the real Kent Oranski. And I only trust him in broad daylight with both hands in plain view. Now go. I've got work to do. Why don't you hit on that cute museum tour guide and let me get this shoot wrapped up?"

"She was cute, wasn't she?" Kent shoved a reporter's notebook into his back pants pocket, straightened his tie and ran a hand over his carefully moussed hair. "Bet she'd be a big help with my story, wouldn't she?"

"Thank goodness," Katherine murmured as he retreated in search of damsels more susceptible to his rescue techniques. Kent never seemed to tire of making futile passes at her; she wondered, sometimes, what it would take to convince him that no meant no.

It wasn't that she automatically turned men down. Goodness knows, after she'd finally adjusted her thinking and made up her mind that all men weren't like Jerry, she'd tried to get on with her life. And that meant, in addition to pursuing her career with a fervor that none of her old friends or family understood, reintroducing herself to the opposite sex.

During the years she'd lived in Des Moines, she'd met a number of men who had been interesting and fun to be around. But she'd learned quickly that it was hard to find a man who fitted her lifestyle. Invariably, it seemed, they were fathers already, looking for someone to assume the role of part-time stepmother, or they wanted to settle down to the old-fashioned values of hearth and home. And children.

Men with children. They either had them or they wanted them. And if she'd still wanted children in her life, it wasn't a viable option as far as Katherine was concerned. She couldn't have her own. And with her anxiety attacks finally under control, she didn't need anything to upset her hard-won equilibrium.

Only one man had been special enough to make Katherine question her adamant refusal to allow children into her life. Buddy had been a sweetheart, a teddy bear in the body of a burly high school football coach. They had met when his team broke every state high school football record in Iowa, making him good magazine material.

As she had captured him on film during practice, at a championship game and in the quiet of his home, Katherine had been convinced that Buddy might be different. So convinced that when he asked her to meet his little boy and spend the weekend with them, Katherine had said yes. Not without apprehension, of course. But she'd felt, somehow, that Buddy and his son were the answer to something in herself that still felt empty. Maybe, she'd told herself, she had been wrong all those years when she'd been so sure that she didn't want children in her life. Wasn't she in control again? So she'd said yes.

They'd started the day at the zoo. The boy, a tiny, round-eyed version of his husky dad, had been one of the cutest things she'd ever seen. But the moment Katherine picked him up, she'd known she was in over her head.

In less time than it takes a toddler to drop an ice-cream cone on a clean T-shirt, Katherine had fallen apart. Trembling, her insides constricting in pain, she had been gripped by the beginnings of her first anxiety attack in years.

She had controlled herself, but only by erecting an unbridgeable emotional barrier between herself and Buddy's three-year-old son. No one but Katherine knew what had almost happened. But the trip to the zoo was a short one anyway, with Buddy growing more confused as Katherine grew more distant.

"I thought you two would like each other," Buddy had said stiffly when he walked her back to her front door. "Most people like the little guy. I'm sorry you didn't."

"It isn't that, Buddy." Her words had come out in a breathless rush as she kept her eyes averted from the car, where the small boy was strapped into his car seat. "It's nothing personal."

"Nothing personal?" Buddy's voice had been soft but incredulous. "How can you say it's nothing personal when it was obvious you didn't even want to get near my son today?"

"I did. I did want to be near him. It's just..." Katherine had cringed at the hurt in his eyes. How to explain the unexplainable? Sometimes she was convinced that only those who had been through the dehumanizing experiences that went with infertility could understand. Buddy had seemed to understand, when she told him. But then he looked hurt and defensive.

"But he's not yours, right? So maybe he's not good enough. Right?"

"No, Buddy. It's just that being around children is...it's become pretty traumatic for me." Her mouth had been dry, her palms damp. *Why is this happening,* she'd wondered, *the one time I try to be normal again?* "Finding out you can't have children makes you feel...not quite human. Like something's been left out. Like there's a hole where something..."

When she stole a look at Buddy's face, Katherine had realized that attempts to explain were futile. The painful words died on her lips.

"Right." He had taken a step backward, the look in his eyes still defensive. "I guess it's just not a good idea for you to be around children. Sorry I put you through this."

Looking around the gallery for her next shot, Katherine rewound a roll of film and pulled out a fresh roll. *What is it,* she wondered, *that keeps pulling me toward men who can't possibly fit into my life?*

Men like Hank Weisbecker—a man with not just one daughter, but two. A man who hadn't already learned the hard way that Katherine Barnett and children didn't mix. She shuddered when she thought of how close she'd come to repeating her fiasco with Buddy's son when Hank's daughters had settled down on the blanket with them at the Shakespeare festival Saturday night. If it hadn't been for the mind-and-body control techniques she had learned through yoga, she would have made a fool of herself all over again.

And there was no guarantee it wouldn't happen the next time.

When Hank had called later that same night, Katherine had almost wished he could see firsthand why she couldn't give in to her attraction for him. Once he saw how his daughters really affected her, a man like Hank wouldn't be calling again.

LETTING HER CAMERA BAG slide into the hotel room chair, Katherine used both hands to massage the tension out of her neck and shoulders. First, a quick, hot shower. Then she would be refreshed enough to run out and grab a quick salad somewhere, plump up the pillows on the king-sized hotel bed and read the horror novel she had picked up at the airport.

Adjusting the water in the shower until it was as hot as she could stand it, Katherine steamed the remaining tension out of her shoulders. Revived, she toweled off and slipped on a denim skirt and cotton sweater. As she towel-dried her hair, the telephone rang.

She didn't recognize the stranger's voice at the other end. "Ms. Barnett, I'm sorry to bother you at the end of a long day. But your editor told me how to reach you. I'm Bill Kowalski with the University of Nebraska Press. We thought you'd want to know that we've got the go-ahead for your photo book on Midwestern workers."

The towel dropped out of Katherine's hand. "You're kidding!"

The laugh on the other end was friendly and pleased. "Not at all. We're really quite excited about the project and can't wait to discuss it in more detail."

Katherine listened, half dazed, as the University Press editor outlined the details of the contract. The advance wouldn't make her rich, and neither would the sales, but it was another feather in her cap. Another indication that her life had borne the fruit of accomplishment. A book of her photography, with narrative by one of the foremost poets in the region.

Making notes on the pad beside the telephone, Katherine found it hard to keep a check on her soaring emotions.

After hanging up, she could hardly contain her happiness. *This calls for champagne,* she told herself, whirling in a circle and clapping her hands. Dashing to the mirror, she pulled her hair back in a ponytail and looked in bemusement at the clothes she wore. Denim and cotton. Not exactly celebration clothes.

Hands trembling, Katherine considered calling Kent and offering to take him to dinner. Not a good idea, she warned herself. But she had to share her exciting news with someone.

Snapping her fingers in sudden inspiration, Katherine went back to the phone and dialed. Her heart pounded as she listened to the ring of the phone hundreds of miles away. A soft, familiar drawl answered. Katherine took a deep breath.

"Mother? It's me. Katherine."

"Katie!" The surprise and pleasure in her mother's voice gave Katherine a pang of guilt.

"Katie, how good to hear from you! Where are you, honey?"

"In Memphis, Mother. Working on a shoot for the magazine. Mother, I—"

"That's too bad, honey. That job doesn't leave you much time to enjoy yourself, does it? You've hardly been at home to enjoy your new house, have you? Are you getting all settled in? I was telling your father last night that I should pull some of those curtains out of the attic, just in case..."

Anyone who thought all Southerners spoke like molasses in January had never had a conversation with Eudelle Barnett. Katherine jumped into the brief pause. "Thanks, Mother, but I really don't need the curtains. I called with some news."

"You did? Oh, honey, that reminds me. We've got some good news, too. I've been meaning to call, but I never know when you're home. Seems like I always get that machine. You haven't talked to Frankie and Barb, have you?''

Katherine saw no point in telling her mother that she hadn't talked to her brother and his wife since Christmas. Family was still important to the Barnetts of Sylvester, Texas. But for Katherine, work had replaced those sentimental ties.

''Well, we're all so excited. They're expecting again. And we just know it's going to be a girl this time. After three boys, it's just got to be a girl, don't you think? I'm getting tired of waiting for a granddaughter. Those brothers of yours needn't think they can get away with nothing but sons.''

Eudelle laughed and the sound conjured for Katherine an instant picture of her mother's face—a face that was so much like her own.

''I've already been shopping for pink, that's how sure I am. And Barb's doctor said...''

Katherine sat on the edge of the bed and let her mother prattle on. She tuned out the words. Soon, she thought, she'll slow down long enough for me to give her *my* news.

Fiddling with the edge of the notepad, Katherine let her eyes scan the details she'd scrawled on the small, square sheet—details that had seemed earthshakingly significant just moments before. Now, her enthusiasm for the project that had been so lovingly conceived was beginning to fizzle.

''...Gone on so long, I forgot you had some news for us. What is it, Katie?''

The anticipation in her mother's voice told Katherine that what she had to say would fall short of her family's expectations. They had waited for years for news of remarriage. She knew that her fast rise in her profession hadn't been a suitable substitute, even though no one had spoken the words.

"Oh. Well, it's nothing much, Mother." Katherine turned the pad facedown. "I'm just going to do a photo book for a university press. Nothing—"

"A photo book?" Katherine could hear the lack of comprehension in her mother's voice. "Well, that's nice, dear. Your dad will be real proud, I know."

"Thanks, Mother. But...listen, just tell Frankie and Barb that I'm..." The words almost choked her. "Tell them I'm real glad for them. I'll be pulling for a girl."

Hanging up, Katherine caught another glimpse of herself in the mirror. Now, the dull denim and the bland cotton sweater matched her mood perfectly. All thought of celebration was ludicrous. After all, what did she really have to celebrate? Another sterile achievement.

Hearing once again her mother's unenthusiastic response to the accomplishment that had seemed so stellar just moments before, Katherine turned away from the mirror. What, she wondered bitterly, was the big deal about fertilizing another seed and having it grow into another crying, red-faced baby? People did that every day.

Some people did that every day, she reminded herself. Others had to settle for developing film.

Suddenly angry with herself, Katherine whirled back to face the mirror. Fists clenched, she confronted the face, splotchy with controlled anger.

"You're not settling for anything!" she cried. "You've got what you want out of life. You didn't just do what the world expects of you. You got to make better choices!"

The face in the mirror stared at her, blurred by tears that Katherine blinked back in angry determination.

Struck by the futility of convincing her unhappy reflection, she turned away once again.

No longer hungry, Katherine took off her clothes, hung them neatly and put on a worn gray sweat suit. She pushed aside a small table and chair to clear a spot on the orange carpet and settled down. Legs bent, arms relaxed, back straight, she breathed deeply. Every soothing breath settled into the emptiness at the core of her being. When the breath had filled the hollowness at her core, it spread outward, taking the emptiness with it. It seeped slowly into her muscles, into her lungs, into her heart, into every tiny recess where the emptiness hadn't been before.

Soon, the emptiness was no longer a small knot at the core of her being. Soon, it was everywhere.

SOME MISTAKES, Hank thought as he checked his watch, *you live with forever.*

Tammi, her bare toes peeking out of the wool blanket in which she'd enshrouded herself, huddled on the couch watching MTV. The smell of mentholated medication and cherry-flavored cough syrup emanated from that part of the room, as it had for the past week. Hank had quickly discovered how much he preferred an eight-hour day of sweating and straining to a twenty-four-hour day of nursing an eight-year-old with the flu.

What he hadn't realized was that it would get even worse once Tammi was well enough to be restless but not well enough to go back to school.

"You're going to sleep in one hour, right?" Hank reminded Tammi as he tucked the blanket around her toes again. "No whining?"

Tammi's eyes widened in a look of innocence Hank didn't trust for one second. "No whining, Daddy. I promise."

Hank checked his watch again. Where the hell was Heather? She'd promised to be back from the mall in plenty of time for him to pick up Vickie Andersen for their date. Hank frowned and squirmed against the discomfort of his necktie. He almost preferred the thought of sitting home with the kids tonight to the thought of his blind date.

Ten minutes later, just as Hank had decided he would have to cancel on Vickie once again, Heather sauntered in. Hank took one look at her, and every bit of frustration he'd just been feeling exploded into unreasonable anger.

"What do you think you've done to yourself?" he demanded, taking in the bright colors rimming her eyes and the unnatural shade of raspberry that flamed on her lips and cheeks.

"Whaddya mean?" She did a creditable imitation of the innocent look Tammi had favored him with earlier.

"All that makeup. What are you doing with all that stuff on your face?" Her bored shrug served only to turn up his anger another notch. "You've got enough stuff on your face to keep the Miss America pageant supplied for the next year!"

Heather rolled her eyes in exaggerated boredom and shrugged past him on her way to her room.

"I want you to wash your face right now. And don't you ever go out of this house looking like that."

Before entering her bedroom, Heather turned back and smiled at him, a smile that held no humor. "What planet do you live on these days? You don't have a clue what's going on in this world, did you know that?"

TWO HOURS LATER, Hank had to agree with his older daughter's assessment.

Two hours later, he wondered if he wouldn't have had a better chance carrying on a conversation with his older daughter than he was having with Vickie Andersen.

His fantasy of a robust, wholesome farm girl had disappeared the moment Vickie opened the front door at her Uncle Jessie's. Tall and blond she was. But that's where reality and fantasy parted ways.

The real Vickie was all funky sophistication, like something out of a fashion magazine. Blond hair tumbled wildly to her shoulders, tucked over her ear on one side by an oversized turquoise-and-blue plastic fish. Matching earrings dangled almost to her shoulders. They were large enough to win the crappie tournament back home most years, thought Hank.

Her dress was some kind of stretchy stuff, he supposed. Turquoise with glittery silver threads all through it. It was about the size of a respectable T-shirt, which meant that it left plenty of long leg in plain view. And it was cut low in front and back. Hank had more than a few uncomfortable moments pondering what kind of undergarments permitted such lavish exposure of flesh in front and back. The only obvious solution made his discomfort even more acute.

"I'd love moving to Omaha just for the concerts," she was saying as she tackled the grilled mahimahi on her plate. One of the swankest steak houses in Omaha, and she had ordered seafood. Seafood with some kind of fancy name, at that. "You get some wonderful acts here. Some of the best in the business."

Hank dragged his attention back to the conversation as she ticked off the names of musicians he didn't even recognize. New-age jazz or something, he supposed. "Umm, yeah, that's true."

"I came up last year for a couple of concerts," she said. "What have you been to lately?"

"Me?" Hank felt certain everyone in the restaurant was looking at him and wondering what he was doing with such an uptown dish. Jessie hadn't told him she looked like a cover girl. Or that she acted like one. "I...I don't go to many concerts."

A forkful of rice pilaf paused on the way to her lips as she contemplated that answer. "Oh. Well, you can get such great sound on CDs these days that lots of folks would rather listen at home. Right?"

Hank saw no point in telling her he didn't have a CD player either. In fact, he saw no point in continuing the evening. As soon as he could do so without appearing rude, he planned to pay the tab and deposit the sleek Vickie Andersen back at her Uncle Jessie's front door. This conversation about music was only the latest of many futile attempts to converse.

First, he'd tried to talk about family. Hers bored her. They were more interested in freezing corn and canning tomatoes from the summer's garden than they were in her career aspirations—she was vitally interested in investment banking. "You wouldn't recognize me in my pinstripe suit," she'd said with a wry wink.

Hank was certain she was right about that.

Next, he'd ventured into her years at the University of Nebraska, knowing that Cornhusker football was always fertile conversational ground. Vickie's disdain of the barbaric sport—"It's amazing to me that we're still willing to undermine the male mentality while we continue to glorify the myth of the macho male" —had been fascinating. But it had made Hank wonder why she had agreed to a blind date with a man who worked with his hands.

As Hank did his best to discourage lingering over coffee and dessert, his thoughts drifted back to the last woman he'd talked to like this.

Katherine. Katherine, who had understood when he'd blathered on about living in the country. Katherine, who had even seemed to appreciate the work he did. She'd said she might use him in a book, hadn't she? Katherine, who had savored the flavor of spiced cider and cool autumn evenings.

"You like apple cider?" Hank didn't realize until he had spoken that he'd interrupted Vickie in the middle of her treatise on the effects of AIDS on small-town society.

"What?"

"Apple cider. Hot. With spices in it?"

She smiled patiently. "Yes, it's okay. Did you want some?"

Hank shook his head and slipped a casual glance at his watch. With any luck, he could be home in time to catch the last quarter in the replay of the Nebraska-UCLA game on the sports channel.

And try not to wonder if he would ever figure out women.

CHAPTER SEVEN

KATHERINE PAUSED halfway down the long table laden with casserole dishes and platters of food. Her plate was already full, and she could still see a mine field of baked macaroni and cheese, savoury goulash and homemade yeast rolls waiting to ambush her as she made her way to the iced tea.

"I've got to get out of here," she whispered to Penny. "You didn't tell me this was the neighborhood association for the terminally overfed."

Penny laughed as she scooped up a spoonful of red cabbage. "Enjoy. You can fast tomorrow. You can't tell me you get a chance to eat this well very often when you spend so much time on the road."

The memory of the fish fillet sandwich and salty fries she'd picked up at a drive-thru window for her dinner the night before flashed before Katherine's eyes. She reached for a yeast roll and perched it on top of kielbasa and peppers.

"Hope you haven't filled up," Penny said a few moments later as they balanced their plates on their knees. "I've just spotted the yummiest thing in the whole room."

"Don't tempt me." Katherine's eyes followed the direction of Penny's gaze. Her knees quivered in response; she barely caught her plastic plate before it slid off her lap. It was Hank. She narrowed her eyes at her friend's suggestive smile. "Cute, Penny. Very cute."

"Uh-huh." Penny nodded her head. "Much more than cute. Definitely yummy. What say we take a poll? I'll bet that 83.5 percent of the women here will agree that Hank Weisbecker is the yummiest thing in this room, coconut cream pie notwithstanding."

"The same percentage will agree that you're a big buttinski," Katherine said, pleased with how well she was playing the part of disinterested bystander. And it wasn't easy—the way Hank Weisbecker looked in a blue plaid shirt, yellow suspenders and a pair of slim-fitting cords should be outlawed. Or rated R, at the very least, and banned from neighborhood meetings.

Katherine kept quiet. She knew she wouldn't stand a chance against Penny's persistence if her neighbor knew that hardly a day had passed when she hadn't thought of Hank. She'd even caught herself trying to structure arguments in favor of a relationship with a weekend father.

"And you're a chicken," Penny countered, suddenly snapping her fingers. "Come on. I've just had a great idea. If you're so immune to his blond hair and blue eyes, come with me while I talk to Hank."

"You go ahead. I'm still eating."

As Penny crossed the junior high gymnasium, Katherine tried to start up a conversation with a woman sitting in the folding chair beside her. Fortunately, the woman was a chatterer and barely noticed that Katherine's attention was elsewhere.

Out of the corner of her eyes, she saw Penny and Hank talking. Smiling. For a moment, Katherine felt a twinge of pique at her neighbor. *If she's so eager for me to fall for Hank, what's she doing flirting with him?* she wondered.

Well, a man like Hank is the last thing on my mind right now, she told herself as she got up to throw away her plate. *Or at least, the last thing that should be on my mind.*

She had to get busy on her photo book. She had to call the poet to confirm all the details. Then she had to start scheduling all the photos she had outlined in the book proposal. There was the rodeo manager in Burwell, the irrigation expert in Loup City, the cattlemen in Nebraska who still held an old-fashioned roundup every year and the cooperative of women laborers in Oklahoma, who did everything from plumbing to painting.

She had plenty to keep her busy without wasting energy thinking about a man who didn't fit into her lifestyle. Why, then, had she done just that?

Penny returned a few minutes later, uncharacteristically quiet but sporting a Cheshire cat smile. Refusing to take part in whatever little game Penny was playing, Katherine said nothing about Hank.

"Come on," she said instead, steering her tall friend back to the rows of folding chairs facing the microphone and table at the end of the gym. "Things are about to start. Now, what's going on here that's so important tonight?"

As they settled onto metal chairs, Penny filled her in on some of the issues in which the neighborhood association was involved.

"He's going to talk about a drug education program we're thinking about participating in with the school system," Penny leaned over to whisper as she gestured in the direction of the association president.

Katherine inclined her head in that general direction, but her eyes were skimming the far corners of the gym. She saw no blue plaid shirt.

"The next issue is that weekend cleanup I was telling you about," Penny volunteered after the group took its vote. "Will you be in town to help?"

"Hmm?" Katherine leaned over to reposition her purse under her seat, taking the opportunity to glance toward the back of the room. A flash of blue plaid caught her eye. She straightened up. "Oh. The litter cleanup. In two weeks? Is that what you said?"

As she made vague promises, Katherine took another casual look toward the back of the room in the direction of the blue plaid blur. It was easy to spot. It was sitting on the back row, beside a cloud of flame-red curls. Close beside.

"This is the part I wanted you to hear," Penny whispered.

Katherine pointed her chin toward the front and focused her eyes on the speaker. But she heard only disjointed scraps of the discussion centering around the association's efforts to work with the city government on improvements to a park that bordered the neighborhood.

She was too antsy to sit still for long. "How about a refill on your drink?" she asked Penny.

"Not now. You need to hear this."

"I'm listening." But she wasn't. She picked up their cups and headed for the drink table along the side of the gym. Voices droned all around her, but she had no idea what they were saying. Her attention was riveted on the splotches of blue and red in the back row.

Katherine hurried back to her seat.

"...we have right here in this room the expertise and the connections we need to make the city sit up and take notice of the conditions in the park," Penny, now on her feet beside her chair, was saying. "Katherine Barnett, one of our newest neighbors, is an award-winning photographer. Even if we can't get the city council to visit this park and see the disgraceful condition it's in firsthand, I know Katherine has the skills to show them."

For the first time, Katherine zeroed in on the events of the meeting. She smiled and groaned all at once. She might have known that Penny's insistence that she get involved with the association's work wouldn't end with mere encouragement.

"But will they really listen?" someone else in the audience asked. "Even if they can see for themselves?"

Penny nodded in agreement. "Not necessarily. That's why I suggest that Katherine team up with Hank Weisbecker for this project. As you know, he works for the city's landscaping department and..."

Katherine almost dropped her drink. There was more to Penny Gray's scheming than even she had imagined. She tugged on her friend's jacket, but Penny's voice never slowed.

"Penny!" she hissed. "Don't you dare!"

Penny ignored her and continued to talk, easily convincing the association members that Hank and Katherine were the perfect team to carry the project to successful completion.

Among the voices from around the room that finally joined the conversation was a deep one Katherine recognized. "I'm not sure it would be appropriate, since I work for the city...."

Bulldozing over Hank's objections in her usual fashion, Penny soon convinced everyone in the room that Hank could offer his professional assistance and advice without jeopardizing his position with the city. Within minutes, the group had voted. Katherine and Hank were now a team.

A reluctant team, it appeared. But a team nevertheless.

"How could you do that to me?" Katherine asked her neighbor a few minutes later. "What if he thinks this was my idea?"

"Good. Then he'll know you're interested."

"I am not interested. And if I were, why would I want him to know?"

Penny looked down at her with a distinct lack of comprehension. "Why in the world wouldn't you want him to know?"

Katherine sighed as she put on her coat. "Forget it. Let's just get out of here before you rope me into anything else."

"Not yet. I've got to talk to the president about an idea I've got. What do you think of a neighborhood home tour this spring?"

Katherine backed off and shook her head. "Oh, no, you don't. I'm getting out of here before you rope me into that, too."

"Actually, your house would be—"

"I'm gone. Now. Forget you ever met me." She laughed and turned away from her still-scheming friend.

As she stepped out into the crisp October chill, Katherine contemplated all the ways she could gracefully bow out of this project.

Maybe, she thought wryly, she would simply pass a camera to Hank's red-haired sidekick.

THE REDHEAD'S GRIP was like a boa constrictor around Hank's biceps. Tearing his eyes away from Katherine's retreating backside—yep, it was just as round and cute as he'd remembered—Hank turned back to the woman who lived two doors down from him.

"Lettie, it's been real nice talking to you..." he started and saw a miffed expression cross her face.

"You're not going to run off on me, are you, Hank?" Hiding the flash of anger, Lettie feigned a pout. It was supposed to look girlishly alluring, Hank knew, but it just looked silly. "I thought we could walk home together."

"I'd like to, Lettie. I really would," he lied, reaching down to pry a finger from his arm. "But I think I need to talk to Ms. Barnett. About the park project. You know—get coordinated."

"But, Hank..." Her fingers loosened reluctantly.

"I knew you'd understand. See you later."

Breaking into a slow jog, he caught up with Katherine about a block away from the school building. He slowed to fall into step beside her. Was the thick cloud of perfume Lettie had worn still clinging to him? He hoped not.

"I'm not even going to ask this time," he said, grinning as she looked up at him in dismayed surprise.

"What do you mean?"

"If I can walk you home. Just gives you a chance to turn me down."

She hesitated for a step. "Listen, Hank, there's no need—"

"Oh, but there is." He took her arm and linked it through his. It felt good there. Small, but not defenseless. Her tension was palpable, as if she refused to give in to the protectiveness in the gesture. "We've got this project to do together and..."

She slipped her hand away and shoved it into the pocket of her ski jacket. "Why don't I just take the photos, bring them to you and let you take it from there? Simple."

Hank shook his head. "Won't work. You need me to tell you what shots to take. I know what the boys downtown need to see to convince them this park needs some work. You don't. No, we definitely need to do this together."

"Did you put Penny up to this?"

Hank looked down at her in surprise. "No. I was hoping you had."

"You're the one who had a little tête-à-tête with her right before the meeting began."

The tightness in her voice pleased him. He grinned. "Jealous?"

Katherine opened her mouth, then clamped it tightly shut. Hank realized he had gone too far. Nothing he did with this woman was the right thing, it seemed. "You don't like me very much, do you?"

Her shoulders drooped, the defensiveness that had kept them rigidly squared suddenly gone. "It isn't that, Hank."

"Good. That's a start." He stopped and turned her toward him, lifting her chin to look her in the eyes. "Then what is it?"

Her eyes shifted and fluttered closed. She was trying hard not to look at him squarely. He sighed and let her chin drop. "Ah, I know that look. It's the same one my daughter gives me when she has no intention of telling me what I want to know."

Her smile had been given unwillingly, he realized. "Hank, I'm just not sure this is a good idea."

"You don't like me."

"I told you that's not it."

"You find me physically repulsive."

Now her soft laugh was a bit more relaxed. "That's not it, either."

"Your mother told you to stay away from men who wear suspenders."

Now she laughed outright. "That's it."

"Fine." He reached inside the waistband of his cords, unbuttoned the yellow suspenders and shoved them into a back pocket. "Problem solved. Now, what time should I pick you up tomorrow for our mission?"

"Don't you ever give up?" Her voice had thawed, so he took her hand and once again tucked it into the crook of his arm as they started down the sidewalk.

"No. I told you that from the beginning. Tell me it's impossible and all you're doing is forcing me to prove you wrong." He unconsciously compared her to the cloying redhead who had leeched onto him for most of the evening. Except there was no comparison. A fuzzy beret covered Katherine's soft brown hair. And if she wore makeup, it wasn't apparent. Under her sleeveless ski jacket, she was trim in her slim jeans and cable-knit sweater. "So, what do you say, about nine in the morning?"

"Nine? Sure."

They walked. Hank decided to try a detour down a long block leading away from Katherine's house and was pleased when she didn't reroute him toward the most direct path home. Her hand stayed where he had placed it, but it didn't stop feeling deliciously foreign there. It continued to tingle right through the flannel of his shirt long after it should have felt commonplace.

"You must enjoy what you do if you don't mind helping out during your off hours just to benefit the neighborhood," Katherine said.

Was he mistaken, or had her fingers squeezed his forearm? Just barely, of course. But hadn't that been a little squeeze? "I do enjoy it. I always helped Mother in the garden. My brother always liked working with Dad, helping out with the livestock. I just liked seeing things grow."

"Why?"

"There's a miracle in it." Hank realized he'd never felt brave enough to say these things to anyone else except Doris. "You can take dirt and water and sunshine and nothing but a tiny seed, and it'll grow into something that will feed or shelter you. Somebody said only God could make a tree, and that's true. But He lets me help. And that feels . . ."

He stopped, embarrassed, and wondered if he'd gone too far.

"Feels what?"

Her eyes were soft with what he could only interpret as acceptance and understanding of what he was saying. Something in his chest expanded, making way for all kinds of feelings he couldn't quite identify.

"It feels like you're creating life. You know what I mean?"

She looked down. "Yes, I . . . I think so."

"You must feel that way sometimes with your camera. Like you're creating life on film."

A shadowy smile flickered across her face and was gone. He thought for a moment there had been a hint of bitterness in the smile; he must have been wrong.

There was no bitterness in her voice when she spoke, but there was something else.... Resignation? He couldn't tell.

"No. I only get to reflect images of life. I don't get to do the actual creating."

"Lots of people would disagree. Didn't you tell me you might be doing a book? That's pretty creative, if you ask me."

Her smile looked almost grateful. "I am doing the book. It's been accepted."

"That's wonderful!" He turned toward her and swept her into his arms, planting a light kiss on her forehead. He released her quickly, realizing instantly that it wasn't safe to take her into his arms for a friendly, congratulatory kiss. The spontaneous contact had fired up all kinds of reactions in him, all of them dangerous. "Tell me about it."

"Not much to tell," she said, filling him in on a few of the details. "By the way, you promised to be one of my subjects. Are you still game now that it's more than just talk?"

By the time they reached her front door, they had discussed the kinds of shots she wanted and the best time to get them. Although Hank found the discussion a little intimidating, he also felt a surge of excitement. Could he handle himself with such a self-sufficient woman?

Hank wasn't sure he was ready to travel in that kind of company. Doris had been completely different. Her secretarial work had been merely an interruption of her career as wife and mother. She had depended on Hank to make all the decisions. And she hadn't doubted any of those decisions, even if they hadn't always been right.

Life would never be that simple with a woman like Katherine Barnett. But something about the prospect of trying to please her was exciting. It might be impossible for a guy like him, but his stubborn streak made him want to give it his best shot anyway.

"How about a little coffee before you head home in this cold?" she was asking as she unlocked her front door. The house, dark except for the golden glow of the overhead light in the entry hall, beckoned with warmth and intimacy. The night behind him did, indeed, feel cold and just a trifle empty as he anticipated heading for home alone. Besides, Heather wasn't due in for almost an hour and Tammi was sleeping over at her den mother's with the other girls in her Brownie troop. No reason to rush home to an empty house.

"Sounds great."

Katherine draped her jacket on an elaborately carved oak hall tree and Hank followed her to the kitchen. She stopped to talk to two squawking birds whose cage hung from a carved brass stand in the living room and to give the Pekinese a hug.

While Katherine measured coffee into a four-cup coffeemaker, Hank tried to find something to distract him. He was painfully aware of the intimacy of being alone with her. He was equally aware of the sudden intensity of his need to reestablish physical contact between them. He felt, without her hand hooked through his arm, like Samson shorn of his hair.

Hoping to take his mind off the urge to walk up behind her and stroke the back of her neck, where a few soft waves of hair feathered loose from her ponytail, Hank surveyed the kitchen. Like the rest of the house, it looked palatial to him, compared to his condo.

"You picked a big place for one person," he said, trying to focus on the neat row of old-fashioned, multicolored dishes lining a shelf over a drop leaf table. Anything to keep his mind off the deft movement of her fingers as they lined up coffee mugs and sugar bowl and spoons. "You must be planning on a big family."

She fumbled with the turquoise sugar bowl, sending it clattering to the floor. The curved finger-hold snapped off, and a small heap of sugar lay beside it. As she stared down at the mess, her lower lip trembled. Hank knelt at the same time she did. Their hands met at the broken crockery.

"I...I'm sorry," she said, her soft voice quavery. "What a klutz."

Hank closed one hand around hers. With the other, he picked up the sugar bowl and handle. "It's a clean break. No chips. I can fix it for you."

Her sorrowful eyes were still on the broken sugar bowl in his hand. He pulled her to her feet and set the bowl on the counter. "It'll be just like new, honest. Presto-chango, and you'll never know it happened. I'm a magician—practically. Didn't I ever tell you that?"

Looking up at him, Katherine smiled faintly. "No, you never told me that."

The grains of sugar crunched beneath the soles of his shoes as he moved closer. "Well, now you know. So there's nothing to worry about, is there? You have your very own prestidigitator at your beck and call."

"I'm not sure I believe in magic."

Her eyes told him she was only half teasing him. She obviously doubted that he could supply whatever magic she was missing in her life. He made up his mind to prove her wrong.

"You don't believe in magic?" His voice quietly incredulous, Hank placed his hands on her shoulders—narrow shoulders, tensed in a show of strength. Her arms were crossed beneath her breasts to complete the barrier. He worked his fingers in a slow, gentle massage. "There's all kinds of magic in the world, Katie. You just have to let it in."

"It's not always that easy, Hank."

But he could feel the easing in her muscles, could hear the softening in her voice. He let his softly insistent touch travel down her forearms. Her eyes closed. He knew she would feel the magic, even if she didn't know it yet.

"I know it isn't easy," he admitted, gently unfolding her arms. He held each hand in one of his for a long moment, making circles with his fingers. When a soft sigh escaped her lips, he drew her arms around his waist and pulled her against his chest. Without a protest, she melted against him. He lowered his lips to hers.

The meeting of their lips was tentative, soft. He coaxed her along, gentling his lips against the soft fullness of hers. He felt something fragile in her, something that could send her flying out of his arms at any moment. Fighting back the stronger feelings trying to push their way to the surface, Hank made the touch of his arms around her shoulders, his hands on her back, as soft as the touch of his lips on hers.

Only when her fingers tightened over the muscles in his back did Hank allow himself the luxury of deepening the kiss. He captured her tongue in a lazy dance. Heat grew in him as Katherine pressed herself closer. His hands slid up her side, stopping just below the swell of her breasts. Her heart pounded against the edge of his hand, and he pressed gently against her fullness.

Hoping he hadn't gone too far, Hank raised his head and looked down into bewildered eyes. Taking a deep breath as they loosened their hold on one another, Hank dropped a kiss onto the soft brown waves over her forehead. "See? Some magic is easy."

He heard the uneasiness in her soft laughter. He lightly ran his arms over her shoulders and stepped back to give them both space to recover. Sugar crunched beneath his soles again. He grinned. "Not all magic is easy, however. Making sugar disappear, for example, is not easy."

While they cleaned up the sugar and sipped at the fresh coffee she had brewed, Hank kept a watchful eye on Katherine. The same hesitancy, the same tense wariness that he'd felt in her first kiss was evident in all her movements. In answer to her questions, he told her about his boyhood fascination with magic and the hard-earned summer money that had bought his first ventriloquist's dummy when he was twelve.

But he had the feeling that, instead of being a way to bring him closer, her questions were just another dodge to keep him at a distance. By keeping him talking, she could avoid giving away bits and pieces of herself. But there wasn't time to break down those defenses again. Hank looked reluctantly at his watch. He had just enough time to beat Heather home if he hurried.

"I hate to do this, but I've got to run." He didn't look at her when he said it. He was too afraid of seeing relief in her eyes. "Tammi's spending the night with friends, but Heather will be home any time now. One of the little joys of being a single parent is having to keep the same curfews as your kids."

He grinned and took his mug to the sink. When he turned back to her she was still sitting in her chair, staring at him as if he had just announced his intention to return to Mars for the evening.

"Your . . . your daughters live with you?"

"Yeah. That they do."

"How . . . how does their mother feel about that?"

Hank's grin faded. "Their mother died two years ago."

TWO HOURS LATER, Katherine took small satisfaction from the dozens of strips of film hanging up to dry in her darkroom. It had taken all her concentration just to get the job done right, without adding fixer to the developing tank when she should've been adding developer. The minute she'd let her mind stray, she'd found herself picking up the wrong containers or forgetting to set the timer.

Her shoulders sagging, Katherine trudged upstairs. Although it was now nearly midnight and she was so weary her bones ached, she knew her mind was no closer to letting her sleep than it had been when Hank had walked out the door.

Leaving only one soft light burning, Katherine poured a snifter of brandy and settled into her rocker, making way for Baxter to curl into a warm, comforting ball in her lap. She stroked the dog's soft fur. But Baxter, like everything else, reminded her of what she most wanted to forget.

Her lips, too, reminded her. The warmth hadn't left her. The melting softness that had eased through her held on tenaciously, refusing to let her rest. She tried burning it away with a long swallow of brandy.

Developing film hadn't done the job; neither did the brandy. She could still feel Hank's arms around her. And the gut-wrenching fear she'd experienced when she realized that Hank wasn't a weekend father at all. He was a full-time father, and a relationship with Hank brought the inevitability of a relationship with his children.

That was something Katherine couldn't handle. Keeping her emotions on an even keel, she told herself, was tough enough without muddying things up with someone else's children.

Katherine closed her eyes against the sting of unwelcome tears. *How could I have made such a mistake? And what am I going to do about it now?*

CHAPTER EIGHT

HANK POINTED toward the rotting tree trunk wedged into a creekbed, blocking the stream of clear water.

"You need to get a couple of shots of that," he said, casting a wary glance at Katherine.

She nodded without changing the pleasant but oddly unrevealing expression with which she'd greeted him at her front door at nine. Their morning at the park wasn't quite living up to Hank's fantasies of an outdoor adventure. Katherine was smiling and agreeable, but she was totally out of reach.

All the vulnerability of the night before had vanished. Hank had a hunch he could pull a rabbit out of the battered baseball cap she wore a lot more easily than he could pull any genuine emotions from Katherine Barnett.

"Did I do something wrong?" he asked as she switched from a long lens to a shorter one. For just a moment, her hands stilled, then she resumed her task with a deliberateness that seemed exaggerated. But she didn't look at him, didn't raise her eyes as she slipped the long lens into its case.

"Don't be silly."

Her impish smile was as cute as ever except for one small thing—it was completely phony. He could see it in her eyes. Or, more to the point, he couldn't see it in her eyes; not a hint of a smile lived in those gray-green depths. Whatever emotion they held was too far beneath the surface.

"Isn't it a shame they've let this park go downhill? Why in the world would they do that?" she asked too brightly.

Hank fought for control of his rising temper. "You're not playing fair."

Her eyebrows rose, the perfect facsimile of confusion and consternation. "Hank, I don't know what you're talking about. Are you feeling all right this morning?"

Biting back a hostile reply, Hank guided her closer to the most visible signs of decay in the large tree trunk. "Let's get a couple of close-ups. I want them to see what happens when you ignore things too long."

If he'd hoped for a reaction, he was disappointed. She continued to volunteer only insipidly pleasant comments. Hank had just about made up his mind that women were as hard to figure out as teenagers. *Or maybe,* he thought, *that's the whole problem with Heather. It's not that she's becoming a hardheaded teenager, she's just turning into a damned impossible woman.*

So many times he'd thought Katherine was as interested in him as he was in her, but something always seemed to come up. Like that night at the park when they'd been having so much fun until his kids showed up. Then last night she'd acted kind of strange after she broke the sugar bowl. But when he'd announced that he had to go home to his kids, she had really frozen.

As he pondered the two separate events, watching her limber form climb over rocks and hills in search of the best angle for her photos, Hank was suddenly struck by a new thought.

His kids. Could Katherine's mood swings have something to do with his kids?

It didn't make sense, he thought, but it did add up. Things had followed the same pattern right from the beginning, since their first meeting. Hadn't she been plenty flirty that first time they met in the grocery store? But when he went to her house the next day, with Tammi, she had built some kind of wall around herself that he'd never quite been able to scale.

Looking toward the ramshackle playground equipment, Hank decided to play his hunch.

"That should do us for nature photography," he said. "Now let's show 'em what kind of rotten shape the playground is in."

"Good idea." She started purposefully toward the rusting swings and unsteady sliding board, shoving her hands into her jeans pockets and letting her camera equipment swing freely from her shoulder.

Knowing Katherine needed no help in spotting the problems with the equipment, Hank simply watched while she took the necessary shots. He concentrated on coming up with a subtle way of testing his theory that Katherine was one of those single career women who didn't know much about kids.

"I'll bet you don't take photographs of empty playgrounds very often, do you?" Hank realized right away that was a weak ploy; he shifted to a more direct approach. "I mean, I'll bet you photograph kids a lot, don't you?"

He watched expectantly, but the reward was small. Her only reaction was to stop for a moment to brace her elbow against her abdomen for a steadier shot.

"Not a lot."

"No? I'd think kids would make great subjects. Don't you think so?"

She flashed him a quick smile. Too quick for him to be sure that it had trembled around the edges. "I like shooting old people better," she said. "Lots of character in their faces."

"But kids are so much fun," he persisted. "Don't you think looking at cute kids makes everybody feel happy?"

She paused for a moment to blot her forehead with the back of her hand before covering her face with the camera once again. Feeling the cool morning breeze, Hank was surprised she was perspiring. Taking pictures didn't look that strenuous.

"I'm sure you're right," she said at last.

This time Hank knew he had to be imagining things. Why in the world would her voice quiver? No, this subtlety was getting him nowhere fast. Directness. That was more his style.

"I saw on the cover of a magazine at the grocery store last week that lots of career women these days are finally starting to have families," he said. "Do you plan to have children?"

As soon as the words were out of his mouth, a sense of déjà vu pickaxed him between the eyes. And when he realized that Katherine's hands were suddenly shaking so badly she couldn't control the camera, Hank knew he was right. Last night, he remembered with a start, she had dropped the sugar bowl right after he'd said something about having a big family.

He didn't know quite what he'd discovered, but it seemed that for once his instincts about a woman were on the money.

With casual deliberateness, Katherine slid the camera into the top of the open camera bag on the ground. She turned to face Hank; her eyes were like the tips of an iceberg. Hank knew the coldness he saw there went far deeper than what he could see.

"Hank, my biological clock isn't ticking." Her words were clipped and controlled, but Hank was certain he heard an underlying trembling. "The spring on that particular clock broke years ago. Am I making myself clear?"

"Listen, it's nothing to me if you don't want children. I was just..."

Her whole body was shaking now, but whether with the effort to control herself or with something else, Hank couldn't be sure.

"I...it's..." She struggled to speak. Her shoulders finally sagged and she turned to a wooden bench and dropped onto it heavily.

"Are you okay?" Hank rushed to her side and took her hand. It was cold and clammy and trembled in his. "Katie, what's wrong?"

She shook her head. This close, he could see the tiny beads of perspiration that dotted her upper lip and forehead. "N-nothing. J-just feeling a little shaky."

He put an arm around her shoulder and pulled her protectively against his chest. He could feel the shudders running through her entire body. "Katie, you're shaking all over. What's happening? It's no big deal if you don't want to have kids. Heck, I've got two of my own and sometimes even I don't want kids."

She closed her eyes and leaned her head against his shoulder. Without thinking, Hank brushed a kiss over the soft hair feathering against his cheek.

"I just...caught a chill, I guess." The quiver in her voice was fading now, but she still sounded unsteady.

Confused and afraid, Hank simply held her close. He could feel her steadiness slowly return as she drew a series of long, ragged breaths. The trembling stopped. With an instinct born of tenderness he usually reserved for his children, Hank continued to drop a series of tiny kisses on the top of her head. When she finally straightened up, he loosened the arm around her shoulders but didn't let her slip out of his protective hold.

"I'm fine now." Her voice was steady but weak. She didn't look up at him. Her face was still alarmingly pale.

"Kate, you really had me worried." Hank framed her heart-shaped face with his hands, hoping to restore its usual pink glow with the warmth of his palms. The corners of her lips tipped up in a weak smile. Her lids lowered over her eyes.

Hank bent closer to drop a kiss on each lid. Her face, still cradled in his hands, moved fractions of an inch into the kiss. He tried another, on her cheek. She turned her face to his, almost imperceptibly, as if seeking the comfort he offered. He smiled and drew her lips to his.

They were cold at first, and dry. But they drew from the warmth of his lips and were soon as soft and pliant as they had been the previous evening. He kissed her tenderly, still cautious of the trembling woman she had been just moments before. He slipped his hands away from her face. One cupped her head, tilting it to bring her lips more fully to his. The other traced the curve of her shoulder, grateful for the sleeveless ski vest that left the slender muscles of her upper arm free for him to explore. She felt strong, but he knew now that something far stronger than her well-toned body could render her helpless.

She pressed closer to him, but the padding of her quilted vest made it impossible for him to feel the curves and swells he knew were there. He hungered for more but satisfied himself with the leisurely awakening of Katherine's own passion. His tongue traced the outline of her lips, and he heard the breath catch in her throat. Response throbbed through Hank, deep, dark and demanding, but he instinctively knew he could not act on it here and now. He had to keep it under control until Katherine was ready to give a lot more than she could give at the moment.

He pulled back, gradually loosening his hold on her and easing his mouth from hers. She was too vulnerable right now. He wanted her to want him, but not because she needed reassurance.

"Katie, what happened?" he asked softly, planting another gentle kiss on her cheek.

"I told you, Hank. Just a chill." She pulled away slightly. It was time for the wall to go up again.

"It wasn't just a chill. What is it, Katie?"

"Do you mind if I come back some other time to finish the photos?"

Afraid of precipitating a recurrence of whatever had happened, Hank decided to let it drop. But stubbornness hardened his resolve. Whatever was bugging Katherine Barnett, he wasn't going to let it stop him.

HEATHER SHOVED one work shirt after another into the washer. She knew she was supposed to squirt stain remover onto any grass or mud spots first, but that took twice as long. Her dad would just have to learn not to be so messy when he worked.

She had raised a real ruckus when he had told her to do the laundry and stay with Tammi today while he worked on some kind of neighborhood project. Heather frowned as she reset the water and temperature levels, then pulled a load of towels out of the dryer. Actually, she hadn't minded having an excuse to stay home today. She'd never tell her dad that, but it was true.

Marty's folks had gone to the game in Lincoln, so he was having everyone over. That was okay, but Heather worried about being in the house with Marty when there were no grown-ups around. He'd been pretty pushy lately. She knew what he was expecting of her—at least, she kind of knew—and she didn't know how to say no. The last time he'd kissed her, it had been pretty gross. And she'd had a hard time getting him to stop, too.

She shivered. Still, Marty was the coolest dude in the group, and if he liked her that must mean she was okay. Most of the time, she even liked it when he kissed her— until he got so…heavy-duty about it. And he was cute. All the girls said so.

She lugged the basket of towels into the living room. Looking over Tammi's shoulder at the morning cartoons, she sat on the couch and pulled out a washcloth to fold.

"Hey, twerp, how about helping with the towels?"

"Do I have to?"

"Yes, you have to."

Without taking her eyes from the frenetic action on the TV screen, Tammi slid across the floor and pulled a kitchen towel out of the basket. She had finished two towels when the doorbell rang.

"I'll get it!" Tammi jumped up, knocking the stack of towels off the coffee table.

"No, you pick up the towels." Heather took satisfaction in calling the shots. "You know you're supposed to let me get the door when we're here by
ourselves."

She peered through the peephole. It was a woman, so
she opened the door but left the chain on, the way her
dad had taught her to do when he wasn't home.

"Yeah?" She didn't recognize the woman, but she
liked her right away. She was dressed in a really cool
pair of safari pants with about a million pockets. And
her sweater was big and floppy and funky.

"Heather, I'm Penny Gray. I live in the neighborhood and your dad said I could come by and talk to you
today."

Vaguely, Heather remembered her dad saying something about a woman from the neighborhood association coming by. But at the time she'd been wondering
how she could keep him from seeing her next report
card and hadn't really paid attention. She slipped the
chain off and let the woman in.

"I run a real estate agency out of my home, just a few
blocks from here," Penny said when they were seated in
the living room. Tammi had lost interest in folding
clothes and was once again sprawled on the floor in
front of the TV. "I've been looking for someone to help
me out in the afternoons and on weekends, and your
dad said you might be interested."

"You mean a job?"

Penny Gray smiled. She had a nice smile—not like a
lot of grown-ups. She looked like she meant it, not as
if she was just trying to snow you.

"That's right. You won't get rich, but it'll put some
spending money in your pocket."

Listening to the hourly rate and the number of hours Penny suggested, Heather quickly calculated in her head how much money she could earn. For once she was grateful that she was better in math than her report cards indicated. She could buy a lot of neat stuff with that much money. Nevertheless, it would also cut into time with her friends.

"On weekends? You mean like all day on Saturday?"

"Well, that's up to you," Penny said. "A half day would probably be plenty."

Heather was tempted. "What will I have to do?"

"Answer the phone, take messages, open the mail." Penny laughed at the long face Heather pulled. "You're right. It is pretty boring. Why do you think I don't want to do it?"

Heather had to smile at that.

Penny leaned forward, her face turning serious, and Heather knew it was lecture time. Grown-ups couldn't resist lecture time, apparently even grown-ups who looked as cool as this Penny Gray.

"I remember when I was a little older than you," Penny started. "I'd been having all kinds of problems with my folks. You know. They didn't trust me, didn't like my friends, thought I stayed out too late." She suddenly broke into a grin. "Well, maybe they were right about that. Anyway, I started working for a beauty shop in the neighborhood. Running errands, making appointments, that kind of thing. You know what happened?"

Heather wanted to be skeptical of whatever point Penny was trying to make, but the woman's big green eyes held too much honesty. Heather could tell. This woman wouldn't try to feed her a lot of junk. "What happened?"

"Well, my parents still didn't like my friends. And they still thought I stayed out too late." They exchanged a smile that reflected shared history. "But they stopped carping at me so much. It was like they trusted me more. Like they thought I'd suddenly turned into Miss Maturity just because I could hold down a job."

"Yeah?"

"Yeah."

Heather shrugged but couldn't stifle the enthusiastic grin that spread across her face. "Okay. Let's give it a shot."

"Awright!" Penny stood and extended her hand in a high five.

Feeling a surge of excitement, Heather slapped hands with the woman.

"I think we'll be a good team. Can you start Monday?"

"Sure," Heather told her, suddenly anxious to begin. As she showed her new boss to the door and returned to the dull task of folding sheets, excitement fluttered in her chest. She wanted to be cool about this, but she couldn't stop the fantasies that popped into her head.

I'll bet Penny is a lot like Mom would've been, she thought, slam-dunking a pair of socks into the laundry basket. *Mom would've been cool, too.*

BY THE TIME he hit the front door around lunchtime, Hank had his plan in place.

If Katherine Barnett had a problem with kids, he'd find plenty of time for them to get to know each other before he complicated their relationship with his two.

Then, after they knew each other and she realized he wasn't looking for a mother for Tammi and Heather—and he wasn't, he assured himself as he tossed his jacket into the front closet—she would also realize that his having kids didn't matter.

Staring into the chaos of his living room, Hank momentarily doubted the truth of that statement. Heather was slumped on the couch, a pile of freshly washed work shirts piled up on one side of her, a tangle of clotheshangers on the other. Her foot tapped to the beat of a tune coming from the TV. A bag of chips had been ripped wide open on the coffee table. Only crumbs remained. Crumbs in the bag. Crumbs on the table. Crumbs on the floor. Tammi danced, simulating the sultry moves of the singer on the tube. Her high voice was raised in tuneless imitation.

Yes, Hank assured himself, he was batting a thousand. Keeping the girls out of Katherine's hair while they got to know each other better had to be a winning strategy.

"Daddy!" Tammi squealed when she saw him, running and flinging her arms around his waist. "Is it lunchtime yet? I'm hungry."

"It sure is, Scooter." He gave her a hug in return. "Why don't you and Heather go in and start on some PB&Js while I make a phone call. I'll be right in."

Heather gave him a withering look as she followed her younger sister into the kitchen. "I do not eat peanut butter and jelly."

"I'm easy." Hank smiled. Heather would not lure him into a sniper attack today. If he'd figured out Katherine Barnett this easily, who knows? He might even find a solution to the Attack of the Killer Teenager. "Have a ham and cheese. It's on me."

"We're outta cheese," she grumbled.

Hank took a deep breath. *No return fire,* he coached himself, and turned toward the phone. Within seconds, he heard the reassuring sound of his mother's voice. After catching up on the latest news—his dad's high blood pressure and the success of his mother's church bazaar the Saturday before—Hank got on with the business at hand.

"Listen, I was wondering if I could bring the kids down next weekend?"

He never doubted for a minute the kind of reception that would get.

"Henry, that would be wonderful! You know we always love to have the girls." Hank listened patiently as his mother covered the mouthpiece and shouted the good news to his father. She was laughing when she came back on the line. "Your father wants to know what the big occasion is. He said you must have a hot date lined up."

Hank laughed. "That's close. I *have* met this woman and..." The words froze in his throat as he looked up into the angry glare of his older daughter. She stood in the door, lower lip thrust out belligerently, already shaking her head and mouthing an insistent "no."

Hank closed the conversation quickly, reluctant to risk Heather's explosion while he was talking to his parents. He hadn't been able to bring himself to tell them about Heather's metamorphosis and he wasn't eager to introduce them to it via a long-distance knockdown, drag-out fight.

"I'm not going," Heather stated as soon as the receiver hit the cradle.

"This is not an optional extracurricular activity, Heather," he said just as decisively. "You are going to your grandparents' next weekend."

"So you can fool around with some chick. That's not fair!"

Tammi came to stand beside them, big-eyed, a spoon and a jar of grape jelly in her hand. Solemnly, she lifted a spoonful into her mouth, her eyes moving from her sister to her father as the volley of words escalated.

"Katherine Barnett is not 'some chick.'" Hank told himself he would not get hot this time. He would remain firm. In control. He would not lose his temper. "She's a nice woman and, yes, I hope to spend some time with her."

"Well, I can't go."

"You'll go if I say you're going."

"No, I can't. I have a job."

"A what?"

"A job. With Penny Gray. She came by today. She said you told her it was okay." The announcement held a note of triumph.

Hank remembered now. The real estate agent had asked him last night if she could offer Heather a job. Thinking it might teach his daughter some responsibility, Hank had agreed to give it a try. He sighed. Complications. Always complications.

"You'll just have to tell her you can't make it next Saturday. Tell her you already have plans."

"I can't do that!" The shrill note in her voice told Hank she was about to move out of the controlled animosity stage of the battle into full-scale frontal attack. "She'll hire somebody else! I won't go!"

"Heather, you'll do what I—"

"No, I won't! I won't ruin my new job just because you've got the hots for some chick who hates kids!"

The wind rushed out of Hank's lungs. He resisted the urge to respond to Heather's accusation that Katherine hated kids. Heather didn't understand, he told himself, ignoring the fact that he didn't understand himself.

"This isn't going to ruin your job, Heather."

Giving him a long, malicious glare, Heather finally raised her chin in haughty unconcern. "Fine. I'll go. In fact, maybe I'll just stay. If you're so interested in a woman like her, it might be better if I go live with Grandma and Grandpa—all the time."

The look in her eyes told Hank she knew she had scored a direct hit. While he was still reeling from the blow, she turned and walked out the front door. It didn't even slam behind her. That's how confident she was of her victory.

CHAPTER NINE

KATHERINE FINGERED the thin Yellow Pages. Physicians & Surgeons, Cardiovascular Disease. Physicians & Surgeons, Hematology. Neurology. Orthopedics. Psychiatry.

She glanced away from the page. The broken sugar bowl caught her eye. She looked back at the page and touched the column of type. No single name in the columns sent a signal that it was the right one.

"Suppose any of these shrinks have the answers, Baxter?" She forced a breezy flippancy into her voice. Baxter whimpered, his tail swishing against her ankles. She bent to pick him up. He peered at the telephone book opened on the kitchen table but seemed no more moved to action than Katherine was.

"Nah, I didn't think so, either." The dog looked up at her with sorrowful brown eyes. Katherine pressed her cheek to his silky head, feeling a bleakness of soul that was at odds with the afternoon sunshine, glaringly cheerful as it poured between the kitchen curtains.

"I need help," she whispered. "I can't let this get the better of me. Not again, Baxter. Not again."

He turned his pug nose in her direction and gave the side of her neck a lap with his tongue. Seeing her solemn expression, he propped his front paws on her chest and wagged his tail vigorously. His funny little face seemed to grin as an energetic yip burst forth.

Katherine laughed, hugging the dog to her chest. "Can we, Baxter? Can we beat this together?" He yipped again, even more enthusiastically. He was practically bouncing in her lap now. "Okay, okay. You're right. Together, we can lick the world. No pun intended."

She laughed again, somewhat shakily, as his active tongue told her that he took her statement quite literally.

HANK CONSIDERED the likelihood that anything in his grocery bags would melt or spoil while Tammi dawdled over gathering her toys from the cabbage rose rug on Mrs. Whitesides's living room floor.

"I'm so glad you asked me," the elderly woman said, taking Tammi's jacket from the foyer closet. "Keeping Tammi after school will give this old soul something to look forward to every day."

"I really appreciate that, Mrs. Whitesides," Hank replied, his relief at her agreement somewhat overshadowed by Heather's parting threat. His daughter had never seemed so cool after one of their skirmishes. He, on the other hand, was terrified. Heather was just volatile enough to make good on her threat. He glanced at his watch, wondering if she would be home when he and Tammi returned. Or would she be, as he had imagined while pushing his cart around the store, plotting to leave home?

He swallowed the taste of fear, hoping his voice sounded normal. "This after-school job is important to Heather. But if Tammi gets to be too much to handle..."

A hand on his forearm stopped him. "Don't even think it, Mr. Weisbecker. This little girl of yours is the sweetest thing I've ever seen. After my own grand-babies, of course." She gave him a wink. "And with the park right outside the door, nothing is more restful in the afternoons than sitting on the porch and watching her play."

"Still, she can be a handful," Hank said, taking the small hand Tammi offered now that all her toys were stuffed into her backpack. He wondered if Mrs. Whitesides had ever been subjected to a restful after-noon of MTV.

"She's delightful," Mrs. Whitesides insisted, her wrinkled hand smoothing Tammi's untidy hair back from her face. "No one could resist her."

Thinking of Katherine as he and his daughter walked out the front door, Hank wished it were truly that sim-ple.

HEATHER HESITATED at the door. She didn't want to go in, but could think of no way out. If she left now, all the kids would think she was weird. She pretended her in-securities were no more important than a chalkboard full of algebra. With a quick mental swipe, she erased her worries and swaggered into the room.

"Yo, guys!"

The basement, which had been outfitted as a rec room, was filled with cigarette smoke. Heather wanted to gag from the smell. Beer bottles were sweating rings onto the coffee table and chair arms. Music pulsated loudly through the windowless room. She had heard it when she walked up the sidewalk. Heather's heart picked up the beat, a rhythm that was wildly out of control.

She thumped her friends on the head or gave their feet a nonchalant nudge with her toe as she passed.

They nudged her back or waved, with a lift of the hand that barely counted as movement. A few grunted out welcomes that were unintelligible over the music.

Marty was playing pool in the back of the room, pool cue gripped in his fist and propped on his shoulder while he waited his turn. He grinned as she approached, then turned his attention to the balls on the table. He gave the cue ball a vicious shove, slamming a striped ball against the far edge of the table before it rolled to the other end and dropped into a corner pocket.

Marty was too cool to acknowledge the enthusiastic reaction to his shot. He pocketed three more balls before missing. Then, while his opponent shot, he feigned mild interest in Heather.

"Decided to show up, didja, kid?" He took a long draw on a cigarette. He was hunkier than anything on TV or at the movies, Heather reminded herself. Blakely had said so last week at the mall. His sleeveless T-shirt exposed his biceps to full view. He had junky-looking tattoos on them, but Heather told herself she wasn't cool enough to appreciate them. It was his face that was really cool. He could slay you with his face, looking over you like you were dirt and he was doing you a favor to glance in your direction.

Heather wondered sometimes if that was true. After all, who was she? Just a dorky junior high school kid who was lucky enough to hang around with the kids in senior high.

"Yeah." She tried to look as cocky and sure of herself as he did. "Thought I'd see what you guys were up to."

He grinned as if he knew something Heather didn't. He pulled her close and ran his hand down her back.

Heather held her breath. She was grateful when he turned back to the pool table. "Watch this, kid. I've got him right where I want him."

Marty was right. The game was over in moments. His opponent racked up the balls for another. Marty reached behind him for the beer bottle growing warm on the bookcase. "Want some?"

Something clogged Heather's throat so she had to swallow hard to speak. "Nah. I had a big lunch. I'm pretty full. Maybe later."

Marty laughed. Heather could tell she hadn't fooled him. She felt a moment of panic. What if he got tired of her?

Placing the bottle back on the shelf, Marty pulled her to him again, pressing her against the length of him. She could smell the beer and cigarettes on his breath. She held herself rigid. If he really held her close, he would realize that she wasn't nearly as filled out as most of the older girls.

Marty leaned forward and brought his lips down over hers. Heather didn't like the taste. She knew how she was supposed to feel—she'd seen it in movies. But what she felt she recognized as fear, which was something else again. She waited for him to stop. When he did, he looked down at her with displeasure in his eyes.

"You gotta grow up, babe. You wanna hang around with me, you're gonna have to start acting like you've got a clue what's going on. You read me?"

"Sure, Marty." She lowered her eyes. She was embarrassed by his chiding and searched her mind for a way to win back his approval. "Guess what, Marty? I got a job!"

He dropped his arms from around her and reached for his pool cue. "A job?"

"Yeah. Working for a real estate company after school." He didn't look impressed. "I'll be practically running the office."

Marty rolled his eyes. He definitely wasn't impressed. He was even less impressed, Heather realized, with the fact that she was.

For the next few minutes, Marty divided his attention between the pool game and his bottle of beer, barely glancing in Heather's direction. One look from him, she thought, and she would cry. She just knew she would. When he was engrossed in his next shot, she sauntered toward the stairs. With a quick backward glance to make sure no one was paying attention, she dashed away.

Hurt and confused, Heather stumbled through the living room and out the front door. She walked slowly at first, hoping no one from Marty's house would come upstairs to see her escape, but as she neared the street corner, her footsteps grew quicker. By the time she turned the corner, she was running. She ran for six blocks before she slowed down.

As she dropped to the ground beneath a tree, Heather didn't even realize what she had murmured over and over since leaving the house. "Mommy," she pleaded softly. "Mommy?"

It was a while before she admitted to herself that there would be no answer.

KATHERINE CLOSED the book with a satisfying thunk. She held it up and waved it in the direction of Fibber's and Molly's cage. "Confront your problems, it said. Seize them by the throat and conquer them by taking charge."

She jumped up from the chair and dropped the book onto the table, on top of a stack of three other library books.

"Two books in four days," she announced as she fed the chattering birds. "And they all say the same thing. Anxiety attacks are triggered by anything and nothing. And the only way to rid yourself of the nuisance is to come to grips with the underlying problem."

She snapped her fingers, causing Baxter to raise his chin from the floor. "Piece of cake. I'll just come to grips with the underlying problem."

She looked around at the two birds, then down at the dog, and contemplated the problem that had been festering and eating her alive for almost a decade. She gave a shaky laugh. "Piece of cake. Right."

Katherine walked to the bay window and dropped onto the chintz-covered window seat. The sky was gray. Gloomy. It spoke of winter just around the corner. After half a decade in this part of the country, she should be accustomed to winters that started in November and ended in April, but she wasn't. She sometimes still missed the oppressive steaminess of a Texas summer and the winters that were milder than a midwestern autumn.

Texas. A part of the underlying problem. Instead of facing it, she had left Texas like a fugitive, barely looking behind her as she ran. *So maybe that's where you have to start,* she told herself. *Back in Texas.*

She stared out the window for another quarter hour, barely seeing the clouds scudding across the dingy sky or the leaves swirling and gathering in depressing brown heaps. At last, she stood and headed upstairs. In the bottom drawer of her desk, she found her brocade-covered address book, a birthday gift from a mother

who had never realized that Katherine was not a bro-
cade kind of person. She flipped through it, found the
number she was looking for and dialed.

The soft drawl on the other end was almost a stranger's voice, tired but sweet. Katherine breathed deeply.
"Barb? This is Katherine. How are you?"

Her sister-in-law, in the tradition of Southern polite-
ness at all costs, hesitated only slightly before greeting
Katherine as if they had just spoken a few weeks earlier. "Katherine! Why, I'm just wonderful. And how
are you? It's so good to hear from you!"

"I just wanted to... I talked to Mother a few weeks
ago and she... I heard the good news. About
the...baby. I wanted to congratulate you and Frankie."

Another silence on the other end told Katherine her
sister-in-law was having trouble digesting this surpris-
ing turn of events. "Well, thank you. We sure are happy
about it."

Gulping in a big lungful of air, Katherine pushed
forward. "I hear you're rooting for a girl this time."

As Barb warmed to her subject and talked about their
plans for the new baby girl, Katherine listened only
enough to catch the pauses that demanded a response
from her. Her mind swirled with a confusing mish-
mash of images. Her brother's first baby, pink and
smelling of talcum and milk. Kittens being born in a
dark corner of the barn. Her best friend's baby shower.
The sometimes painful, always impersonal probes of
strangers attempting to discover why she hadn't been
able to do the most natural thing in the world. The
confusion in a pair of three-year-old eyes as she'd sat on
a bench at a Des Moines zoo, trying to hang onto her
sanity. A small body, trusting and warm, pressed
against hers on a blanket in the park.

And a gentle kiss that made her want to believe she could be whole someday.

Dreams and nightmares. Katherine's womb contracted in empty pain. Only the nightmares were real. Katherine Barnett could never be whole. No amount of magic could change that.

TAMMI SKIPPED ALONG an imaginary hopscotch figure on the sidewalk, chattering away to her father about the chessboard in Mrs. Whitesides's parlor.

"She said it belonged to her husband—he died a long time ago—and I could learn to play it with her if I wanted to," Tammi said, hopping on her right leg from one imaginary square to the next. "Chess is *so* radical. It looks like checkers, but it's better 'cause you have kings and queens and horses and stuff to play with, and not just little circles."

Hank smiled. He was beginning to realize what a big favor Penny Gray had done for him. Heather had been more subdued in the week she'd been working in the real estate office. And Mrs. Whitesides was wonderful with Tammi. Instead of flopping down in front of the TV every afternoon when she and Heather came home from school, the youngster was now actually learning to play the way kids used to play. Mrs. Whitesides had turned her front sidewalk into a hopscotch board. One afternoon they had baked gingerbread men—gingerbread people, Mrs. Whitesides had called them, in honor of the equal rights of the gingerbread sexes.

Hank had no doubt that Tammi would be able to take him in chess before the month was out.

"Know what Mrs. Whitesides said?" Tammi dropped into step behind him as they headed for home.

"What did Mrs. Whitesides say?" The short walk back home from the sitter's every afternoon was turning into one of Hank's favorite times of the day. He wished he could think of some way to get the same kind of time with Heather.

"She said before I started staying with her she was lonesome sometimes. 'Cause she lives alone." Tammi looked up at him with solemn brown eyes; Hank could see the beginnings of a softheartedness inherited from her mother. He felt a bittersweet tug at his own heart.

"Living alone isn't always easy," he said, knowing Tammi would never understand that sometimes even Hank felt as if he lived alone. Even with two noisy, active girls in the house, he sometimes felt alone.

Tammi nodded and stared down at her feet. "Katie lives alone."

"That's true." He'd thought of her, alone with whatever it was she hid from so assiduously, over and over during the past week. He'd wanted to go to her; he'd wanted to show her, with his gentleness, that she didn't have to hide out any longer.

Tammi looked up at him impatiently, as if he were being uncommonly slow to catch on. "She lives alone, so she's probably lonesome, too—just like Mrs. Whitesides. Don't you think?"

"Could be." A good possibility, Hank thought, but he didn't have a clue what to do about it.

"So we should stop by and see her. She could fix us dinner. I bet she'd like somebody to fix dinner for. Mrs. Whitesides said she misses having somebody to cook for."

Hank had to laugh at that. Not having someone to cook for was probably the last thing a career woman like Katherine Barnett missed. "She's too busy to fix dinner for us, Scooter."

Tammi looked skeptical. "Well, we should still go see her. So she won't be lonesome all night."

As he looked down into his daughter's intense brown eyes, he could find little fault with her conclusion. He admitted to himself, even as he spoke, that he was simply letting himself be talked into something he'd been wanting to do for a whole week. Dinner could wait. Heather wouldn't be home from work for another hour anyway.

He took Tammi by the hand. "You're a pretty smart young lady, you know that?"

IRRITATED AT THE SOUND of the doorbell, Katherine clipped the dripping roll of film up to dry, wiped her hands on her jeans and took the stairs two at a time.

She was even more irritated when she opened the door. Irritated with herself for the little flutter of excitement that died a cold death when she realized Hank wasn't alone. At the end of his arm was a dark-haired, all-smiles little girl.

"Hi!" Tammi stepped forward. Katherine noticed that her front tooth was growing in just the least bit crooked and softened as she remembered her own years in braces. "We were in the neighborhood."

Katherine almost laughed at the grown-up manner of the little girl's enthusiastic pronouncement. But the laughter stuck in her throat. She wasn't sure, right now, which prospect was more intimidating—being around Tammi or being around her father.

"Well, that's..." Hank started dubiously. His smile was almost apologetic.

Katherine wanted to throw her arms around him. And slam the door in his face.

"Actually, I guess that's just about right," he continued. "We were walking home from the sitter's and just wanted to say hi."

Katherine stepped back from the door to make way for them to come in. Bouncing into the entry hall, Tammi snatched her knit hat off her head, peeled off her coat and thrust them both at Katherine. "We won't stay long. Unless you want us to have..."

"Tammi." Hank's voice was a threat, but Katherine looked around in time to see the amusement in his eyes. "We won't stay long is exactly the right thing to say."

Tammi giggled. As Katherine draped their coats and hats over the hall tree and led them into the living room, she realized she was almost smiling herself at the infectious sound. She searched her mind for casual conversation as they sat. One look at Hank confirmed that he was doing the same. His searching look also confirmed that, if Tammi hadn't been in the room, he had plenty of things he'd want to discuss.

Katherine couldn't believe she was actually grateful for the presence of a child.

"Do you have a chessboard?" Tammi asked. She was perched primly on the edge of the Victorian loveseat, her legs swinging far above the floor.

"No. I'm afraid not."

"Oh. I guess that's 'cause you don't have anybody to play it with, huh?"

Katherine sucked in her breath. Hank cleared his throat. "Tammi's sitter is teaching her to play chess. Right now, it rivals video games for riveting her attention."

"Yeah. But you know what the best thing about chess is?" Tammi leaned forward, elbows on her knees, and looked Katherine squarely in the eyes.

The elfin little face was so full of mischief, Katherine found it almost impossible to resist. She told herself the slight racing of her heart was simply a reaction to the newness of the situation, not incipient anxiety. She understood her problem better now and she could control it. There would be no panic attack today. She smiled her encouragement. "What's the best thing about chess?"

"If you're losing—" Tammi's voice lowered almost to a whisper "—your knee can bump the board and knock everything over. Then you have to forfeit the game and start all over."

Looking absolutely delighted with herself for the strategy she'd discovered, Tammi rolled back against the couch and giggled. Before she realized what had happened, Katherine found herself laughing, too. Hank joined the laughter as Tammi then proceeded to explain how she had also made a few adjustments in the setup of the pawns and knights while Mrs. Whitesides answered a telephone call earlier in the afternoon.

"I can see we need to have a serious father-daughter discussion on ethics," Hank said as their laughter subsided.

Tammi shook her head. "We already did ethnics in school. Marisa brought in stuff from Mexico, 'cause that's where her grandmother lives. And Jimmy showed us Africa stuff—his great-great-great-great-great-somebody was a warrior. Isn't that way cool? What ethics background am I, Daddy?"

Hank raised an eyebrow at Katherine, his bemused smile telling her that he sometimes had trouble keeping Tammi on track long enough to straighten her out.

"Your great-great-grandparents came from Germany, a long time ago," he said patiently.

"Before I was born?"

Katherine warmed to the patience with which Hank spoke to his daughter.

"A long time before even I was born, Scooter." They both smiled at Tammi's wide-eyed reaction. "But that's your *ethnic* background. Ethics is something different. Ethics is about being honest and not cheating."

Tammi regarded him seriously before a wide grin brightened her face. "Then I like ethnics better. You should have seen all the pictures of African warriors the teacher showed us. It was way cool." She turned suddenly to Katherine. "Can I play with Baxter now?"

Following Katherine's directions, Tammi disappeared into the dining room in search of the Pekinese. Within moments, they heard her delightful chatter and the dog's yipped responses.

Katherine looked at Hank. His eyes were soft with concern. She wanted to wipe out the concern, but she didn't want to talk about the things that had caused it. She didn't want to feel that vulnerable right now.

"I'm really looking forward to shooting you at work with your crew in a couple of weeks," she said, grasping at the first safe topic that came to mind. "I did some shooting at a cattle ranch out west earlier this week. It was great."

She thought for a moment that he wasn't going to respond.

"My stuff won't seem very exciting compared to cattle ranching," he said slowly.

"You'll look wonderful." Katherine smiled at his deepening skin tone. "You will. I'm the pro here. I know what I'm talking about. I want to be sure to go out with you when we get our first ice storm this year, too. That has good possibilities."

She could already envision a black-and-white study contrasting Hank's strength and power with the fragility of the frozen world.

They heard the sound of Baxter's rubber ball bouncing against hardwood floor. Hank frowned. "Tammi, you be careful in there," he called out. "Don't bounce the ball. Roll it."

"Yes, sir, Daddy."

He smiled at the sound of the little girl's voice and Katherine almost wished she could handle a series of photos on father and daughter. Her heart did an unpleasant two-step at the thought, and a fine mist of perspiration broke out just along her hairline. She turned her thoughts back to the study of Hank on the job. Impulsively, she leaned forward in her chair and took one of his hands in hers.

"I want to do close-ups of you." Her fingers ran softly over the square cut of his hands, the creases on his palms, the ridges of rough flesh. She told herself it was the photographer in her growing excited. But the feel of his skin on hers aroused feelings she'd never experienced behind a camera viewfinder. Her breasts ached for the touch of those rough and gentle hands. She spoke before she realized how husky her voice had grown. "I want to show your hands. Big, tough hands."

Their eyes met. Her heart did another little two-step. This time, it was anything but unpleasant. "You won't mind if I do close-ups, will you?"

His face moved closer. She drank in the scent of his maleness, felt herself turn warm and soft as he spoke.

"Not at all. How close would you need to get?"

"Oh, pretty close. About..." she eased another inch closer to his lips. "Like..." And another. "This."

Their lips met. Long and slow and gentle. Then less gentle, not quite so slowly. She leaned toward him until she was barely touching the edge of her seat, hungrily devouring and being devoured.

While their lips mated, the hand that had held his moved slowly up his arm. The hard sinews of his forearm flexed beneath the sleeve of his work shirt. His hand was at her waist, his fingers playing over her rib cage, grazing the taut tip of her breast.

A soft thunk from the other room penetrated the haze that had settled over them. Baxter's rubber ball. They sprang apart.

The friendly glimmer in Hank's eyes had darkened to passion. "I'd like to do that some more. A lot more."

"So would I."

"Soon." They were content to stare into one another's eyes for a few moments, absorbing the sensations crackling between them.

"Katherine, about the other day, in the park..."

"Oh, I'm glad you brought that up," she jumped in, not glad at all. "I've been pretty swamped this week, but I've just developed the film. I'll have something you can use by tomorrow."

"By tomorrow. That's good. But what I—"

A loud crash interrupted him. They both jumped up and went quickly to the hall. "Tammi?"

"Yes, Daddy?" A timid voice floated up the stairs from the direction of the darkroom.

Katherine led the way. When they reached the bottom of the stairs, they discovered Tammi standing back from a spreading pool of developing fluid. In the middle of it lay a half-dozen strips of newly developed negatives, bent and crumpled and soaking up the fluid.

Katherine's heart went out to the forlorn-looking child who gazed up at them. The urge to comfort was quickly displaced by an acute pain in the region of Katherine's abdomen. Involuntarily, she pressed her hand against the pain.

"Tammi, what in the—"

"I'm sorry, Daddy. I didn't mean to. It was an accident." Tears pooled in the little girl's round, brown eyes. Katherine fought against the urge to double over against the intensity of the pain slicing through her midsection.

Hank bent over to begin picking up the film. "Sorry is not good enough, young lady. You've just—"

"It's all right." Katherine felt close to blacking out. She had to get these two people out of her house. She had to lie down before she fell down. "It's nothing. Just . . . just leave it."

"Nothing doing," Hank protested. "We'll clean it up and—"

"No!" Katherine knew her voice was sharp, but she couldn't help it. The entire room was losing focus, turning black. "It's not a big deal. I'll do it myself. Just get Tammi out of here . . . before she . . . before she gets some of the solution on her."

"Daddy, I'm sorry. Baxter's ball bounced down the stairs and we came after it. I didn't mean to knock anything over."

The tearful plea for forgiveness registered in Katherine's pain-fogged brain. Ignoring her discomfort, she dropped to her knees and reached for the girl, enveloping her in a hug. "It's all right, sweetheart. It doesn't matter."

Tammi sniffled, but snuggled deep into the hug. "I made a terrible mess."

"We'll clean it up. It happens all the time," Katherine crooned into the youngster's ear.

"Are you sure?"

"Sure I'm sure." She let Tammi go, but didn't rise. She wasn't sure she could. "Now, Tammi, will you take Baxter upstairs? If he licks up the stuff on the floor, he'll be sick."

Tammi disappeared up the stairs, coaxing the dog along with her. Hank knelt beside Katherine. "*You're* sick. Katie, you have to tell me what's wrong. You're scaring me."

Even through the haze of her pain, the concern in his eyes touched her, started to soothe the latest wave of hurt. "I'm sorry. It's really nothing. Nothing physical, anyway." A bubble of hysterical laughter rose in her throat and rippled out. "Guess you could say I'm just a little unstable."

She slumped onto the floor and squeezed her eyes shut until the latest pain died. Hank sat beside her and pulled her against the comforting hardness of his chest. "What are you talking about? You're in pain."

She laughed again, a small sound that seemed to come from somewhere else, somewhere far away. "But that's unstable if there's nothing wrong with you."

"But what do you . . ."

"Panic attacks." The seizures of pain were easing now. She willed the tension out of her body. Hank felt so good. She felt safe. "They just . . . come . . . out of nowhere."

He was silent. She melted into him, refusing to contemplate the irony of being brought to her knees by something so closely akin to labor pains.

His rough hand was gentle against her perspiring forehead. His lips followed. "Something must cause this, Katie."

"Daddy?" Tammi's frightened voice floated down to them.

Katherine straightened, seized with a sudden fear that Tammi would see her again and realize something was wrong. "I'm fine now, Hank. Please go. Please."

"I can't leave you like this."

"Hank, go. Now. Please."

He rose reluctantly and began to mount the stairs, turning back every few steps. "I'll take Tammi home, then come back."

"No!" How could she tell him that she only turned into a basket case when he was around? "I don't want you to come back, Hank. I'm fine. Just...leave."

"But..."

"Please, Hank. I need to be alone."

"I could help."

Unreasonably, she felt he could. But experience had so far proven otherwise. "Not now, Hank. I'll be fine."

By the time she heard the front door closing behind them, she was able to pull herself to her feet. Her knees were still shaky. She stared down at the spreading, sticky puddle.

She laughed, a shaky laugh quivering on the edge of tears. "So much for coming to grips with the underlying problem."

CHAPTER TEN

KATHERINE'S FINGERS felt numb, clumsy. She rang Hank's doorbell, telling herself she would be in and out in minutes. In fact, maybe she wouldn't go in at all. She could just . . .

The face confronting her when the door opened was hostile. Young and hostile and so much like Hank's it made her smile. The girl didn't change her expression.

Katherine ignored the tightening in the region of her stomach. "You're Heather, right? I'm Katherine Barnett. We met at the Shakespeare Festival." Only the slightest of nods indicated that she'd even heard Katherine. "Is your dad in?"

"Yeah."

The girl stepped back and opened the door wider—but not very wide. Not wide enough to be welcoming. Katherine combed through her memories, trying to recall if she had ever been such a sullen teen. Her only impression was that she'd spent the years from thirteen to sixteen up to her ears in good-natured mischief. But then, she reminded herself as she followed Heather into the condo, she hadn't faced her teen years without a mother.

Hank, a damp kitchen towel tucked into the front of his jeans and a slotted wooden spoon in one hand, came out of the kitchen. The worry on his face was a dead giveaway that he, too, remembered their last meeting.

Heather sprawled on the couch and glared at them over the top of a textbook.

"Sorry. I guess I've come at a bad time." She wanted to touch his forehead, ease away the worried crease. As she contemplated the touch, she realized she wanted more than that. She glanced down at his makeshift apron and tried to make her tentative smile teasing. "Tofu soufflé, I presume."

Relief washed over his tense face. "No, but you can sample the spaghetti sauce. It came in a jar, but Tammi and I are positive we can improve on it."

"I really can't stay." She held up the manila envelope in her hand. "I brought the park photos. You're all set for your meeting with the bureaucrats."

"Great. But I thought the film was ruined."

"No, these negatives were already dry and in jackets." She started to hand him the envelope, but he took the opportunity instead to grab her by the wrist and pull her toward the kitchen. The same melting heat she'd felt the day before flowed through her, weakening her knees as she followed.

"That's good news. Now come in and sample Mama Tammi's spaghetti sauce."

"I really shouldn't..."

"You really shouldn't miss this," he finished for her, taking the envelope out of her hand and stashing it on top of the refrigerator, safely away from the disaster that had descended on the small kitchen.

Tammi, a bibbed apron that reached below her knees draped over her jeans and sweatshirt, was standing on a folding chair, stirring the contents of a black iron Dutch oven. The rich red of tomato sauce had dripped over the edges of the pot, dotted the stove top, splattered Tammi's apron and, even more obviously, ringed the edges of the eight-year-old's wide grin.

"Hi! Did you bring Baxter?"

"No, I sure didn't." Reviewing in her mind the platitudes she'd forced herself to memorize from the psychology books the night before, Katherine walked over to the stove and leaned over for a whiff of the sauce. "Mmmm. That smells terrific. What are you doing to it?"

"Making it special. Instead of putting in hamburger, Daddy bought Italian sausage and we put that in. He said it's like sausage you have for breakfast, only better. And..." she paused for dramatic effect "we have garlic bread. A whole loaf."

"Looks like you're doing a great job."

Tammi looked over her shoulder. Her bright smile faded as she received a silent message from Hank. "Oh, yeah. I'm real sorry about making a mess at your house yesterday. It was an accident and I'll never do it again."

"You want to know a secret?"

The little girl nodded solemnly.

"I've done the same thing myself. It's not a big deal."

"Thanks, Katie."

Before Katherine could respond, the little girl wrapped both arms around her neck and squeezed. Tamping down the whirl of feelings the hug generated—longing and tenderness and fear and wonder—Katherine returned the squeeze and stepped out of reach as quickly as possible.

"Watch out, Scooter." Hank stepped up with a towel and wiped Tammi's hands. "You'll have more sauce on Katie than we'll have for our spaghetti."

"We'll have plenty." Tammi peered into the steaming pot. "In fact, you can stay for dinner, Katie. You could even go get Baxter and we'd have plenty for him, too."

Katherine laughed in spite of herself. "I'm sure Baxter would be thrilled. But I really have to go."

Hank moved in to stand between the two, draping his arms over their shoulders. "Tammi, I think you're right. Katie should stay for dinner. What do you suppose we can do to convince her?"

Katherine looked up at Hank, hoping for understanding. But the weight of his arm seemed to weave a magic spell around her. A spell made up of desire and comfort and strength. A spell that almost convinced her she could sit down like any normal person and have dinner with these two people she was learning to like so well.

But she couldn't, she knew, give in to the black magic Hank's presence always seemed to work on her. "Hank, I really—"

"I've got it!" Hank winked at Tammi. "We'll cut the cards for it. You get the high card, you go home and do whatever it is photographers do at night. I get the high card, you stay for dinner. Deal?"

"I don't think so, Hank."

Hank and Tammi shook their heads. "Tammi, she's a chicken. I never would have thought it, would you? Too big a coward to take a little bet."

Tammi dropped the wooden spoon onto the stove and jumped off the folding chair. "I'll get the cards."

"But I'm not going to—"

Hank held a finger to her lips to shush her. "She'll be right back. What have you got to lose?"

Katherine lowered her voice. "Hank, remember what I told you yesterday. You don't understand. I can't control it. It just happens. It could happen right now. It could—''

''If it does, I'll hold you close. I'll put you on the couch and cover you with the afghan my mother made for my birthday last year. I'll rub your feet. I'll wave my magic wand over you and make it disappear. I'll take care of you. Don't worry about it.''

She wanted to argue, wanted somehow to make him understand. But how could she? How could she possibly tell him that it was his own daughter who was most often the source of her distress?

''Here we are.'' Tammi slapped the cards down on the kitchen table.

Hank took Katherine's hand and led her the two steps across the room. Rolling up his sleeves to demonstrate that there was nothing concealed in them, Hank picked up the deck and adroitly shuffled them.

''Why do I feel as if I'm being set up?'' Katherine asked as she took in the view of Hank's well-toned forearms. They were dusted in golden hair. Like his chest? she wondered.

''Tammi, I think we've been accused of cheating.''

Tammi giggled at Hank's stern pronouncement.

''Tell the woman, Tammi. Does the Great Weisbecker cheat?''

Tammi's eyes gleamed. ''Never. But he always lets me win.''

Katherine looked down at the deck Hank had just stacked neatly on the table. ''He does, huh?''

''Yep.'' Tammi watched as Katherine cut the deck. ''Except when it's time for me to go to sleep at night.''

''Um-hmm. I thought as much.'' Katherine turned the stack of cards up to reveal a queen of hearts. Her smile was smug. ''Looks like the Great Weisbecker *needs* a few cards up his sleeve. A queen is tough to beat."

Closing his eyes and waving his hands over the deck of cards, Hank played up the hocus-pocus for all it was worth. Then he reached down and palmed a portion of the deck. He held the cards between his hands, prolonging the moment.

"If you're feeling lucky, we could up the ante."

"What did you have in mind?"

Hank took a deep breath and glanced at his daughter. "Not in mixed company."

"Then keep your mind on the business at hand."

With a confident smile, Hank raised one palm off the other to reveal the king of hearts.

Tammi clapped her hands gleefully. "I knew it! I knew it! He always gets the king of hearts."

The youngster dashed to the stove, dragged the folding chair to the china cabinet and climbed up to pull down another plate. Then, with extra utensils and a paper napkin, she headed into the dining room.

Katherine gave Hank a hard stare, softened by a smile she couldn't hide. "I think I've been bamboozled."

"You can't say I didn't warn you. Telling me something is impossible is the surest way to get me to make up my mind to do it. Remember?"

"I remember."

He traced the hollow of her throat with his thumb. "I'm just sorry we didn't up the ante."

She couldn't stop herself. His devilish smile and the swirl of feelings radiating out from his barely-there touch were enough to make her forget her reputation as Katherine the Cold. Lowering her lids in what she hoped was a half-successful stab at Hollywood sultry, Katherine turned slowly and looked back at him over one shoulder. "Nevertheless, I feel compelled to warn you, I never fool around with men who wear aprons."

HEATHER'S HEART felt lighter the moment she walked onto Penny Gray's porch. She'd managed to cut a class today and slip over to the mall without getting caught. And her dad had even abandoned his plans to banish her for the weekend when he found out Grandpa wasn't feeling too hot. Mostly, things were working out great.

Walking around to the side door that led to the small suite of rooms Penny used as her office, Heather avoided looking in the direction of the big pink house next door. She had spent all day trying not to think of dinner the night before and she didn't want to be reminded now.

Penny, her lace-up high-heeled boots propped on her desk as she laughed into the telephone, waved and continued her good-natured argument. "Have you looked at the carpets in that place? A dog wouldn't sleep on them. Unless your client wants to do something about the carpeting, there's no way we'll come close to the asking price." She paused, listened, then laughed. "Freddy, do I really look like that kind of woman to you?"

Heather smiled. She liked listening to Penny wrangle her deals on the phone. She was smart and funny and usually got what she wanted.

I'm going to be just like that someday, Heather thought, dropping her schoolbooks onto the floor beside her desk.

Her very own desk. Penny had said she could fix it up any way she wanted to. Heather planned a trip to the mall when she got her first paycheck. Maybe she'd buy one of those name plaques on a little stand.

The mail was waiting for her, so she pulled out the brass letter opener and dug in. Penny had encouraged her to read it as she opened it so she could begin to learn something about the real estate business. So far, she'd learned that it was pretty confusing.

"How's it going?" Penny asked when she finished her call. Her feet still on the desk, she leaned back in her chair. "Exciting stuff at school today?"

Heather grimaced. "Oh, sure. If you like algebra. And Emily Dickinson. What a geek. I can't believe they make you read Emily Dickinson."

"And you think the world is changing."

"What do you mean?"

"I mean twenty years ago I thought Emily Dickinson was a geek, too."

"You did?"

"Did I ever! It was clear to me this woman had never heard rock 'n roll. And what message could possibly interest me from someone who'd never heard rock 'n roll?"

"Exactly. Now come tell that to old man Adkins." In the few days she'd been working for Penny, Heather had been amazed how much Penny seemed to understand about her. She'd even found out that Penny wore two earrings in one of her ears sometimes.

"I'll be at the school tomorrow," Penny quipped, swinging her legs off the desk. "We'll storm the teachers' lounge and force them to listen to rock until they can quote lyrics in their sleep."

Heather giggled, envisioning old man Adkins, with his silly-looking fringe of brown hair and shiny white head, rocking out. Penny was too cool.

"How about it, partner? You ready to learn how to update the listings today?" Penny pulled a three-ring binder off the table behind her desk.

Heather had already learned that the binder was considered the bible for real estate agents in the vicinity of Omaha. There were hundreds of pages showing photos of every house for sale in the area, with prices and square footage and every other detail of interest to potential buyers. Keeping the book current was time-consuming and all-important, Penny had said. And it was to be Heather's job. Her heart raced a little faster. What if she screwed it up?

As Penny put the binder on her desk and explained how it was organized, Heather listened carefully. The way Penny talked about it, everything sounded pretty simple. Something about the way Penny said things always made Heather feel she could handle the job. And so far, Penny hadn't been teed off about anything Heather had done. She hadn't even been all bent out of shape when Heather had misplaced the telephone message from that guy with the condo to sell. She'd just explained how much money could be lost if the wrong telephone message was lost at the wrong time. Comparing that figure to what she earned, Heather had made up her mind it would never happen again. Especially since Penny had been so cool about it. She hadn't even yelled.

That was the way her mom had always been, Heather remembered as she parroted Penny's instructions. Whatever happened, Mom had been cool about it. And she'd made you feel like, no matter what happened, you wouldn't want to disappoint her again.

"Sounds like you've got it," Penny said, stepping back. "I'm going to leave it in your capable hands while

I go convince the most exasperating woman in Omaha that we can't look at every house in two states before she makes up her mind.''

"You mean you're leaving?" Heather was suddenly struck with apprehension. She really didn't want to mess this up.

"Duty calls, partner. You can handle it. But I probably won't be back before you leave." Penny ducked out into the hall and came back with a suede cape that swirled past her knees. It was a killer cape, Heather decided the moment she saw it. Someday, she wanted to dress just like Penny. "So lock up. And don't worry if you don't finish this today. Sometimes it takes a while."

"But . . . what if I don't understand something?"

Penny grabbed her oversized leather tote, topped her sandy hair with a wide-brimmed suede hat and paused at the door. "You'll probably have questions. Just put anything like that aside and we'll figure it out together tomorrow."

And she was gone. Heather smiled after her. She made everything sound simple.

Wouldn't it be cool, she thought as she pulled out old sheets and inserted updates, *if Dad fell in love with somebody like Penny Gray?*

Her hand froze over a page of newly constructed split-levels. Why couldn't her dad fall in love with someone like Penny Gray? Penny might be a few years older, but nobody minded that these days.

As the idea grew in her mind, Heather could barely sit still. Penny Gray would make a killer stepmother, that was for sure. Heather remembered walking around Penny's house her first day on the job, envious of the big, airy rooms. *Wouldn't it be neat to live here?* she thought, letting a sheet of listings float back to her desk as she daydreamed, her eyes focusing distantly.

The daydream took solid shape in her imagination. She would have a big room with lots of windows. Penny wouldn't make them eat oatmeal and junk like that for breakfast. They would shop together, and Penny would tell her how to act around guys.

The fantasy soared until something in the distance brought Heather's attention back to earth. The pink house. She could see the turret of the pink house through the window. And inside the pink house was the woman her dad actually had in mind to be their stepmother. He hadn't said so, but she knew it.

She'd seen the way they'd looked at each other the night before at dinner. Like nobody else was in the room. Like they would fall all over each other if everybody in the room left. The Barnett woman had acted nice enough, smiling and kind of joking around. But Heather didn't like her. There was something in her eyes that Heather didn't trust. It was almost like the Barnett woman wanted to look at her without seeing her. Like if she just didn't see Heather or Tammi, everything would be okay.

Heather contemplated the possibility of redirecting her dad's attention. *Surely,* she thought, *I can do something to make him like Penny better than that other woman.*

"WEISBECKER, I don't see any problem with the plan you've outlined here," the parks commissioner said, once again leafing through the glossy prints Katherine had brought the night before. "You've thought this out well. And I especially like what you have in mind about funding the work. If you hadn't brought that up, I would've had to put you off until the next budget year. But I think this will work."

Hank sat back in the chair across from J.T. Lansky. He'd done a little more than the neighborhood association asked him to and he was glad. He'd had a strong hunch that, if he brought problems and no solutions, he would have had bad news to report.

"How soon do you think this could be worked into the schedule?" Lansky asked.

"Probably not until spring. We've got plenty to keep us busy before winter hits."

"Fine. Plug it into the calendar. In the meantime, I'll get the maintenance people on the playground equipment." As Hank stood to go, Lansky waved him back into a chair. "Hang on a minute. I've got something else I want to discuss."

Hank sank back into the chair. He was eager to get out of the office, where he felt acutely conscious of his khaki work clothes.

"Weisbecker, I've been looking for another place in the operation for you for quite some time." Lansky looked him squarely in the eye. "I think I've found the place."

"I beg your pardon?"

"We're establishing a training manager's position. Someone to work with new employees, get them ready to hit the streets. Someone to keep up with what's new in the field, plan training programs to keep the men on top of those developments." Lansky smiled. "I think you're the man for the job."

"Well, thanks. But I've never done anything like that. I—"

"I know you haven't. But I've watched you train your new men. And I know you make it a point to keep

up with what's going on in your field." Lansky leaned
forward. "You're a leader, Weisbecker. And we're
wasting you out there trimming trees." He waited for
that to sink in. "The job carries a pretty substantial
raise. You'll be in the office next door. It's a smart move
for you. You won't regret it."

Hank's head was spinning. He listened as Lansky
continued to sell him on the new job. Hank was flattered, but the more Lansky talked, the worse the job
sounded. An office right in the middle of all the bureaucrats. He knew what that meant. A white shirt and
tie every day, dress shoes, lunch with the big boys,
game-playing, politics, telephone messages and meetings.

The only thing that sounded sweet about the whole
deal was the money. With a raise like that, he could
certainly make a dent in his bills. Maybe even think
about that college fund he'd been putting off.

As he thanked Lansky and promised to get back to
him about the new job, Hank was torn. The new job
sounded awful, like his worst nightmare, but how could
he turn down that kind of money? He owed it to the
girls, didn't he?

When you're a father, he told himself, *you have to do
what you're supposed to do, whether it makes you
happy or not.*

Katherine Barnett came to mind. *Sometimes even
fathers get to do what makes them happy,* he argued
with himself.

But as he swung into the driver's seat of the city truck
amid the banter of his men, Hank wondered if he
should consider the job. Maybe he did owe it to the
girls.

And maybe, he accused himself as he stole a glance at his troubled eyes in the rearview mirror, *you're feeling guilty about falling for a woman who's clearly not stepmother material.*

CHAPTER ELEVEN

HANK'S VOICE on the telephone might have been nothing more than a continuation of all the fantasies Katherine had entertained that day. While handling some shoots across the state line in Iowa, she had found it impossible to banish thoughts of Hank. He had laughed over her shoulder and winked at her aggravations and teased her while she fought traffic.

So his call that evening, just after she'd finished a half hour of yoga, didn't surprise her.

"Thought you'd want to know that your photos were just what we needed to make our point," he said after filling her in on his meeting.

"Thanks, Hank. But I'm sure your persuasiveness had a lot more to do with it than my photos." *Are you flirting?* she asked herself. *And are you prepared to do something about it if he responds?*

"So I'm persuasive, huh?" His voice took on a teasing tone. She could picture his face when he used that tone of voice. Those blue-on-blue eyes would crinkle at the edges. The little-boy shyness of his smile would be at odds with the glimmer of seduction in his eyes. "You're not fooling me, woman. Now that you've sampled my spaghetti sauce, you're just hoping I'll reissue my invitation for tofu soufflé. How about this weekend?"

Katherine's spirits plummeted. "I can't, Hank. I've got some shoots scheduled."

She heard his hesitation and knew he was wondering if her excuse was just another way to avoid him. She rushed on to explain. "I usually don't work on the weekends, but this was the only time they could schedule it. And since it's my fault we had to reschedule..."

"Is this the stuff Tammi ruined?"

"Hank, it's really not a big deal."

"It is, isn't it?"

"Yes, it is, but..."

"Then I'll come, too."

Resting her back against the wall, Katherine slid down to the floor and sat, knees bent to provide a resting place for her chin. She wanted to say, "Yes, yes, yes." But the words came hard. She didn't often say yes to life's unplanned pleasures. "Hank, that's not—"

"I'm a good helper. You'll see. I can help you drive, fetch your equipment, move your chair so it's right behind you whenever you want to sit..."

She chuckled. "I'm a photographer, not a director. Photographers don't have assistants."

But she let him talk her into it. And by the time she hung up, all the peace of mind that had come with her yoga had disappeared. She danced around the room, delivering a noisy thump to the birdcage and swooping Baxter up off the floor to become her partner in an awkward imitation of a waltz.

She felt like a teenager. Eager. Excited. And anxious.

HEATHER WAS so preoccupied with her new plan, she almost swept right through the living room without hearing her dad's telephone conversation.

One phrase caught her ear. "They'll be able to help with the baby."

She knew right away that he was talking to his younger brother, whose wife had just had a baby. She thought she'd escaped one of those deadly dull weekends in the country, but it looked as if her dad had a substitute in mind for a visit with her grandparents.

Not an option, Heather thought as she dropped her books onto the couch. She had no intention of helping her Aunt Elena with a squalling baby anytime soon. She had important things to do. She was learning the real estate business.

She stopped and turned to face her father, who was leaning comfortably against the wall beside the phone. While he finished up the conversation with her Uncle Wes, she tried to picture her dad with Penny Gray. She decided they would make a stunning couple. Her dad was tall and well built, Penny was tall and svelte, not like that shrimpy Barnett woman.

As he hung up, she made up her mind to handle this carefully. With a little Penny Gray savoir faire. If she was going to be a successful matchmaker, she couldn't afford to antagonize her subject.

"Dad, what were you and Uncle Wes talking about?"

She could tell that her calm question surprised him; she could also tell that he was more than a little flustered at being caught. He really was a nice guy, she thought, if only he wouldn't act so much like a dad all the time.

"Now I don't want any argument over this, Heather. I want you and Tammi to spend the weekend with Wes and Elena." He paused. She knew he was waiting for her explosion. She smiled and waited. "I have plans for the weekend."

She knew what those plans were. He had something hot going on with that Barnett woman. She would have to think fast. Surely she could do something to spoil those plans.

"But, Dad, I have a job now. I can't go running off every weekend." She tried to keep her voice rational, the way Penny did on the telephone when she was trying to get her way.

"Ms. Gray won't mind. You only work part-time, and she doesn't expect you to work every free minute."

"Why can't I just stay here? Tammi could go and I could—"

"You're wasting your breath."

He was beginning to irritate her. How did Penny keep her cool when people acted like dork-brains? "But, Dad..."

"This isn't up for discussion, Heather. You're going whether you like it or not. Understand?"

Anger welled up in her so quickly that Heather knew she'd better beat it before her resolve to stay calm deserted her. She wheeled and went to her room. As soon as the door was closed, she slammed her books onto the floor.

Her dad would have to learn that she was too old to push around anymore. This weekend, she would teach him that.

FLATTENING HERSELF against the damp, cool ground, Katherine nosed the end of the 150-millimeter lens under the edge of the wire fence. Across the penned area, man, horse and steer plowed into the wire that restrained them. If they had been on Katherine's side of the fence, the steer's front hoof would have landed just about midway up her forearm before the wire stopped giving.

"Aren't you afraid of getting trampled?" Hank's voice made it apparent that he was afraid for her.

"Of course I am," she grunted, her chin hard against the dirt as she tried to bring into focus the man on horseback barreling after the angry, frustrated steer. "I got a kick in the camera like this once. Thought I'd broken my nose. I'd have to be a fool not to be a little bit afraid."

She squinted into the viewfinder. Man and animals thrashed so rapidly—so violently—in the penned arena that it was almost impossible to keep them in her sights, much less in focus. Especially with her mobility severely hampered by her being forced to shoot from beneath the lower edge of the fence. But the mesh wire marred her shot from above.

"Then why?"

He was lying close beside her on the ground. She tried to block her awareness of him and keep her attention on the pen. She had been incredibly lucky. When she and Hank returned for her reshoot at the western Nebraska cattle ranch that morning, one of the cowhands was practicing for his appearance at the annual Burwell rodeo next summer.

Katherine clicked off a half-dozen rapid shots as the cowboy looped his rope around the horns of the lumbering steer, leaped off his horse and, defying the laws of probability, forced the snorting animal to the ground.

When the action was over for the moment, Katherine rolled onto her side to stretch her knotted back muscles. Her heart pounded wildly from the excitement. When she looked into Hank's eyes, the pounding grew wilder.

"Then why?" he repeated, bending his elbow to prop his head, an easy smile on his face.

"Because it's the next best thing to being on the horse." She knew she should be getting another roll of film ready; the one in the camera would be full soon, but she was enjoying just looking at him. Just seeing him smile at her. Just pretending they were an ordinary, uncomplicated man and woman spending Saturday together. "Because when I'm struggling to capture on film what he's feeling and smelling and hearing and straining against, I'm in his skin. That could be me out there."

She paused and laughed softly. "Only I don't get nearly as many bruises this way."

He didn't laugh with her. She could see in his eyes that what he wanted right now was just what she wanted. He wanted to pull her close. He wanted to kiss her fiercely. He wanted to absorb the excitement that was pulsing through her, just as she wanted to absorb his.

He reached for the collar of her shirt and pulled her toward him. As their lips met, his fingers eased down the V of her shirt. The slight roughness of his knuckles grazed the valley between her breasts. His lips were slow and wet over hers, pulling her closer with the promise of heat. She flicked her tongue against his teeth. She hesitated. And plunged, groaning as his hand closed over her aching breast.

She was flash fire.

When she arched to draw him closer, her camera jabbed her in the belly, reminding her that she had business to finish. She pulled her mouth away, dipping back more than once to brush her lips over his.

"You said you'd help."

"I am helping." His hand traced the buttons down the front of her shirt.

"This isn't helping anything," she accused. Signaled by the sound of the gate opening to admit the cowboy into the pen again, Katherine reluctantly rolled back into position.

"That depends on what you've got your mind set on," Hank drawled, his breath on her hair.

This time, she missed the shot when the cowboy downed the heaving steer.

The rodeo cowboy was the last shot of the day. It was late afternoon by the time they took advantage of the bunkhouse shower, changed clothes, packed up Katherine's gear and loaded it into her VW Bug.

"I can't believe you get to spend all your days like this." Hank shifted to angle his long legs into a comfortable position in the small car.

Pointing the Bug down the mile-long dirt drive leading away from the ranch to the main highway, Katherine waved out the window at the cowboys disappearing in her rearview mirror. "I want no complaints. I told you this wasn't glamorous when you signed on."

"I'm not complaining. It's fun to watch you."

"You're confused. I'm the watcher, not the watchee."

"Not this time. This time, I was the watcher. And you were great."

His words made her uncomfortable. She realized she didn't know how to have this kind of conversation. Not now, when there was no escape. "What's to watch? Me pushing the shutter release. Me changing film. Oh, exciting moment, me switching lenses.''

"I'm not kidding. How about you taking charge. You telling the cowboys what to do. You not caring a whit if you get your hands dirty, as long as you get the job done.''

"My hands, and my clothes, and my face.''

They laughed. "You looked great. Even grimy. But the point is, it was a kick to watch you. I never realized before what the appeal was in strong women.''

As she turned onto the highway, Katherine wondered if she could in all honesty accept his assessment. She knew too well there were a great many battles she hadn't been strong enough to win. Might never be strong enough to win. But she didn't want to talk about that today. She ignored the little twinge of conscience that reminded her she never wanted to talk about it. "So, no women in your past who groveled in the dirt and pushed cowboys around, huh?''

He was silent. When she glanced at him, his eyes were trained on the two-lane highway stretched out in front of them. She knew then that he was battling his own ghosts.

"What was your wife like?''

She asked the question softly, barely able to admit even to herself that it cloaked another question she dared not ask: did he still love her?

Hank hesitated a long time. Katherine wanted to touch him, but right now she felt the presence of the other woman too strongly.

"I'm sorry. You don't have to—''

"No, it's okay.'' His voice was even softer than usual. "I really don't mind talking about it. Especially to you.

It's just . . . Hell, I don't know. Maybe I do mind talking about it.''

She glanced over at his rueful half smile. "Then don't." Who was she to ask someone to talk about what they wanted to avoid?

He sighed heavily as she turned back to face the road. Katherine wondered if he often felt as trapped in his silence as she felt in her own.

"Doris was wonderful." His voice broke into the vacuum that had been building around her, drawing her back to him. "Sweet and patient and reliable. But she wasn't exactly . . . she was still a little old-fashioned. All she really wanted was to be a wife and mother, but she went back to work to earn some extra money. One night she didn't make it home. Her car went out of control during a storm."

Katherine pursed her lips, her hands tightening their grip on the steering wheel. "I'm sorry."

"I guess for a long time, I've been looking for someone to replace her, to be the mother our children lost."

She wanted to tell him there was nothing wrong with that, but the words stuck in her throat. The only thing wrong was that it would never be her. Even if she wanted it to be, Katherine knew she could never fill those shoes.

But maybe, just for today, that didn't matter. Maybe, just for today, he could be persuaded to think of something besides a woman who could mother his children.

He changed the subject before she could find a response that wouldn't sound bitter. "Say, you're not hungry, are you?"

"Oh, I wouldn't say I was hungry, exactly. Starved, maybe. But where are we going to find food? If my map is correct, we're about fifty miles north of nowhere."

"No problem. This is my old stomping ground. I grew up about a hundred miles from here. Western Nebraska doesn't have a lot to keep you busy, so we spent lots of weekends cruising the highways." She caught his grin from the corner of her eye. "Looking for trouble mostly."

"I suppose you found it?"

"I have to confess, if we didn't find it, we made it. I'm ashamed to say that more than once the highlight of our Saturday night was a concerted effort to disturb the peace in our little burg." He grew suddenly silent.

"Feeling guilty?"

"Maybe. Mostly thinking it's all coming back to haunt me."

"What do you mean?" But she knew before he answered. She'd seen his moody, sullen teenaged daughter for herself and had learned from Penny exactly why she'd hired the fourteen-year-old.

"Heather. She seems to have inherited all my tendencies for being a teenaged hell-raiser."

Katherine decided to try her hand at one of those regular, commonplace conversations everyone in the world except her knew how to have. "Except she's a girl and it worries you more?"

Hank shook his head. "Except things are a lot different now than they were when I was growing up on a farm fifty miles north of nowhere."

"You're right."

"And it's tough when you're doing it all by yourself."

His wistful tone made her suddenly jealous and, at the same time, sad. Sad for Hank. Sad for his daughters. Sad for their wife and mother. It occurred to her that, with all the dirty tricks life had played on her, it had played an even dirtier trick on Hank's wife. It had given her children, then stolen the years she deserved to enjoy them.

Katherine tried to imagine the anguish of having someone snatched away so suddenly. She couldn't. "I'm sorry, Hank."

"It was hardest on the girls."

"And that makes it harder on you," she said softly.

He nodded. "You got that right. For a while, they wanted to talk about it all the time. I had to learn to cope real fast. So I could take care of them without falling apart."

"I understand." And she did. The terror of falling apart was an anguish she could understand only too well.

"Anyway, the worst is over now." From the corner of her eye, she saw him fidgeting with the button that opened the glove compartment. "Not a day passes that I don't think of Doris, miss something about her. But it's not tearing my guts out any more."

"Are you sure?"

"I'm sure, Katie. I'm sure."

She believed him. There was conviction in his voice. She was almost glad she didn't have to look into his eyes as he said it, however. She had the feeling his eyes held a message she wasn't ready to see.

She reached over to touch the knuckles that were clenched around the edge of the car seat. They relaxed with her touch. She heard him let out the breath he'd been holding. His fingers gripped hers briefly, fiercely, before freeing her hand so she could return it to the steering wheel.

They fell silent. For the next few miles, Katherine knew Hank must be thinking about his wife, but somehow she didn't feel left out.

She was startled when he spoke again.

"I guess we've all got problems of one kind or another, don't we?"

She hoped he didn't notice that she'd swallowed hard. "Sure."

"Tell me about yours."

She glanced at him. Tall and broad, looking almost cramped in her tiny front seat, he was smiling encouragingly. A smile that said he would listen. A smile that said he cared. She wanted to pull over to the side of the road and kiss that smile.

She turned her eyes back to the road. What she didn't want to do was spoil their closeness with a discussion that was sure to hurt. Hank might be that brave. But she wasn't ready for it. Not yet.

"Not now, Hank."

"You can tell me about it, Katie. I don't bite."

She knew that without his saying it. Hadn't he been tender and concerned before, when she'd gone to pieces in front of him? He hadn't seemed to think she was crazy. He'd been calm and nonjudgmental and supportive.

But she wasn't ready to test him further yet. Today, she simply wanted to enjoy.

"Would you mind if I...if we just... Not right now, Hank. Okay?"

He drew a deep breath. "How long are you going to shut me out, Katie?"

She realized she was gripping the steering wheel like a lifeline in a storm. She forced herself to loosen her hold. "Please, Hank. Just for today. Give me one day when I don't have to worry about . . . anything."

"Wish granted." He leaned across the front seat and brushed her cheek with a kiss. "I guess we should really head for home. I know you're hungry, but by the time we hit Omaha, it'll be way past dark as it is."

"I guess you're right." Katherine hesitated. Chances to make Hank just a little bit hers wouldn't come very often. She wanted him to be. Even if just a little bit. "Unless . . . there's a great little inn in Grand Island, right on our way. Surely we have time for a quick meal."

Neither of them mentioned that by the time they finished dinner, it would be awfully late to drive the rest of the way home.

CHAPTER TWELVE

THE CASTING DIRECTOR had made a big mistake, Katherine thought. Romantic lead was not supposed to be her role.

In her khaki slacks and cableknit sweater, she knew she needed another run through the wardrobe room before she could even come close to playing the part. And if Hank's uneasy glances around the intimate, dimly lit dining room of the inn were any indication, he felt the same.

"Maybe this isn't such a great idea," Katherine said, lowering her menu and glancing over the top of the flickering candle in the middle of their table. "I've only been here for lunch and I didn't realize it was quite so...ritzy...at dinner. We don't have to stay."

Hank's blue eyes were dark in the low light. His smile was soft. "What? Just because I got the distinct impression the maître d' has a rule against cowboy boots in his dining room?"

"We might be a little underdressed."

"Don't worry about it. It'll keep them humble, having a guy in jeans ordering pâté and truffles. They'll just wonder if we're rich and eccentric."

"Is that what you're going to order?"

He frowned in disbelief. "Are you kidding? They've got steak, don't they? Some plain old Nebraska beef?"

"We can leave, you know."

"Nah. You're too pretty in the candlelight."

She thanked him with her eyes and found she couldn't look away. His eyes were doing some talking, too. They were asking for things that weren't on the menu. A tremor started deep inside her and shimmied its way to the surface.

It appeared she was cast as the romantic lead whether she was dressed for the part or not. She pulled her eyes back to the menu but suddenly realized it would be difficult to swallow a single bite.

"Don't look now," Hank whispered, "but I think the maître d' and the head waiter are plotting to get us out of here. They'll never take me without creating a scene."

Katherine smothered her laugh and looked up into the devilish gleam in his eyes. "I hate to play into their hands, but why don't we blow out of here? I'm not feeling stuffy enough for this place tonight."

"Want to go someplace where we can hold hands?"

"And eat with our fingers?"

"At last. My kind of woman."

They walked out of the dining room and back through the lobby of the inn. Katherine kept her eyes averted from the registration desk. Hank's steps slowed as they passed; Katherine's heart raced. One look from her was all that was needed, she knew. What they both wanted wasn't on the inn's menu. It waited upstairs, in a high four-poster in one of the small, quaint rooms.

They walked past the desk, not stopping until they were safely off the wraparound front porch and in her car. They drove for less than ten minutes before they spotted a drive-in burger joint on South Locust, exchanged looks and pulled Katherine's VW into a spot beside a microphone. They ordered burgers, a double order of onion rings and root beer in frosty mugs.

"This is more like it," Hank said.

"Definitely. I'll bet they used to have girls on roller skates working here."

"That's what my dad says. You may not realize this, but he was the original cruiser."

She returned his grin. "The original cruiser?"

"Yep. He started the whole thing—about 1953. Someday, somebody'll get smart and immortalize the old man."

"So you followed in your father's footsteps."

"Tire tracks, actually." When he turned in his seat to face her, their knees met. "I'll bet I know what you were like in high school."

Her smile felt wobbly. She felt wobbly all over, in fact. She gave herself permission to relive their kiss earlier in the day and the confidence with which he'd touched her. Her nipples grew hard. The memory was a physical sensation, throbbing through her. She knew she couldn't speak without sounding breathless. "Betcha don't."

The challenge in her words and the huskiness in her voice weren't lost on him. She was sure of that from the sudden fire burning in his eyes. The rim of dark blue seemed to smolder and spread, swallowing up the softer pale blue at the centers of his irises.

"Sure I do." He took the hand she had draped over the steering wheel and traced her fingers with the same sure strokes he'd used to touch her breast that morning. "You were serious. Made straight *A*'s, and never wore jeans to school and turned your nose up at the guys who were known troublemakers."

She forced herself to talk over the tightening in her chest. "Actually, I was a known troublemaker myself."

"Naw. Not Katherine Barnett. You had to be the prissy type."

As he said it, his free hand trailed up her arm to rest on her neck. The teasing look in his eyes dared her to prove him wrong by leaving his hand, warm and intimate, right where he'd left it.

She retaliated by giving him a playful pinch to the inner flesh of his palm. He chuckled.

"Prissy? I'll have you know I grew up determined to be even more delinquent than my three brothers."

"Ooh, I like that. Does that mean you make out on the first date?"

The word jarred her. This wasn't a date, was it?

She brushed her cheek over the hand at her neck. "Wise guy. I'll have you know I was far too imaginative to settle for being fast and loose with the guys. My most heralded escapade was hot-wiring the science teacher's car for my science project and moving it to the parking lot of the elementary school. Deputy Tatum found it that night when he made his rounds and matched the tag number with the stolen car report."

"Not bad. I'll bet you were ready to hop a freight train when the truth about that one finally came out."

"Actually, no. I outlined the whole thing in the science report I turned in the next day. I thought it was a sure A."

"And?"

Right now, she was ready to give Hank an A in seduction, but she forced her thoughts back to the conversation. "Mr. Watkins was not impressed with my scientific skills. Deputy Tatum, however, was quite impressed. So impressed he let me clean litter off the town square for twelve straight Saturdays.''

He studied her, apparently intent on finding something else in her story. ''What happened to that Katie?''

''What do you mean?''

''That doesn't sound like the kind of person you are today.''

She shifted her eyes away from his, pretending to look toward the building for some sign of their order. ''You're right. I'm a reformed hot-wirer.''

''That's not what I mean. You seem more serious now. Almost like... like life isn't that much fun for you.'' He tugged on her ponytail to recapture her attention. ''You laugh a lot and joke around a lot, but it's not very convincing.''

''No, that's not... I have lots of fun. But things change, Hank. People grow up.''

''Katherine, what is it? What made you grow up?''

She shifted away from him. ''Oh, you know. Marriage. Divorce. I don't suppose divorce is as hard as... some things... but it still leaves you different.''

''What happened to your marriage? Was it because you weren't ready to have children?''

She laughed and knew the sound was brittle. She took a deep breath, trying not to give in to her urge to talk to him when what she really wanted was to spill everything out, to let him see things in her that no one had ever seen. He would understand, she knew. And his understanding might help her work some magic that she hadn't been able to work alone.

Or it might simply take all the magic out of their evening together.

If his present couldn't spoil this night, she decided, neither could her past. She called up a big, teasing smile. "Hank, if my divorce is the most romantic topic you can think of, you've been out of circulation far too long."

His face was expressionless for a moment. He wasn't going to be satisfied for long with her evasiveness, she could see that. Then he returned her smile. It was reluctant but genuine.

"You want romantic? In a car that's smaller than my bathtub, you want romantic?"

She leaned closer to him, brushing her lips over his. Anything more and she wouldn't care if their burgers never arrived. "Does that mean you've never experienced the romantic possibilities of a bathtub?"

He groaned. "You are a troublemaker, aren't you?"

After they finished their burgers, they didn't even mention driving back to Omaha. At Hank's direction, she pointed her VW once again in the direction of the Platte River.

"Is that a road?" She slowed the car and looked skeptically down the dark, narrow opening in the cornfields, where he'd told her to turn off one of the gravel roads outside of town.

"Close enough."

She did as he said and, after much winding along the narrow, bumpy path, they found themselves in a small copse of trees along the bank of the river.

"Park here and let's walk—or talk."

She was grateful for the reprieve that allowed her to forget she was sealing a fate she wasn't certain she was even ready to face. The longer they stayed, the less likely they were to head for home tonight—and the more likely she would have to make a decision about just how involved she planned to get with Hank.

And his girls.

She banished the thought. "I know your type, Hank Weisbecker. You've heard I'm a troublemaker and you're just trying to find out if I can be kissed on the first date."

Their eyes locked. "That's right. But not here. Come on."

He reached behind the seat for the blanket she had stashed there after the photo shoots. She followed him, the moonlight reflected off the water lighting their way to a small clearing that was guarded by a thick stand of shrubs and trees.

The night was cooler, the sky cloudless and dotted with stars. They spread the blanket and Hank pulled her down beside him. Moonlight sparkled in his eyes, glowed white on his pale hair.

"This is nice," she murmured, feeling the warm length of his body alongside hers. "How'd you know it was here?"

"Fishing. Camping." She looked at him with a taunting smile. "Okay, okay. Parking with girls. The Platte has lots of places like this."

"Isn't the country nice? We're just minutes out of town, but we might be hundreds of miles from anyone else."

"Then what are we doing living in town?"

"I don't know. I ask myself that sometimes." Her breath caught on the last word as he placed a warm hand at her waist. "The city's a good place to be anonymous, I guess."

"To hide?" He pulled her onto her side, so they were facing each other. "Is that what you mean?"

She could barely speak for his closeness. He was inches from her, his chest radiating heat, his breath mingling with hers. "I thought you wanted to kiss."

He smiled as he lowered his lips to hers. "Well, for starters, anyway."

His lips covered hers, gentle but hungry. They warmed her, then heated her, coaxing into full flower the passion that had danced around the edges of her senses all day. As their mouths clung, tasting and probing and demanding, Katherine insinuated her body closer to his. He made her feel small and protected, but not weak and defenseless, as she sometimes felt. The emotion surging up in her was nothing if not powerful.

Her breasts pressed to his hard, broad chest, Katherine wrapped her arms around his lean waist. He was hard, warm, strong. She tangled her legs in his, sighing as the hardness of his thighs weighed her down. She felt the heat at the juncture of his thighs and thrust the softness of her belly against it. He groaned. His maleness leaped against her. Every ounce of the strength she'd absorbed from his touch melted in the heat of his desire.

His hand slipped beneath her jacket, pulled her shirt from the waistband of her jeans and found warm flesh. His hand was hot, rising quickly up her slender rib cage to her breast. A whimpering cry rose in her throat as his hand closed over her breast, capturing the beat of her heart and the taut response of her aching nipple.

He eased his lips away from hers. "We should stop."

"Not yet," she whispered. She fumbled with his buttons, wanting more of their flesh to meet.

"Then not at all."

She smiled at him, pausing again to enjoy the glow of moonlight on his face. Then she eased on her back, rolling him with her until his body covered hers. She slipped a leg over his, until he nestled between her thighs.

"It's no bathtub," she whispered. "But I think we can make it work."

His eyes, now shadowed in the darkness, burned into hers. "I can...make sure everything is...safe."

She closed her eyes, a little too tightly, refusing to relinquish her hold on the magic shivering through her. "Not to worry. Everything is...taken care of."

"You're sure?" She heard the apprehension in his voice. "I've been...I've made that mistake once in my life already and..."

"I'm sure."

When she pulled his lips to hers again, her kiss held more fierceness, more urgency. Hank responded with an ever-increasing urgency of his own. She let the heat in him engulf her, let it consume the moment of emptiness that had come with the irony of his concern for birth control. His lips covered hers. His chest covered hers. He pressed hard against the softness at the juncture of her thighs. His need filled her, replacing the empty longing that had tormented her for so long with a new yearning, one only he could satisfy.

Hank pulled away briefly to rid them both of their jeans. Katherine lay back, enjoying the gleam of his strong thighs and the eager power of his arousal. When he lowered himself to her again, he pulled the corner of the blanket up to cover them. She cried out as the silken tip of his erection caressed her, teased against her softness. He was soft and hard, gentle and demanding.

He rested his weight on elbows and knees, delaying their union while he pushed aside her clothes to reveal one small, round breast. Like a man dying of hunger, he lowered his face to it and caressed it with his cheek. At the gentle rasp of his end-of-day whiskers, she arched into him. His erection slipped inside her softness.

He called out her name, then pulled back to look into her eyes as he completed the slow movement that joined them. They moved together, and for the first time Katherine forgot she had anything to hide. As Hank swelled against her, she felt the involuntary contractions that told her she was just inches from the edge, in danger of slipping over.

"Oh, please," she sighed, closing her eyes against the powerful emotion she read in his eyes. He rocked against her, forcing her to quaking climax. She clutched at him, holding fiercely to his shoulders, her whispering cries incoherent but unmistakable in their message.

He slowed while she slowed, regaining a steady rhythm only when she was ready. Breathless and weak, she felt the inexorable pull of her senses in response to his thrusts. The tension built in her once again as she felt it grow in him. Linked to him by some current of emotion and sensation, she felt his response intensify. Their movements quickened as their desire consumed them. Then she felt his climax, rising from somewhere deep within him. She gave herself up to it, let herself absorb the power of his surging completion. Together, they shared the shower of exploding sensations.

They lay in silence for a long while, letting their heartbeats slow, letting the stars return to the sky and the shimmer of the moonlight on the river make its presence known again.

"Okay, I believe you," he whispered at last.

"About what?"

"You're not prissy. I swear, I'll never call you prissy again."

She laughed, grateful for the lightness in his tone. Right now, her emotions were too close to the surface. If he'd tried to engage her in some serious conversation, she would have gone to pieces. And she wasn't ready to give up what she held in her possession. Right now, for the first time in almost a decade, she felt whole and content and strong, inside and out. It was only an illusion, she knew. A sleight of hand Hank had somehow conjured out of moonlight and kisses. And it could vanish just as quickly.

But while she had it, she planned to savor the feeling. Tomorrow could take care of itself.

STIFLING A YAWN and reaching a hand into the shower, Katherine tested the temperature of the water. Hot. Steaming hot. She thought longingly of the deep, footed tub at home, and the scented oils on her shelf.

Next time, she thought, refusing to acknowledge her fears that there might not be a next time. Last night, with her suggestion that they return to the inn and stay overnight, she had fulfilled her decision that Hank would be hers for at least one night. He could belong to his daughters and their life together later. But for last night, deep in the feather pillows and muslin sheets on the old-fashioned four-poster, he had been hers.

And this morning, they would have to make do with the shower. She thought hungrily of his strong body slick with water and steam and soap. An entire night of feeding their passion had done nothing but increase her hunger.

Wrapping one of the oversized towels around her sarong-style, she turned back to the bedroom, anticipating the fun of rousing Hank out of his sleep and dragging him with her to the shower.

But Hank didn't need rousing. He was sitting on the side of the bed, clutching the telephone and staring at the far wall. He looked up at her, panic in his eyes.

"It's Heather. She's gone."

CHAPTER THIRTEEN

THE LOOK ON HANK'S FACE would haunt her forever, Katherine thought as she opened a can of soup.

His eyes had been filled with fear as they had hurriedly thrown their things into her car that morning. Fear and confusion and guilt.

"What am I going to do?" He ran one hand through his hair, the other fanning the air helplessly. "What if something's happened to her? Do you know what could happen—"

"We'll have to take it one step at a time." She hoped, as she took his hand, that her own fear didn't show. "Your brother's already called the authorities. They're on the lookout for her. All we can do right now is pick up Tammi and see if they've learned anything else."

"But Wes's place is hours from here. I can't just—"

"Hank, Tammi needs you now, too. That's all we can do."

He had covered his face with his hands. "But I feel so helpless. I should find her. I should know where she is. I should..."

Katherine had put her arms around him, wishing she could do something to banish his anguish.

"You should go to Tammi. Then we'll decide from there."

When they arrived at his brother's farm, they had learned that a band of volunteers from the church were helping local authorities scour the countryside. The highway patrol had Heather's description.

"The best thing you can do is go home and wait," Wes Weisbecker said to his older brother.

"Wait? Just sit there and wait? I can't do that. I've got to—"

"She's probably headed for Omaha, man. You need to be there."

Hank had nodded. But thinking of Heather setting out on the hundred-mile trip back to Omaha had done nothing to wipe the fear out of his eyes.

They'd stopped at virtually every freeway exit along Interstate 80, to ask if anyone had seen her. And with each negative reply, Hank's anxiety level went up. Tammi, solemn-faced with fear, grew fretful and teary as the trip dragged on.

"Daddy?" she'd finally whimpered, sitting in Hank's lap on the passenger side of the VW. "Daddy, why did Heather go away?"

From the corner of her eye, Katherine saw the tension in Hank's face. His voice was strained. "I don't know, Scooter. She was mad at me, I think."

"Daddy, she won't go away forever, will she?" Tammi's voice dropped to a whisper. "Like Mommy did?"

Katherine swallowed hard at the sound of Hank strangling back a sob. "Tammi, don't worry, honey. She'll probably be waiting for us at home when we get there."

But she wasn't. Katherine went up with them when she dropped them off, but the condo was empty. Sensing that Hank wanted to be alone with Tammi, Katherine had returned to her own house.

She had paced the silent, still house for hours. She wanted to call Hank, but didn't want to tie up the

phones. She wanted to go to him, but didn't want to
intrude. She wanted to remember something besides the
look in his eyes, but his bleakness was more powerful
than anything she had ever seen.

Even memories of their lovemaking didn't warm her
as the sun went down on the bitterly cold day. Such a
change from the day before, when it had been sunny
and crisp, she thought as her soup heated in the microwave. But today, the portent of winter chilled her to the
bone. The sky was gray and the wind roared across the
plains with fierce determination. The first snow of
winter couldn't be far away.

She glanced at the kitchen calendar as the microwave dinged. Three weeks until Thanksgiving. The
prospect was already discouraging.

She ate the soup without appetite, thinking ahead to
another gloomy holiday season. At least her single
friends at the magazine, many of them also separated
from home and family, had always made the holidays
easier to get through. There were plenty of parties, and
someone in the crowd always had Thanksgiving and
Christmas dinner for those whose families were far
from Des Moines.

This year held no such promise.

Wandering from kitchen to living room, she couldn't
help but think of Thanksgiving dinner at the Weisbecker home. They'd probably have a big turkey, and
the house would be full of the savory smell of stuffing
and cranberries and pumpkin pie. At the head of the
table would be a man who made her body—and her
heart—sing. A man who had, for a short time, made
her celebrate the possibilities of life again.

"Right," she told Fibber, who had started to scold
her roundly from his cage. "And me at the other end of

the table, starting to shake and sweat and double over in pain. Happy holidays.''

She set her half-empty bowl of soup on the table and drew her legs up underneath her in the rocker. No, a family holiday with that particular family wasn't in the cards. She closed her eyes and rocked. She couldn't rid herself of the feeling that she should be there for Hank and Tammi right now. She wanted to comfort them both. She even wanted, when all this was over, to try to make friends with Heather. The girl obviously needed a woman in her life, to give her some of the things she was missing out on because of her mother's death.

Katherine thought with longing of all the fun she'd had with her own mother when she was a teen, shopping for school clothes and learning how to drive. As the images played out in her memory, the faces suddenly changed. In her mind, she could see Heather and herself searching the racks for the perfect jean skirt.

Katherine smiled. She would do it. She had driven all the way home with Tammi in the car today without a sign of anxiety. She was getting the upper hand with this problem and was well on her way to conquering it. Tonight, she could take the next step. She could take something to Hank's for dinner. They had to eat, and she could whip up something and take it to them.

She dashed into the kitchen, her heart suddenly light. As she eyed the contents of the refrigerator for something suitable, she thought of Hank's words as he had come back to the car from one of his futile stops at a service station off the freeway.

His blue eyes had gleamed brightly from tears he refused to shed. Rocking a drowsing Tammi against his shoulder, he had looked through the windshield into a place Katherine knew she couldn't see. ''What if I lose her?'' he had whispered. "I don't think I can stand it if I lose her."

Katherine's hand froze as it reached for the ears of corn in the vegetable bin. What if she lost Hank and his girls? What if her affair with Hank never grew into anything more? What if she fell in love, not just with Hank, but with his two girls as well, only they didn't fall in love with her?

With an instant and irrational horror, Katherine realized that if her relationship with Hank didn't work out, she would also have to face the pain of losing two children who weren't even rightfully hers to love.

Her hand started to shake. She dropped it to her side and slammed the refrigerator door.

Better, she told herself, not even to risk it.

HEATHER WAVED GOODBYE to the elderly couple, then pulled her coat more tightly around her. It was cold. Bitingly cold. The sun was almost down, and the wind whipped against her so hard she could barely walk into it. It raised tears in her eyes; she had to squint to see.

"Dumb idea," she told herself, surprised when the wind whipped the words away so quickly she barely heard them. "Megadumb."

Leaving her Uncle Wes's had seemed like a cool idea. She would hitchhike back to Omaha, maybe go to Penny's until her dad got home from his hot date, maybe even call Blakely about going to a movie. But it hadn't turned out to be such a great plan after all.

For one thing, it was cold. Finger-numbing cold. Especially on the highway, when cars whipped by. Sometimes the wind almost knocked her over, it was so strong. Then, she'd realized that some of the people who stopped to offer her a ride were kind of scary. Like the guy in the souped-up car. He'd smelled like beer and looked at her the way Marty sometimes did, with half-closed eyes and a movie-love-scene smile. It had given her the creeps, so she'd walked a while longer.

When the old couple had pulled over in their station wagon and offered her a lift, she'd actually been grateful.

By the time she got back to her own neighborhood, Heather's feet were numb with the cold and her legs were aching and tired. She wanted something hot to drink. She wanted to sit down. She didn't want to hear anybody chew her out, and she had a very strong hunch that was exactly what was going to happen when she walked into the condo.

She paused. Unless she didn't go straight home. She looked in the direction of Penny's house. Maybe, if she went to Penny's first, her dad wouldn't give her a lot of grief when he came after her.

Better still, maybe Penny could talk to him. Explain to him how kids had rights, too, and that it wasn't fair to force them to do things they didn't want to do just because you were the parent.

Maybe her dad would see how cool Penny was. Maybe, just maybe, all this could have a happy ending after all.

Energized by her new fantasy, she ran the last two blocks to Penny's.

KATHERINE STARED at the cheery light spilling from Penny's windows. Large rectangles of inviting brightness warmed the yard between the two houses. Behind those lace curtains, Katherine knew, she would find an equally cheery, equally bright face.

"Come on, Baxter," she said, turning toward the foyer. "Let's make like neighbors. If I sit here any longer, I'll go stir crazy."

She grabbed her ski jacket for the short walk and hooked Baxter to his leash. The bright-eyed dog scampered excitedly. She thought of Tammi and the first day they had met in the park. She leaned over and gave the dog a squeeze before they headed out the front door.

She knew as soon as Penny answered the door that something was off kilter. Her always-smiling friend looked grim. "Come on in," Penny said, waving her arm toward the living room. "The whole neighborhood will be here soon."

"Oh, if you've got company..."

"Not exactly company. More like a stray."

Confused, Katherine followed her friend into the living room. There, looking uncomfortable and irritable as she cupped her hands around a steaming mug, was Heather.

"Thank goodness, Heather!" She went to the girl, giving in to the impulse to put her arm around her. Heather turned rigid and inched closer to the fire. Katherine dropped her arm, embarrassed. "We were so worried about you."

Heather shrugged and turned toward the crackling blaze. "What's the big deal? I'm fine. I'm not exactly a kid anymore, you know?"

Katherine lowered her eyes. Pained by Heather's brush-off, she realized that because of her own altered thinking, she had foolishly expected some kind of automatic intimacy between them. Spending the night with the girl's father hardly made for some kind of bond between Heather and her.

"We were just so worried. Your father and I..."

"Don't rub it in!" The girl whirled to face her, splashing hot chocolate onto the hearth. "I know you think you've got your hooks into him! Well, forget it. I don't need a new mother, so stay away from him! If you don't, everybody's going to be really sorry. Catch my drift?"

Katherine stared at the angry young face. The words tore into her where she was most vulnerable. Without waiting to listen to Penny's outraged response to the teen, Katherine turned and ran toward the front door, with Baxter dragging behind her.

"Katherine!"

She didn't turn back at Penny's call. She felt as if every inch of her body were on red alert. She dashed out the front door and down the steps, where she collided with a solid warmth. Strong hands grasped her shoulders.

"Katie, what's wrong?"

She looked up into Hank's face. It looked tired from worry, but his arms still offered her refuge. She wanted to sink into them, to let him absorb the hurt his daughter had just inflicted.

She knew, though, that she couldn't afford that luxury. Heather had made herself very clear. This whole day, every minute of agony Heather had inflicted on Hank, had been a protest. A teenager's way of getting the grown-ups in her life to listen. Heather didn't want Katherine around. The venom in the girl's eyes and words left no room for doubt. If Katherine didn't pay attention, Heather would take more drastic action to make her point the next time.

"I've just talked to your daughter." She forced steadiness into her voice. "I know why she did this. Don't worry, it won't happen again."

"What are you talking about? What did she say?"

"It's me, Hank. She ran away because of me."

"I don't..."

"But don't worry. She won't have any reason to do it again."

Jerking away from Hank's touch, Katherine turned and ran to the safety of her own front porch. She fumbled with the key, praying Hank wouldn't follow, grateful that a greater crisis would command his attention.

Without turning out any of her downstairs lights, Katherine unhooked Baxter from his leash, then ran upstairs and slammed the bedroom door behind her. Undressing in the dark, she pulled her oldest, most familiar flannel nightgown over her head and crawled into bed. When the phone rang, she didn't answer it. And a few minutes later, when someone rang her front bell, she simply pulled the covers over her head.

She had been right all along. Withdrawing from the situation was the only answer. The only way to stave off the certain pain of trying to force her way into a family that was better off without her.

DURING THE DRIVE BACK to the condo, Heather warmed herself with the memory of the look in her dad's eyes when he'd walked into Penny's living room.

She had expected him to be angry. She had expected a lecture. She had been fully prepared for him to play the role of outraged father to the hilt. But he'd done none of that; instead, he had looked relieved. He had walked right up to her and hugged her close. Held tightly against his chest, Heather had felt some of her stress evaporate.

Maybe, she thought as she hung her coat in the closet and dragged herself toward her room, *even at fourteen you can be a little girl sometimes.*

She'd never say that to any of her new friends, of course, but tonight there was some comfort in it.

Hank's voice stopped her as she was about to close her bedroom door. It didn't sound the way it usually sounded, there was a note of fatigue and something else.

"Heather, why did you run away? Didn't you know we'd all be scared to death?"

She let her backpack drop onto the carpet, then flopped onto the bed, facedown, forehead on her crossed arms. He sounded scared. That was it. He sounded scared and unsure of himself. She didn't want him to sound that way. For once, she wanted him to act the way he always did. As if he had all the answers.

"I'm sorry," she muttered into the bedspread. "I know it was dumb."

"But why?"

She took a deep breath, then turned onto her back. She didn't look at him, but put her hands behind her head and stared at the ceiling. "I don't know. I just felt like...like nobody cared what happened to me. Like I'm just in the way."

Hank pulled the chair away from her desk and sat by the side of her bed, directly in her line of vision. He was looking at her intently, but she was still too afraid to look him in the eyes in case his concern turned to anger. Tonight, if he yelled at her, she might just cry, and she wasn't about to be a crybaby.

"Heather, all of us care what happens to you. Did you know that more than two dozen people from Uncle Wes's church spent the whole day looking for you?"

"They did?"

"They sure did. I could hardly think straight all day, worrying about what I would do if anything... anything happened to you."

"I'm sorry, Dad. I just...I just felt so lonely. It's like I feel that way all the time, now."

"I get lonely, too," he told her candidly.

Heather shifted uncomfortably. She knew what he was doing about his loneliness these days, and she wasn't happy with his solution. She wished he would stop, but he kept talking.

"When you feel that way, let me know. We'll talk. You and...your mom used to talk. No reason why we can't talk, too."

Finally, she looked at him. He had a hopeful smile on his face. She tried smiling back but was afraid it hadn't been a very successful attempt. "I know. But sometimes... I don't know. Sometimes I just wish...if I just had someone who could be like a mother. You know what I mean?"

He stared down at his hands. She remembered how safe she'd felt with his arms wrapped around her. She knew it had been silly, but all the way home she'd been jealous of Tammi, because Tammi was holding hands with their dad and she had only been able to wish for that much comfort.

"I know what you mean. Maybe someday we'll find someone who can be like a mother to you."

Heather decided she had better speak up before her dad voiced ideas of his own. "Penny's kind of like that. She's real good to talk to. I think she'd make a great stepmother."

He didn't speak for a long time. The events of the day started swirling through Heather's head. She was so tired, but they wouldn't stop playing themselves out in her mind. Most of them she wanted to forget.

"Heather, I think it's great you and Penny are friends, but I don't think it's very likely she'll ever be your stepmother."

It was all wasted. Everything she'd tried to do. Heather rolled onto her side and faced the wall. "I'm tired now. I think I'll go to sleep."

But Hank didn't leave. Heather's heart started to pound heavily. He had something else on his mind and she wasn't sure she wanted to hear it.

"What did you say to Katherine?"

She might've known that Barnett woman would blab. She bit her lower lip. "That's between her and me."

"It's between you and me if you're trying to run my life."

"You try to run mine all the time!"

The silence stretched out. Maybe he would just leave.

"You're my daughter. That's my job, running your life." He waited for a response, but Heather decided to freeze him out. "I like Katherine, and if you have a problem with that, you talk to me about it. You don't threaten her and you don't pull stunts like the one you pulled today. Is that clear?"

Heather felt the tears she had been squelching all night rise up in her eyes.

"Heather, you have to understand..."

"I understand. Now is it okay if we can the rest of the lecture for now?"

She heard him sigh deeply, but he didn't move. When he finally stood, he leaned over her and kissed her on the forehead before he left the room and closed the door behind him.

Tears trickled down the side of Heather's face and dampened her pillow. She understood. He didn't want a new mother for Tammi and her. He wanted some cute little babe. Someone else to steal his time. Someone else he could love more than he could ever love a tall, skinny, troublemaking teenager.

CHAPTER FOURTEEN

KATHERINE CAME TO DREAD the ringing of the telephone in the week that followed. Too often, it was Hank. And she was running out of excuses.

"Katie, I think you're avoiding me." After his third attempt to get her to agree to go out with him, she could hear him straining to keep the teasing note in his voice. "I wouldn't have pegged you for the love 'em and leave 'em type."

Katherine's smile was wan, but it wouldn't be stopped. Like magic, Hank could always produce a smile, even when she felt her lowest. But whatever legerdemain he employed, she reminded herself, he couldn't make her anxiety disappear. Or his daughter's animosity.

Katherine's smile faded to wistfulness. "I warned you, I'm a reformed delinquent. You should've known better."

"Be serious. Just for one minute. That's all—one minute. And tell me why."

She hesitated. "Because it won't work. I'm not cut out to be around kids. Even Heather can see that."

"Heather's going through a stage. You can't listen to—"

"I have to listen to what she says. And you should, too, unless you want a repeat of last weekend."

The conversation ended quickly. Even Hank couldn't argue with that.

The rest of the afternoon was long. A slow but steady rain and gray skies were the perfect match for her mood. She worked diligently, lining up shoots for subsequent issues of the magazine and getting the slides and prints in order for the current one. As she wandered through the living room after making herself a cup of Formosa Oolong tea, she peered out the window, wondering if the clouds would clear long enough for her to make a trek to the post office to overnight her assignments. A tiny slip of brightness peeked through dingy clouds, but she held little hope.

"Trapped," she announced to Fibber and Molly as she shook fresh seeds into their feeder. "Caged. No escape for yours truly today. And you don't have a bit of sympathy, do you?"

Fibber squawked gleefully. Molly honored her with a disdainful look.

"Don't look down your beak at me. I'll show you both. I'll go anyway. Gene Kelly, here I come."

Covering up in her green vinyl slicker and the funny matching hat brightened her mood even before the sliver of tentative sunshine started to spread. Oblivious to the stares of others as she purposely stomped through puddles, she walked the four blocks to the neighborhood post office, her package of photos tucked under her raincoat. As an experiment, she even tried thinking back on her weekend with Hank, to see if she could remember the good parts without aching for what she had lost. It was still too soon.

By the time she came out of the post office, the rain had stopped. Sunshine peeked out between clouds and was spreading itself like a slow grin across the sky.

Katherine started to whistle. Unladylike, her mother had always said. But good for the spirits, Katherine told herself.

It was when she decided to cut through the park near the Corner Market that she stopped midwhistle. There, in almost the same spot where Katherine had first seen her, was Tammi, jumping rope. While Katherine stood, mesmerized by the youngster's attempts to get in more than two repetitions without tangling her feet in the rope, Tammi realized she was being watched. When she turned and saw Katherine, her face brightened as visibly as the sky.

"Hi." When Katherine spoke, Tammi dropped the rope, ran to her and hugged her around the waist. Katherine cautiously felt around her emotions for other reactions. Neurotic reactions. None so far. "You're doing pretty good with your rope jumping."

Tammi shrugged, but her smile reflected her pleasure at the compliment. "I'm just learning. I'll get lots better if I practice. Wanna practice?"

Laughter bubbled up in Katherine. "I'm a little old for that, I'm afraid. But I'd love to watch you."

"That's what Daddy said. He's too old. I think he's just pouting."

"What do you mean?"

"You know. Pouting. Like he tells me not to do. He just walks around every day now with a sad face." Tammi reached down for her jump rope, then looked back up. "How come it's okay for him to pout but not okay for me?"

Katherine's good mood dripped right into one of the puddles on the sidewalk. Her heart ached. Hank didn't deserve to hurt over all this. Not Hank, of all people.

"Do you think he's still sad because Heather ran away?" Tammi asked, poising herself for another go at jumping rope.

"That could be it." And that was part of it, she told herself. Maybe that was most of it. Why should she be vain enough to think Hank's sad face had anything to do with her?

But she knew it did. Just as the sad face she'd worn all day had much more to do with Hank than it did with the dismal weather.

She looked down at Tammi, who was splashing in a puddle in much the same way Katherine had been just minutes before. "Are you sure you should be playing in the rain?"

"Mrs. Whitesides said I could. I got tired of coloring and playing chess." Her foot tangled in the rope, Tammi stumbled to a stop. "Besides, it's not raining anymore. Look, there's a rainbow to prove it."

Heart lurching, Katherine looked in the direction where the tiny finger was pointing. Sure enough, over the trees of the park, a pale rainbow glittered in the rays of sunshine.

"By golly, you're right," she whispered, pursing her lips against emotion. A rainbow of promise. A promise she hadn't kept. She had shut herself off from the people who cared about her most, simply because she couldn't confront her own fears. Her own disappointments.

And she was still doing it.

"Two of my favorite girls." Hank's deep, mellow voice broke into Katherine's thoughts, startling her. "Imagine being that lucky."

"Daddy!" Tammi squealed in delight. "It's because of the rainbow. That's why you're lucky."

Katherine turned to see Hank swing the little girl up in his arms for a big hug. "I'll bet you're right, Scooter. Rainbows have magic, you know."

"They do?"

"They sure do." But he looked at Katherine when he spoke. "Rainbows appear only when things that aren't happy are about to turn..." he waved a hand behind Tammi's ear and retrieved a papier-mâché flower, "happy again."

Tammi squealed in delight and reached for the bright red flower. "Is it time to go home, Daddy?" When he nodded, she wiggled down out of his arms. "Can I show Mrs. Whitesides my flower first? And get my book bag?"

The little girl dashed off, leaving them alone.

"Do you believe in magic, little girl?" He closed the distance between them. They were close enough to touch.

Katherine felt the magic, flowing from him to her and back again. "No. I don't."

He gave his head one rueful shake. "I don't believe that."

"Listen, Hank..."

"Do you believe in rainbows?"

She opened her mouth to speak, but his words had reduced her to speechlessness. His blue-sky eyes seemed to glimmer with the reflection of the rainbow arcing across the sky behind her. It was all illusion, she knew. What she wanted to believe, she saw. She knew that. But she wanted to grab hold of it anyway.

"I know all about the scientific explanation for rainbows." But she smiled anyway. His eyes were too bright, his smile too gentle, to do anything but return it.

"Yeah, me, too. That's the part I don't believe." He grabbed her hand and whirled her around to face the rainbow, pulling her back against his chest. "Look at that rainbow, Katie, and tell me you don't see the magic."

She closed her eyes against tears she wouldn't have him see. Damn him for being a starry-eyed romantic! Double damn him for making her want to be the same! "The only magic I'd put any money on is black magic."

His arms tightened around her, as if he could force her to feel what he felt.

"Daddy, I'm ready. And I've got a really neat idea."

Katherine moved to pull away at the sound of the young voice at their side, but Hank held her captive, his strong arms curved around hers, warming her back against the breadth of his chest.

"What's that, Scooter?"

"Well, you told Heather she could stay and have dinner with her new boss tonight, right?"

"Right." When he spoke, Katherine felt the rumble in his chest vibrate against her. Her reactions didn't belong in the company of an eight-year-old.

"So I think we should get to eat out tonight, too. We could go get pizza. Okay?"

"Only on one condition."

Tammi looked up at him hopefully. "What condition?"

"That Katie go with us."

Tammi started to jump up and down, her book bag bouncing with her. "Yeah! That's a great idea, Daddy. You'll go with us, won't you, Katie? Please?"

Caught between two pairs of hopeful eyes, Katherine didn't have the will to refuse.

THE ONLY MAGIC I'd put any money on is black magic.
Her words kept coming back to him while they did away
with the biggest, cheesiest pizza in the neighborhood.

Tammi spent most of the time explaining the strate-
gies necessary to win her favorite video game. Katherine spent most of the time slowly thawing, until she was
at last won over. With a look that bordered on disbelief in her hazel eyes, she had followed Tammi across the
dining room to try her hand at the game.

Hank watched, toying with the last slice of pizza. Still
looking a little unsure of herself, Katherine was following Tammi's enthusiastic instruction. But she was
laughing and looking at his daughter in pleased reaction as the game unfolded. She looked, Hank thought,
younger than he'd ever seen her. Young and vulnerable
and happy.

Black magic. He couldn't help but wish she would let
him in on whatever particular brand of black magic had
put the haunted look in her eyes. Then, perhaps he
could reverse the spell, find a magic potion of his own
to banish that wary look forever.

He downed the last of the soft drink in his glass and
walked over to the video game. Katherine was giving his
daughter a big hug. Tammi was full of giggles.

"Daddy, the stegosaurus gobbled her up!"

"Yeah, but not before I put up a good fight," Katherine protested.

"But you still got gobbled up. In the first round! I
never get gobbled up in the first round." Tammi stood
in the curve of Katherine's arm, her smile just the least
bit tinged with pizza sauce.

"Well, now that we've all gobbled up our pizza, it's
time to get home," Hank said, hating the words.
Wishing he could think of some excuse to prolong the

evening. "I'll bet I know a certain young lady who's got homework to do."

Tammi's smile crinkled into a grimace. "Me?"

"You." He took her by the hand and led them to the door.

"Then I've got another neat idea for tomorrow night," Tammi announced, her young voice confident. "For all three of us."

Hank dared not look too hopeful when he stole a glance at Katherine's face. She looked...he wasn't sure. Excited? Fearful? "I'd like Katie to join us anytime she wants, Scooter. It's up to her."

Now Katherine's expression was easier to interpret. She looked down into the eager young face at her elbow, then back up at Hank's. Her look chided him for putting her on the hot seat.

"I'll need to catch up on my work tomorrow night, Tammi," she started. "Maybe we can make it some other time."

"But tomorrow night's the festival. Isn't it, Daddy? Tomorrow night they have the German festival in town. You can listen to music and dance and eat extra-big hot dogs with sauerkraut. Isn't that right, Daddy?"

Hank nodded, seeing the sudden indecision in Katherine's face. "It's true. You can work anytime. But a festival..."

"I don't know..."

"Puh-lease? Pretty puh-lease?"

Hank knew, as he listened to his daughter, that Tammi had suddenly become one of his most effective weapons in the battle to win Katie Barnett.

Now if he only knew how to make sure his older daughter didn't line up on the other side of the battlefield.

KATHERINE FELT an unfamiliar sense of peace steal over her as she got ready for bed that night. As if some healing balm were being poured over the wounds of the last few days.

If there were a healing balm, it was Hank. Hank, who always seemed to have the right words.

"This is a mistake," she had told him earlier as they'd followed Tammi's energetic dash toward the pizza parlor.

"How can you say that?"

His soft voice had made it more than clear exactly what he was thinking of: the lovemaking that had seemed only too right. Katherine ignored the sensations that washed over her. "What about Heather?"

"I'm sorry about what Heather said to you." He had pulled her hand into his. "But I can't let a bullheaded teenager rule my life. She'll get over it."

She wanted to believe him. She wanted to believe in everything that had happened since she left the house earlier in the day, feeling more than a little discouraged and lonely. Tammi's bright smile and effervescent way of looking at life were infectious. Hank's touch was intoxicating. Even the weather had responded, clearing the way for sunshine and rainbows.

Rainbows.

Katherine realized she had stopped by her desk and was fingering the old-fashioned rotary dial on her telephone. Rainbows and promises. Maybe they did add up to magic, as Hank seemed to believe.

She took a deep cleansing breath and felt the healing sift deeper, past fresh wounds to the old scars below. She picked up the telephone and dialed directory assistance in Texas. Minutes later, her heart thudded as she listened to the ringing.

A high young voice answered. Katherine's heart fluttered out of control. "Is your mommy home?"

She waited again. *It isn't too late to hang up,* she told herself. Her heartbeat was a roar in her ears. Then she heard the other voice. The voice that had chided her memories.

"Sita?"

Her old friend's voice was cautiously questioning. "Katie? Oh, please, let this be Katie?" There was no mistaking the break in the voice as Luisita spoke her friend's name the second time.

Katherine struggled to keep her voice steady. "Sita, I saw a rainbow today."

CITY BLOCKS had been transformed from a busy urban area into a bustling German village. Katherine looked around in delight, wondering how she had missed this annual festival in her travels for *Midwesterner*. Nothing she saw looked like a twentieth-century city. From street level, glass and concrete buildings had been disguised to simulate stone cottages and a simpler time in the history of Eastern Europe. Festival volunteers wandered the streets in period costume, and every corner had become a beer garden or a polka palace.

"Daddy, let's make a polka!" Tammi pointed at one of the bandstands, where musicians were thumping out a boisterous tune. In front of the bandstand, hundreds of people danced to the distinctive beat.

Turning to look at Katherine, Hank said, "But Katie might get tired of being alone."

At first, Katherine took his remark at face value. But a long look from him convinced her he was thinking about more than Tammi's dancing arrangements. She looked him squarely in the eye. "Being alone doesn't bother me, Hank." She turned to Tammi, who seemed to be considering the situation carefully. "Besides, it'll be fun to watch you."

"I've got it," said Tammi, who was almost hyperactive with the excitement of the festival and the promise of spending the night with one of the girls in her Brownie troop. "First I'll dance with Daddy. Then you can dance with Daddy."

"That's my girl. Full of good ideas, just like her old man." Straightening an imaginary tie, Hank bowed regally from the waist and extended a hand to his daughter. "*Liebling,* may I have the pleasure of this dance?"

Tammi giggled but followed his lead by executing a wobbly but well-formed curtsy. "Certainly, sir."

Before Katherine could protest that she didn't polka, Hank had winked at her, then steered Tammi to the edge of the crowd of dancers. He took one of the young girl's hands, placed her other hand on his waist and away they went. They whirled to the steady music and, without realizing it, Katherine found herself laughing at the gleeful look on Tammi's face.

When another couple left one of the round, white beer-garden tables along the sidewalk free, Katherine sat down, still keeping her eye on the twosome. She wouldn't have believed it, but they were actually quite good. Tammi knew the steps to the energetic dance and did them with confidence.

When the music ended briefly, Hank and Tammi made their way back to Katherine.

"Now it's your turn," Tammi announced, the words tumbling out on a breathless half giggle.

"You two go again," Katherine protested. "I don't polka anyway and—"

"Aha!" Father and daughter spoke in unison, looking at each other as if they'd heard this story before. Nodding at one another, each reached for one of Katherine's hands.

"You just happen to be in the company of the best polka instructors in all of Omaha," Hank said, his big, warm hand pulling her gently out of her seat.

"The world!" Tammi countered, her tug less subtle but equally persuasive.

"But I..." Katherine looked from one set of laughing eyes to the other. There was no denying them. There was no looking into them without feeling the laughter sparkle right up into her own eyes. "I warn you, guys, I have two left feet."

"That's okay," Tammi said sagely. "That's what Grandma said. And you should see her now."

"But I don't have a whit of rhythm." They were at the edge of the crowd now. Katherine could feel the beat of the music beginning to move into her limbs, coaxing them into response.

"Don't be silly," Hank said, moving closer to her and putting her hand onto his shoulder. "I know from personal experience that you have a beautiful sense of rhythm."

Katherine felt herself blushing, felt the heat spread from her face down to her chest. Felt, as his hand spread against the side of her waist, the heat stray to lower regions.

"I think we'd better dance," Hank said as their eyes met.

"All you have to do is follow his steps," Tammi said, stepping back and placing Katherine's other hand in her father's. "You'll see. It's easy."

HEATHER WATCHED, isolation and helplessness bringing a lump to her throat as the three familiar faces in the crowd broke into laughter once again. She leaned against the fake facade of the beer garden, jealousy, betrayal and bitterness swirling inside as rapidly as the dancers spun around the floor.

She shut down the nine-year-old memory. Her mother, a slender woman whose smile sometimes seemed too wide for her face, and her father, who was so gentle with all of them, pulling a youngster out onto the dance floor, coaxing her to take her first awkward steps in time to the music, whirling her around the floor until they were all breathless with laughter.

Heather barely recognized the young girl in her memories.

That's because she doesn't exist anymore, she thought, steeling herself against the hurt conjured up by her remembrance. *She's dead and gone. Just like Mom.*

"This is too geeky." Heather's memories vanished at the sound of Blakely's bored voice. "Let's blow outta here. There's beer at home and we might be able to sneak a couple if we make it home before my old lady. What do you say? You're still staying over, aren't you?"

"Yeah." And Tammi was staying over with one of her friends. That meant her dad and that Barnett woman could be alone. She set her jaw stubbornly against the feeling of loneliness welling up against her will. She jerked her head toward home and started walking. "Yeah, let's blow. This is really dork city."

She didn't look back, but the images were so vivid she could almost imagine the sound of the trio laughing. It didn't diminish as Heather put distance between herself and the three people, who seemed to be mocking her with their fun.

"AH, FREEDOM." Hank filled his lungs with the cool November air.

You're alone with him, Katherine thought, admiring the swell of his chest as he drew a deep breath. She had longed for intimacy throughout the long evening she'd spent with Hank and Tammi. But now that she was alone with him...

She zipped her jacket up to her neck and shoved her hands into the pockets. Despite the chill in the air and the warmth of his body, which had pulled at her all evening, she found herself leaving a few extra inches of sidewalk between them as they left Tammi's friend's house.

"The kids are great," Hank continued.

His voice, even in such matter-of-fact conversation, had a soft, entrancing intimate quality. Without realizing it, she tensed her shoulders against it.

"But when you can get away from being Daddy—even for a few hours—it feels like some kind of reprieve. Like someone's given you permission not to be a grown-up for a while. Do you know what I mean?"

She tried to imagine the weight that came with being the sole decision maker. Even for the moment, even as limited as her abilities to understand were, the weight felt oppressive. "But you're a wonderful father. Anyone could see that."

Closing the distance between them, Hank draped an arm around her shoulder and cuddled her against him. She felt her tension melt away.

"Don't make me be. Not tonight."

She glanced up to see if the expression on his face matched the wistfulness in his voice. Even in the soft glow of the streetlights along the walk in front of her house, she detected a longing there, as if he'd missed something. Something she might be able to help him recapture.

"What do you mean, Hank?"

He looked down and grinned. "I mean tonight, let's forget about anything except having fun." Once again, he straightened his imaginary tie, executed a courtly bow and held out his hand. "May I have this dance, *liebling?*"

"Hank, I don't..."

He grabbed her hand anyway, swept her into his arms and took a long, sprightly polka step up the sidewalk toward her house. Katherine laughed out loud. "Hank, the neighbors are going to—"

He interrupted her with a long, slow kiss. A kiss that left her even more breathless than the lively dance she'd learned that evening. They stopped at the foot of her front steps, lips clinging gently at first, then more urgently. His arms against her back pressed her into him, reminding her of the wholeness that had come with their joining. She gave herself over to the kiss. To the warmth, the dampness, the seeking, the giving.

Reluctantly, he pulled his lips away, but only far enough to speak. "To hell with the neighbors, Miss Priss. We'll give them a show."

Happiness welled up in her throat. Laughter bubbled there, even as he drowned it with another kiss. His tongue was hot and demanding, then tender and cherishing. She raised her hand to his neck, to feel his flesh against her own. His pulse throbbed against her palm. It wasn't enough.

He pulled away again, looking down at her with the midnight eyes that had the power to bend her completely to his will. She knew that now and realized it almost didn't frighten her anymore. Almost.

"Unless you'd like to take the show inside. Upstairs," he whispered. "What do you say, my Katie?"

Her whisper was almost too soft, too hoarse to hear. "Inside."

Slowing themselves with tiny, stolen kisses, they mounted the steps and unlocked her front door. They dropped their coats in the foyer, their hands seeking more intimate contact than had been possible in the circle of light on her front sidewalk.

"And upstairs?" He slipped her sweater over her head. His eyes on her fair skin were as heated as a caress.

"Upstairs?" She grinned at him wickedly, dragging his own sweater up over his head and tossing it onto the heap of coats at the foot of the hall tree. "I can't wait for upstairs."

They kissed and touched and tugged at clothes, giggling with breathless excitement between each scrape of zipper and swish of fabric. Soon, the pile at their feet held everything but their socks. And neither of them felt inclined to pull their lips apart long enough to toss them aside.

Katherine dragged him down with her onto the Persian wool rug running the length of the foyer, becoming the aggressor, letting her kiss press for more, her hands grow demanding. The hardness of him, from arms to chest to thighs, dizzied her. His gasp was a breath against her ear as she explored the soft curling of hair along his tensed thighs, then moved on to more tender flesh. Then silky flesh, frozen to pulsing readiness. He leaped against her hand and she encircled him with a tentative touch.

"Katie, Katie." The groan rose deep from his chest. "The softest touch. Softest I've ever felt."

She smiled, her eyes squeezed shut, unsure she wanted to see the emotion she heard in his voice. She caressed him gently, slowly, wondering at the response she felt from him. She sighed when a pearl-drop of moisture appeared against her palm.

"Tonight you're mine," she whispered, rubbing the moisture against her belly, warm and slick. She slid her hand around his waist to draw him to her. "Mine."

"All yours." He slipped inside her, filling her, his hardness swelling to fill her softness. They moved together. Slowly. Slowly. So slowly she thought she would have to cry out. Even as their emotions built, Hank refused to increase the pace. She matched his rhythm. A rhythm born, she knew, of a need to make their oneness last forever.

Then, they shuddered in one another's arms, feelings flooding over them too quickly, too urgently to stop.

THE CLOCK BESIDE Katherine's bed said 2:00 a.m. when they decided they were famished and went downstairs to make microwave popcorn. He wore only her short kimono, which barely did the job of keeping him decent, and she wore a pair of wool socks and a sweatshirt that had been draped over the rocker in her bedroom. They dashed down, pausing to giggle over the piles of clothes littering the foyer at the bottom of the stairs.

While the bag in the microwave started to puff and pop, Hank pulled her against him, slipping his hand up the back of the sweatshirt to cup her bare bottom. She snuggled her nose against the crisp hairs curling out of the top of her robe.

"Mmm," she murmured, letting the softness feather against her face. "I am hungry. Hungrier than I thought."

"I've got it figured out." She heard the telltale huskiness in his voice and reminded herself that it wouldn't be a good idea to forget the bag popping away at their elbow.

"Got what figured out?" Nevertheless, she trailed her tongue along the hairs curling over his chest. She had enjoyed the discovery that she had the power to move him. His fingers trailing along the lower part of her back made her grateful she had him to lean against.

"You. Us."

She froze. Without meaning to, without being aware of it, her lips stilled against his chest. Her heart began to pump unsteadily. Whatever he might have to say, she wasn't ready to hear it. She wasn't ready to spoil their night. She pressed herself against him more tightly, hoping that the contrast of roughness and smoothness would be as distracting to him as it was to her.

"Let's take the popcorn back upstairs," she whispered, feeling the first stirrings of life that signaled his instinctive response to her.

"Don't you want to know what I've figured out?"

The bell on the microwave sounded, startling Katherine so that she all but jumped out of his arms. It was just as well, she thought, pulling the bag out of the oven. "Don't you want some popcorn?"

He took the bag out of her hand and set it on the counter. She backed away, but he took her shoulders in his hands and refused to let her retreat any farther.

"No. I want you to know that I think we've got something special going. I want you to know that you're starting to mean a lot to me. I want—"

"Hank, isn't this a little premature?" She tried looking him straight in the eyes, but it wasn't easy. His look was so forthright, so honest. And so searching. Hers, she knew, was uncertain and evasive.

"No." His eyes clouded. "I don't take something like this lightly. And I don't think you do, either."

"I'm just not... The kind of relationship you're talking about..." She couldn't figure out where to go with her protests. He deserved her honesty. But how could she be honest with him when it had been so hard to be candid with herself?

"Listen, Katie, I know you've had some problems." She closed her eyes to avoid looking at him. "Damn it, look at me!" Her eyes popped open. All the tenderness in his eyes had been replaced with the hard-headed determination he had warned her about from the start. "That's better. I know you've had some problems. I was there. More than once. Remember?"

"I remember."

"Good. You might also remember that I cared. I care even more now." He gave her shoulders a little shake. "Did you get that, Katie? I care even more now. I think I love you, woman. And if you refuse to admit that you're falling just a little bit in love with me, I think I deserve some answers."

She barely heard anything else after the word "love" spilled from his lips. Love. *You've got to do something right now,* she told herself. *Fast, before this gets out of hand.*

"Hank." Her voice had that strained hoarseness that signaled anxiety. "Hank, I think we'd better talk."

CHAPTER FIFTEEN

HANK PULLED THE KIMONO closed across his chest and brusquely tightened the knot in the belt. "Good. Let's talk."

She backed away and averted her eyes. How did she say this? Where did she start?

"It's simple, really," she said, shrugging to prove to him how casually she took the words she was having so much trouble saying. She forced herself to grin, but the effort almost made her queazy. Could she really joke about this? "As a woman, I'm your basic failure. Missing parts or something. You know, behind the door when the essentials were being handed out."

She heard Hank's heavy, impatient sigh. "Katie, what are you trying to say?"

She pushed away from the counter. With her back to him, she picked up the brightly colored saltshaker on the table and turned it in her hands. "I just thought you'd want to know. Ought to know. I can't have children. I'm sterile. Barren. Infertile." She faced him with a big smile, wondering if she looked as frail as she felt. Could she keep up this act? "In the Reason for Being category for women, I'm a big zero."

As the words spilled out, as breezy as she could make them, Katherine was suddenly struck with a shattering realization. She had never before spoken those words. *I can't have children. I'm sterile. Barren. Infertile.* She had never been able to force them from her lips before. Had talked around it when it was necessary to talk about it at all, as if leaving the words unspoken might somehow make it possible for fate to renege on its dirty trick at some point in the future.

She became light-headed. The room started to spin and Hank's solid form faded into a gray cloud. She clutched the table. *Get a grip,* she chided herself. But the warning sounded weak and faraway.

Hank clutched her shoulders, steadying her. The room started to settle back into place. His face came out of the cloud, although she wouldn't let herself focus on it.

"Is that what all this has been about?"

His air of incredulity stung her. "All what?"

"The dizziness and the pain?"

She wanted to shrug him off, but she needed the steadiness of his touch. "I have anxiety attacks. That's all."

"Because you can't have children?" He didn't even wait for an answer. "And that's why you draw yourself up like a porcupine whenever anyone tries to get close?"

"What if it is?" She wanted to be angry but didn't have the strength. What she really wanted, more than anything, was for Hank to put his arms around her, hold her close and tell her it was okay. Or for him to stalk out the door, leave her alone and never again make her feel the kind of confusion she had felt during the past month.

She imagined him doing just that. Her head grew woozy again at the thought.

Before she realized what was happening, Hank had backed into one of the ladder-back chairs and pulled her down into his lap. He cuddled her tightly against him and she felt his lips against her hair and her face. His hands were comforting. Strong. Greedily, hungrily, she let herself absorb the strength. They sat in silence for a long time, until she felt herself growing clean and strong and almost whole.

When she stirred in his arms, he spoke. "Katie, you're not a big zero. You're not a failure. And the only essential part you're missing is your self-confidence."

They were words she wanted to believe, but they grated against some part of her psyche that was newly raw. "You're saying that because it's the right thing to say," she said, praying for his denial. "Not because you believe it."

"I'm saying it because it's true."

With his arms around her, with his voice crooning soft reassurances to her, the urge to believe was as tempting as an apple in paradise. She squeezed back the tears but lowered her head to his shoulder.

"Tell me again," she said. "Tell me again, Hank."

THE NEXT WEEKS were a kaleidoscope of sensations and emotions and images of Hank.

Whenever he had the chance, Hank denied all the flippantly spoken but deeply held thoughts she had revealed the night of the German festival, as if the repetition could work some magic.

And maybe he was right.

Every moment Katherine could squeeze out of her hectic schedule, she'd spent with Hank. She spent one full day with his crew, furiously shooting photos for her book.

"You're not really going to put Weisbecker in a book, are you?" asked Stu. "Hell, I'm twice the man he is."

"At least twice," Jessie had retorted, giving Stu's paunch a pat. "I think the lady's looking for more man and less packaging, Stuart."

As Katherine watched safely from behind her camera lens, she had to admit that Hank's packaging might have been what initially caught her eye. But it was what came inside the packaging that had made him impossible to resist. The tenderness. The genuine caring. The good humor he used to maintain his sanity.

The previous weekend, having sneaked a peek into the two empty rooms upstairs at her house, Hank had decided his dirty clothes could wait a few more hours and had dragged her to half a dozen out-of-the-way antique shops on the outskirts of Omaha. A sturdy iron bed, which conjured up images of Spartan life on the prairie, and a rustic washstand of weathered cherry went home with them in the back of his station wagon.

"There." Wiping the dust from his hands, Hank stood back from the bed they'd just assembled. "A guest room."

"It looks wonderful." As she looked at the room, she could envision it with simple muslin curtains and a clean but worn rag rug like the ones her mother had made when Katherine was a child.

The image expanded. What if she asked her mother and father to bring one of the rugs in person? At Christmas. She hadn't spent Christmas with them in years.

"Now all you need is a guest." Hank slipped an arm around her waist and nibbled gently at the curve of her ear. "On second thought, maybe we should try it out first. You'd hate to invite somebody to stay over and find out the bed didn't work."

The bed had worked exceptionally well.

She had helped him put new brakes on his station wagon, a task Katherine had helped her brothers accomplish more than once.

"Are you sure the wheels won't fall off?" Hank, his face smeared with grease, had looked up skeptically as she handed him the hubcap.

"Daddy," Tammi had chided, doing her part by putting the tools away. "Trust us. Katie's done this a million times. Right, Katie?"

"Right, Tammi."

Being with the girls had been frightening. When Katherine offered to have Hank and the girls over for dinner—knowing this was a commitment to attempting a relationship with all the Weisbeckers—she had been nervous. Nervous bordering on exactly the kind of reaction she feared most. Just before they were due to arrive, her stomach had tightened. Her knees had weakened. She'd looked at Penny, who had agreed to join the dinner party to make things easier for Heather.

"Don't pull this stunt with Aunt Penny," her neighbor said sternly. "I'm already ticked off that it took you months to come to me with all your confessions. I'm not putting up with any of this anxiety-attack junk. Besides, if I can quit smoking, you can certainly give up anxiety attacks."

"It's not the same thing," Katherine protested.

"You're right." Penny pulled a book of matches out of her pocket and lit the candles on the dining room table. "Quitting smoking is much harder."

And gradually, Katherine had stopped worrying about the anxiety attacks. When she felt one of the familiar reactions, she took as stern a stance with herself as Penny had. More than once, she stopped in front of a mirror and looked herself squarely in the eye and said out loud, "You can't have children. Big deal. You've got a great life anyway."

At first, it had been hard to believe the forced self-confidence staring her back in the mirror. Soon, the face in the mirror almost seemed to believe it.

When she reached that point, she took one of her boldest steps. She invited Heather to join her and Penny on a Saturday afternoon shopping spree. Although the teenager went grudgingly and didn't hold back on her cutting remarks, Katherine felt the day was a success of sorts.

"So, are you divorced or what?" Heather had asked as Katherine paused over yet another rack of denim.

"Yes, I'm divorced." Katherine's mouth went dry.

"Kind of turns you off marriage, doesn't it?"

Katherine caught the smirk that went with the retort, even though Heather had tried to turn away in time to hide it.

"I'm really not looking to get married anytime soon, if that's what you're asking."

The right answer, apparently, for Heather had been much more agreeable after that.

As the changeable Nebraska autumn turned blustery, Katherine felt herself falling under some kind of spell. As if Hank had indeed waved a magic wand over her head and granted a wish she had never dared to make out loud.

The Weisbeckers were beginning to feel like family.

Her family.

The morning she caught herself trying out the sound of "Katherine Weisbecker" in her head, panic struck.

She sat on the kitchen floor, where she had flopped with Baxter after his morning walk. The leash dropped from her hand. The world seemed to have stopped spinning, a top that had hit an unexpected wall and tumbled to its side.

"Oh, my gosh," she whispered. "I've done it. I've fallen in love." She looked down at Baxter, her eyes wide with apprehension. "With Hank. With all three of them. Oh, my gosh! What have I done?"

Baxter seemed pleased with the announcement. He placed his front paws on her knee and grinned at her.

"Oh, sure, you just want a kid of your very own to play with."

Katherine squeezed back the tears misting her eyes and decided it would be okay to put her head in the sand just a little longer. First, she could get used to the idea of being in love. Then, someday she would tell Hank. By then—in another year or so, she reasoned—she might be ready to consider the realities that would come with acting on that admission of love.

"I've come a long way, baby," she said, unhooking the leash. "But not that far. That's too much to even consider."

So she simply gave herself permission to enjoy the fantasy a little longer.

They bought a turkey for Thanksgiving and cleared a space for it in Hank's freezer. They argued over oyster versus cornbread dressing. She clued him in on the mysteries of omelette making. He tried to teach her how to pull Tammi's stuffed rabbit out of his magician's top hat, but she kept coming up empty-handed. She asked his advice on wallpaper and refused to believe him when he said he liked the pattern she had already made up her mind to buy.

And they made love. In front of her fireplace on a windy, blustery Saturday night. One day when he should have been taking a lunch break. In the footed bathtub.

"You were right about the tub," he whispered, running his calloused hand over her wet, soapy breasts as she straddled him in the tub. They responded instantly. "Does this mean we give it a try in your VW next?"

"Only if you wave your magic wand over it and turn it into a nice, roomy van." She moved against him and entwined her fingers in the wet curls across his flat middle.

"Spoilsport."

Katherine smiled, two days later, as the soapsuds hiding her hands in Hank's kitchen sink reminded her of the bathtub escapade.

"Shouldn't be smiling." Heather's admonition startled Katherine back into the present. "If you enjoy it that much, I'll let you finish it yourself."

Embarrassed at being caught, Katherine cast a sideways glance at the girl. It was impossible most of the time to read Heather's true reactions. Even now, her noncommittal expression gave Katherine no clues to her state of mind.

Grateful that Heather was no doubt equally inept at reading hers, Katherine pushed her memories aside and passed the last plate to Heather for rinsing and drying. "No, thanks. Washing dishes is nothing more than a necessary evil."

She wished, as she spoke, that she had Penny's knack for saying the right things in the right way to the teenager. Katherine could tell as soon as her words were out that she sounded too much like a stuffy grown-up. But she didn't seem to know how to loosen up.

Face it, she told herself, *she makes you nervous. You keep waiting for things to blow up in your face when-*

ever she's around. Loving, accepting Tammi had been easy to adjust to; distant, critical Heather kept her always on the verge of... of something she didn't even want to think about.

Drying her hands, Katherine gave the kitchen a final once-over. As she followed Heather out to the living room, she searched for something to talk about. Not school; even she knew that was the all-time stupid adult question. Not work; they had covered that at dinner. Clothes? One look at Katherine's tame clothes and Heather's rock-band-groupie outfit signaled that clothes didn't constitute a shared language.

They stared at one another. At the frankly appraising look in Heather's eyes, Katherine felt her stomach tighten unpleasantly. She cleared her throat.

"I'm history." Heather raised her hand in salute. Katherine stared at her blankly. "I'm gonna plug in and chill out for a while."

"Oh." Katherine wondered if "plugging in" was some activity adults shouldn't approve of. She didn't dare ask. "Well, then..."

Heather made little attempt to hide the smirk on her face. "Don't worry. You guys can't hear it when I'm plugged in."

Understanding began to dawn. Katherine remembered the headset she'd seen tossed onto Heather's desk. Plugged in. Of course. She smiled with a bit more confidence. Heather smiled, too. A knowing smile that gnawed away at Katherine's confidence.

"And as an added bonus, I can't hear you guys when I'm plugged in, either." Heather delivered the message in a conspiratorial whisper. Katherine couldn't stop the flush of color that infused her cheeks.

Looking pleased with the results of her sally, Heather sauntered toward her bedroom.

Katherine took a deep breath and flopped onto the couch. There were some rabbits, she supposed, that even Hank couldn't pull out of his hat. And a teenager without a chip on her shoulder was apparently one of them.

When Hank joined her a few minutes later, she had made up her mind not to brood about Heather. After all, it didn't really matter whether the girl liked her or not. It wasn't as if she planned to be any kind of permanent fixture in her life. At least, not for a long while yet.

"Is everyone duly tucked in and plugged in?" She curled herself against Hank's side as he settled down onto the couch.

With one hand, Hank worked the TV remote control. With the other, he massaged her shoulders. "All's quiet on the home front. So, what kind of mood are you in tonight? Comedy? Romance? Intrigue?"

The strength of his fingers eased away some of her tension. She sighed. "Mmm. Can you come up with something sexy?"

He feigned a villainous laugh. "Can I come up with something sexy?" He pointed the remote control at the set and darkened the screen. "Woman, I *am* something sexy."

She laughed as he swept her into his arms and forced her down onto the couch, covering her face and neck with kisses that started out teasing and light but grew increasingly more serious.

"On second thought, maybe we'd be better off with comedy tonight," she whispered, knowing that neither of them needed the frustration of starting something they couldn't finish with the girls just a few steps away.

Hank pulled back. Slowly, he straightened up to look her squarely in the eyes. "I've got a better idea. Something romantic. Something romantic sounds just right for tonight."

"What did you have in mind?"

He touched her cheek softly, longingly. "How about a declaration of love? How does that sound?"

She stiffened involuntarily; the fingers caressing her cheek stilled in response. She decided to play it for laughs. "Mmm, I don't know, Hank. We might be better off with a horror story."

He didn't smile. "I mean it, Katie. I love you. I love you more every day. I—"

"Hank, I don't think you should—"

"And I don't think you should dismiss me so quickly." He stood and paced halfway across the room before turning to face her. "I'm not saying this on a whim, Katie. I'm saying it because I've thought about it. And I believe you love me, too."

Her hands knotted in her lap. "This has been so much fun, Hank. Why do we have to spoil things now? Why can't we just go on the way it's been?"

"Spoil things?" She heard the irritation in his voice. "By saying I love you? What the hell kind of attitude is that?"

The quivering started deep inside. "I just don't see any point in rushing things."

"I'm not rushing things. I love you. I want you to know. I'd like you to be happy about it. It's that simple. I didn't expect it to be some kind of federal case."

She knew he was hurt and his hurt was coming out as anger. She shoved her hands in her pockets, flattening her damp palms against her pocket linings.

"Okay. You've told me."

"Well, *excuse* me." He drew a deep breath, pursed his lips, then walked over to kneel in front of her. "Katie, I'm not looking for any kind of commitment. That's not why I'm saying this. I just love you. I love you so much it hurts to keep my mouth shut about it."

Katherine fought to keep her breathing steady; it appeared to be a losing battle. "Hank, I'm not ready for this. Can you understand? I'm not ready for this."

"Dammit, Katherine. I'm not asking you to be the mother of my..." He clamped his mouth shut. "I'm sorry. All I meant was, I'm not asking you to set a wedding date or anything like that."

Katherine felt suffocated. She burst away from him and stood to give herself breathing room. Even breathing as deeply as possible, she couldn't find enough air to fill her lungs.

"Is that it? A mother for your children?" She had to raise her voice to keep it steady. "Is that what you're after, Hank?"

"Katie, don't be—"

"Don't patronize me, Hank! And don't push me into a corner. I won't be pushed." She whirled to face him. "I won't get lured into something just because you want a replacement mother for your daughters. I'm not applying for the job. Is that clear?"

His face froze in stunned fury. But the biting words that cut through the room next didn't come from Hank.

"Clear enough for me. How about you, Dad? Does that spell it out for you?"

Katherine gulped for air that wasn't there as she turned toward Heather's voice. All three stood in silence, Hank staring at Katherine, Katherine staring at Heather, Heather feigning nonchalance as her eyes moved from one adult to the other.

"It's okay," Heather said at last. "I can understand why a hotshot career lady like you wouldn't want anything to do with us. Right, Dad?"

Katherine's voice, weak and trembling, carried little conviction. "Heather, it's not like that."

Heather's face was as angry as her words. "Don't give me that garbage. You said what you meant. So don't play games with me. I heard you. Loud and clear."

Hank seemed to recover his voice. "Heather, this is between Katie and me. Why don't you go back to your room?"

"Sounds to me like it's between all of us," Heather muttered as she turned to leave.

"Heather, I'm sorry. I didn't..."

But the girl didn't turn around. As Katherine clenched her fists against their trembling, she realized it wasn't Heather who had turned her back. Katherine had done that herself. With a few careless words, she had turned her back on Heather and Tammi...and Hank.

She knew, better than anyone, how much hurt a few careless words could inflict. She knew, better than anyone, how long it could take for the wounds to heal.

"I'd better go."

Hank didn't even try to stop her.

HEATHER WAITED until she heard no more sound in the house. Then she waited some more. When the little red bars on the face of the clock clicked into position and flashed 1:00 a.m., she rolled out of bed.

At this hour even her dad wouldn't be awake to hear her leave. Which was a good thing. She didn't want to listen to him anymore tonight.

"You shouldn't have stuck your nose into a conversation that had nothing to do with you," he had said, storming into her room just minutes after she heard the front door close.

"Sounded like it had plenty to do with me." She hadn't even looked at him.

He had sighed heavily, the way he always did when he was doing his poor-old-Dad routine.

"Heather, I'm sorry about what you heard. Sometimes when adults are talking, they say things they don't mean."

She had glared at him. Who did he think he was kidding? "She meant what she said. And that's cool with me, because I don't need a replacement mother anyway. Not if it's her!"

He'd tried to smooth things over for a few more minutes, but Heather had decided she was bored with the conversation. When he'd figured out she wasn't going to talk to him any more, he'd left.

And Heather had waited.

Opening her closet carefully, she pulled out two extra pairs of jeans and two sweatshirts. She dumped the contents of her book bag silently onto her bed and stuffed the clothes into it.

As she passed through the living room, she looked through the window onto the street below. Nothing moved. No one was on the street. No moon added to the light from the street lamp.

Six blocks to Blakely's house. Six blocks on dark, deserted streets. She looked back at her father's bedroom door.

She forgot to tiptoe on the way to the front door. She forgot that it creaked unless you opened it very slowly. She looked back again. Still no movement from her father's room.

Not that he'd stop her anyway. He cared more about that Barnett woman than he did about her. So let them have each other.

Taking a deep breath, she closed the door behind her and slung her book bag over her shoulder.

CHAPTER SIXTEEN

HANK'S HEAD hadn't stopped hurting for four days. He could pin it down precisely—the throbbing had started the night Katherine Barnett had closed the door behind her. And it had worsened the next morning when he woke up and found that Heather had also slipped away during the night.

At that point, sheer terror had overshadowed his headache for a few hours. Hank had grown frantic thinking about Heather's flair for such theatrics as hitchhiking home from her uncle's. Memories of his own youthful recklessness intensified his worries. As his trembling fingers dialed every telephone number he could find, Hank had prayed.

He had learned things he hadn't really wanted to know. He had learned that Heather had quit hanging around with her longtime friends months earlier. That she had replaced them with older kids, rougher kids, kids with a reputation for things he didn't want to contemplate. After he talked to Meagan, his knees were shaking worse than his fingers.

Now what? he'd thought, pulling up a chair from the dining room table so his knees wouldn't buckle as he tried to figure out the next step in his search.

He thought of Katherine and wished for her support. He was tempted to call her, but she had made it perfectly clear the night before that serving as substitute mother wasn't her chosen calling.

His elbows on his knees, his face in his hands, Hank tried to chase away the sickness in the pit of his stomach long enough to think. He had to decide what to do now.

Suddenly, a pair of tiny arms had been flung around his neck. "Don't worry, Daddy. Heather'll come back." Hank swallowed the sob that rose in his throat with Tammi's words. She snapped her fingers and he looked up into the young face striving to look back at him with grown-up confidence. "Presto-chango, abracadabra and she'll be back. You'll see. You just have to believe."

Her young chin trembled slightly as she tried to comfort her father. So he smiled back and returned her hug. "You're right, Scooter. Thanks for reminding me."

Her tiny chest had puffed up; she was clearly proud that she'd been the one on the other end of the cheering-up routine for a change. "Did you call her boss yet, Daddy? Maybe she went to her boss's house. That's where she went last time."

Hank grabbed her and gave her a big, smacking kiss on her cheek. "How'd you get so smart?"

Her tip had turned up a lead, the name of one of Heather's new friends. And that lead, after three more telephone calls, resulted in a conversation with a bored-sounding mother who admitted that Heather had slept over at her house. Restraining himself from taking his frustration out on the woman, who hadn't even thought to call him, Hank dashed out of the house. Within a half hour, Tammi was safely in Mrs. Whitesides's care and Hank was pounding on the front door of a tidy-looking Cape Cod.

The middle-aged woman who answered the door looked as bored as she'd sounded. A flannel robe was wrapped carelessly around her, her eyes were red and puffy and she sipped diet soft drink from a can as she slitted her eyes to assess him.

"She doesn't want to see you, mister. Maybe you'd better take a hike till things cool off."

Hank wondered how much trouble he'd be in if he grabbed her by the neck and throttled her. Surely this woman couldn't be the mother of a teenager, not with that kind of complacent attitude. He leaned as close to the partially opened door as he dared, close enough to get a whiff of the alcohol lingering on her breath as she barely managed to stifle a yawn.

"I don't give a damn if she wants to see me or not, lady. I'm her father. And if you don't point me in her direction between now and your next yawn, I'll have the police swarming all over you."

She rolled her eyes. "Okay, okay. Keep your shirt on." She stepped back to admit him, but jabbed a finger into his chest before he'd taken two steps. "And no rough stuff. I'm not havin' this place busted up by some guy trying to prove what a bad dude he can be. Got it?"

What the hell kind of people has Heather taken up with? Hank wondered, barely able to contain his anger. "I don't make a habit of busting up people's homes, lady. But don't push your luck. I'm not in a charitable mood this morning."

He waited in the living room for what seemed like an eternity. The furnishings were expensive and well made, but an air of decay hung in the air. Pillows from the couch were strewn on the floor. Beer cans—enough to see him through a month's worth of poker with the guys—littered the floor and coffee table. Hank turned up his nose at the stale aroma. A single man's shoe rested against the trunk of a ficus tree in a copper planter. Brown leaves curled in a two-inch-deep ring around the base of the planter. The abstract painting over the mantel hung askew; candles in their sconces tipped drunkenly off center.

"Why don't you leave me alone?"

Heather's sharp voice pulled his attention back toward the door. She slouched there, her hair uncombed, her arms folded stubbornly across a T-shirt that sported an off-color message.

"Where did you get that thing?" he demanded, pointing at the T-shirt.

Her jaw muscle tensed in a reaction that was unsettlingly familiar. Hank loosened his own through sheer force of will.

"Is that all you came here for? To yell at me some more? To try and take the heat off yourself?"

He flinched. "I came to take you home."

"I'm not wanted at home."

"That's ridiculous. Now get your things and—"

"No!" Her casual stance abandoned, she made rigid fists at her side. "I'm not wanted at home. You'd rather have that Barnett woman around. I heard what she said, and I don't want her any more than she wants me."

"Katherine Barnett has nothing to do with this." Even as he spoke the words, Hank wondered if he truly believed them.

Heather made a skeptical face. "Right."

By that time, Hank's headache had been a red-hot pain in his temple. "Heather, I don't want to discuss this here. Just get your things and come home."

"I'm not coming home. You can't make me." Her young voice held a challenge that terrified Hank. "You don't want me there anyway, so what's the point of this big act?"

Fear paralyzed Hank. He had gone terribly wrong somewhere, and he couldn't figure out what to say to get back on the right track. As he looked at his belligerent daughter, he could see another young face, square-jawed and blue-eyed, mouth pursed into haughty determination. He remembered staying out all night, drinking beer in a cornfield, just to prove to his parents that they didn't have any power over him. He remembered driving so fast the speedometer on his old Chevy wouldn't register it, just to prove how tough he was.

He remembered. And the memories fueled his fear. The young girl facing him, angry determination in her blue eyes, carried his reckless blood in her veins. How far, he wondered, could he push her before she pulled some irrevocably foolish stunt just to prove he didn't own her?

Hank swallowed hard and tried to contain the anger that had been dictating his reactions. "So what do you think you're going to do? Stay here indefinitely?"

Heather shifted her glance and shrugged. "For a while."

Finally, afraid to push her any more, Hank had agreed to let her stay with her friend. Just until she cooled off, he had told himself. Just until he figured out what to do about it.

Trouble was, he hadn't been able to figure it out. And the headache had just grown worse.

And now, as he answered a summons from his boss, he wondered if the four-day-old pain were about to be compounded.

"Weisbecker, have a seat."

He did. The stuffiness of the closed-in office instantly translated into a new throbbing at the base of his skull.

"I hadn't heard from you in a few weeks, Weisbecker. Wondered if you'd decided about the job we talked about?"

Hank felt like groaning aloud. The promotion. In the contentment of the past few weeks, he had managed to push the threat of a desk job out of his mind. And now, in the middle of all the other turmoil in his life, it was again rearing its ugly head. He could almost feel the necktie tightening around his throat like a noose.

"Yes, I have. And I'm...I really appreciate your thinking about me. It's flattering." Hank saw the frown starting to blister J.T. Lansky's forehead. "But I just don't think I'm cut out for a desk job. I like working outside. With my hands."

"You realize we're talking about a lot more money, Weisbecker." Lansky's voice held a shade of disbelief.

"I know that, sir. And I really do appreciate your having faith in me. But I'm just not cut out to work in an office." Strangely, Hank didn't feel the noose tightening any, even though he was sure he was hanging himself.

Lansky leaned back in his leather chair and looked at Hank thoughtfully. "I see." His brows furrowed. "No changing your mind? You're sure of that?"

Hank forced himself to smile. He had to pull this off without angering anyone—especially the man who turned in his performance evaluations every year and controlled the amount of Hank's merit raises. "I'm pretty sure, sir. I hope you can understand."

Lansky continued to frown. Hank began to enumerate his options if Lansky didn't feel very charitably toward him after this. A new job? He'd always wanted to start his own company, but where would he get the money? What if the station wagon wheezed its last while he was between jobs? What if—

"Dammit, Weisbecker, I do understand." Hank looked up, surprised to discover that the words were accompanied by a small smile. "I can't tell you how many times I've wished I'd never agreed to tie myself to a desk. Believe me, most of the time it's as boring as it looks from the outside."

Hank smiled, too. The pulsing at the base of his skull dulled. Well, he wouldn't be bringing home a raise, but at least he hadn't got himself tossed out on the street.

"Let me know if you change your mind," Lansky said as they shook hands.

Hank left Lansky's office feeling almost lighthearted. But he hadn't taken two steps away from the building when he remembered that he hadn't solved any of his real problems.

He still had a daughter determined to out-stubborn him. And he was still in love with a woman who didn't want anything to do with him and his children.

SNOW BLANKETED the neighborhood, muffling sound and creating an eerie sense of isolation.

"Are you sure there isn't something I can do to change your mind?" Planting her feet solidly in the ankle-deep snow still accumulating on Katherine's sidewalk, Penny looked back at her neighbor. "Threaten your reputation? Hold your birds hostage? Kidnap you at fingerpoint?"

Katherine smiled, hoping the liberal layer of concealer she had used that morning was doing its job. If Penny spotted the circles under her eyes, there would be no getting rid of her. As it was, she had spent the better part of an hour convincing her friend that she was looking forward to her solitary Thanksgiving.

"Go home before you're trapped by a six-foot drift," she warned, shivering at the strong wind threatening to turn her idle threat into reality.

"My son's dying to meet you," Penny tried, refusing to give up. "Besides, with company around for turkey day, maybe we won't argue about his grades."

"Go!"

Penny shrugged and turned to trudge through the snow, calling out over her shoulder, "Okay, but it'll be on your head if we have a fight because he's flunking statistics, and I start smoking again."

Katherine laughed in spite of herself as she closed the door against the cold. Storms this bad were rare so early in the season, but it seemed fitting. The glowing optimism with which she'd plunged into autumn a few weeks earlier had dissipated into glacial disappointment. Why should the weather be any different?

Actually, she had been tempted to accept Penny's invitation to share Thanksgiving dinner. But she had to start rebuilding the solitary existence she had used to fend off her pain for so many years....

She stopped to replenish the food in the birdcage. Fibber and Molly squawked at her, drawing a yipping complaint from Baxter, who was catching a snooze under the loveseat.

"Play nice, you three," she chided, forcing more cheerfulness into her voice than she felt. "We're coming up fast on the holiday season. You wouldn't want Santa putting you on his naughty list, would you?"

Fibber's cranky squawk signaled his lack of concern.

"Yeah, me, too," Katherine admitted, leaving the cage door open so the two birds could roam for a while. "But we're not going to let it get us down. Right?"

Fibber teetered on the edge of the cage, peering around at the wide open spaces awaiting him. Then, with a decided sniff, he retreated to an inside corner.

"Okay, be that way. Crawl up in the corner of your cage and..." She finished limply, clicking the cage shut. "Hide."

But that is not, she told herself, *what I'm doing. I'm rebuilding. Moving forward. I'm putting ... things ... behind me.*

The things she was trying to put behind her, however, had been singularly uncooperative. Hank and Tammi and Heather had remained uppermost in her thoughts all week. Especially after Hank's visit the afternoon after she had walked out of his condo.

"Help me understand this, Katie. I know you can't have children. Does that mean you hate me for having children?"

"Don't be ridiculous."

"Do you hate my girls because they aren't yours?"

She had simply stared at him, making certain her glare conveyed just how inane she considered that comment.

"Then what? Help me understand."

"I don't know if you're capable of understanding, Hank."

"What the hell is that supposed to mean?"

"I can't have children. That simple fact cost me my first marriage. Cost me the life I had planned for myself. Can't you see that?"

"I can see that. But I still can't see why that makes it impossible for you to let someone else's children—no, not just someone's else's children, *my* children, the children of the man who loves you—into your life."

"Because... because... being around kids hurts. Because I spent months breaking into a cold sweat whenever I walked down the baby food aisle at the grocery store. Because crying babies made my knees buckle. Because it took years to convince myself I didn't give a damn about children. Because I can't stand to be around children that aren't mine, that will never be mine." She whirled on him, venting the anger that had built with each helpless word. "Because you're looking for a mother, and it's not something I'm capable of being. Not anymore, Hank. Not after all the energy it took to convince myself motherhood wasn't for me. If you're looking for someone to go to PTA meetings and help with science projects, find yourself another girl. I'm not her!"

"None of that adds up, Katie. I'm not asking you to be a mother for my girls. I'm asking you to be a woman for me."

"It's the same thing. Can't you see that, Hank? Over the long haul, it adds up to the same thing." She hardened her eyes so they wouldn't reveal anything beyond the harshness of the next words. "Unless we don't work out. Then I lose twice. I lose you, I lose the girls. And that puts me right back where I started, Hank. Hurting because I don't have children."

She had laughed. "Only this time the joke's really on me. It won't be imagined children I'll be missing. It'll be real children. Real faces. Real voices. Real arms around my neck. It's bad enough missing children who only exist in your imagination. I'm not ready to find out what it's like falling in love with real live little girls and then losing them, too.''

Hank had seemed to give up after that, Katherine thought as she wandered into the kitchen to take the small Cornish hen out of the freezer to thaw overnight.

"Turkey dinners be damned," she announced, looking down at the tiny, shrink-wrapped bird. "Where is it written that Thanksgiving dinners have to weigh twenty-two pounds?"

WHEN SHE WOKE the next morning, Katherine peered out her bedroom window and tried to convince herself the snowy landscape added to the neighborhood's fairytale charm. This early in the day, with morning-bright sunshine sparkling off the pristine pillows of white covering trees and bushes and streets, the scene stirred a childlike excitement in a Texas girl. Katherine had never seen snow until she was too grown-up for building snowmen or engaging in snowball battles and whatever else it was that children did in the snow.

For grown-up, no-nonsense Katherine, snow was something to dread because it made travel slow and dangerous. It was something you hated shoveling off the sidewalk. It was something you hoped melted soon. But this morning, something fluttered in her chest as she looked out on the Christmas-card scene.

After checking to make sure the Cornish hen in the refrigerator had thawed sufficiently for roasting later in the day, Katherine fixed a cup of hot tea and took it, with a bran muffin, back upstairs to the window seat overlooking her street. Already, the tracks of pedestrians had marred the picture-book scenery. As she munched on her muffin and sipped at the spiced tea, Katherine felt her earlier flutterings of excitement escalate into something more.

Her trigger finger was growing itchy.

Katherine finished eating and showering in record time. Within half an hour, she had bundled up and walked out the front door, cameras over her shoulder—one loaded with color film, the other with black-and-white.

Breathing deeply of the cold, clean air, Katherine added her own tracks to the ones she had observed from the window. Her booted feet were soundless in the powdery snow. An occasional gust of wind whipped up a gauzy wisp of white in her path. It seemed she couldn't walk half a block without pointing her lens at something—a red squirrel, its tail quivering in indignation at being caught unawares; an energetic old woman already heaving snow off her sidewalk, her weather-beaten face crinkled in exertion. And, inevitably, the hillside. The one she'd known she must surely find before she turned back. The hillside full of sledders. Children in bright-colored stocking caps and shiny rubber galoshes, their laughter ringing as clearly as soprano bells in the crisp air.

Katherine's first instinct was to turn away. But wistfulness made her linger, letting the sights and sounds wash over her until the initial pricks of panicky hurt were soothed.

It was then that one of the miniature bundles of energy hurled itself at her.

"Katie! Katie!" Tammi's voice caused the slightest of ripples on the surface of Katherine's calmness. "Come ride on our sled!"

Katherine's breath caught in her throat. Something blossomed inside her at the sight of the little girl who had been so much on her mind during the past week. But when she looked up to see the little girl's father standing a few feet off, her burgeoning spirits shriveled.

"I—I've never ridden on a sled before," she protested to Tammi. But her eyes were on Hank. Hank, who made no move in her direction, whose eyes barely softened in recognition, who made no effort to offer welcome.

And little wonder, she told herself.

"That's okay." Tammi had taken her by the hand and tugged her in Hank's direction before Katherine realized she was moving. "We'll show you. Just like we showed you how to polka. Won't we, Daddy?"

Katherine was afraid to look into his eyes once she stood in front of him. Nothing seemed to deter Tammi's enthusiastic acceptance of anyone and anything life put in her path. But Katherine had thrown Hank's affection back in his face so many times in recent months, that it would be no surprise to learn he'd had his fill.

"Won't we, Daddy?"

"It's up to Katie."

His words were so noncommittal Katherine was forced to look up to read his emotions. Still, even this close, there was no help in his eyes. No anger to signal her to retreat. No warmth to reassure her that she might still be welcome in his family circle. The emptiness Katherine felt bottomed out. And she knew there was only one way to fill herself up again.

"I don't know," she said softly. "I'm not that good at new things."

"Yes, you are!" Tammi turned to Hank again for affirmation. "Remember how great you did the polka?"

"Well, I guess I could try it. Just once." She looked at Hank, her eyes pleading with him for some sign that he was willing to give her one more chance. "I guess."

Tammi squealed happily and started dragging the sled back up the hill. Katherine smiled tentatively at Hank and started to follow the child, but a firm hand on her arm stopped her.

"Just remember," Hank said, fixing her with an unyielding gaze, "once you start down the hill, there's no getting off."

For one quick moment, Katherine had an overwhelming urge to turn and run. Then, one of the young sledders whooshed past, squealing in delight. Raising her eyebrows, Katherine gave Hank a shaky smile.

"Just so you don't expect me to get it right the first time."

"Just so you don't turn and run the first time you take a spill."

"I won't. Not if...not if you'll be there...to help me up."

He leaned toward her and brushed a light kiss over her lips. "I'm always there. If you want me to be."

The first breath-stealing, heart-stopping zip down the hillside left Katherine stunned. She simply sat there, wide-eyed, her cheeks stinging from the cold and the wind, unable to relax the muscles that had held her rigidly in place on the sled. By the time Hank rushed down to her side, she had started to giggle, but she still hadn't changed positions.

"Are you okay?" He leaned down, his voice concerned.

Her words came out in little gulps between giggles. "I don't know. I can't decide whether it was fun or just plain terrifying."

"Maybe a little bit of both?" he asked, reaching for her hand and pulling her up. "Some things are like that."

"Yeah. Maybe a little bit of both. Do you suppose I could do it again?"

For an hour, she and Tammi alternated sliding down the hillside, which grew less powdery and more icy from the traffic. Katherine found herself almost hopping up and down at the top of the hill, impatient for Tammi to finish her run and dash back up with the sled. She laughed and squealed more than the tiniest kid on the hillside.

So at the end of the hour, when Hank and Tammi invited her home for Thanksgiving dinner—the turkey they had bought together—she was too caught up in the fun she always had with Hank to say anything but yes.

The only tense moment came when she discovered that Heather wouldn't be there. Hank busied himself with scooping cranberry sauce out of a can and didn't look her in the eye when he told her.

Tammi was less reticent. "She's been gone a long time. She's staying with a friend now." She folded napkins thoughtfully and put them in place at the table. "But Daddy says she'll be home soon."

Katherine put her hand on Hank's and forced him to look at her. "Is she gone because of what I did? What I said?"

Hank shook his head. "No. Not really. She's gone because of me. Because I haven't figured out how to be a father. Not to a teenaged girl, at least."

Katherine felt her own guilt intensifying with the evidence of Hank's guilt. "I'm sorry, Hank. You'll work it out."

"Sure." He turned to her with a broad smile and handed her the dish of cranberry sauce. "If you'll take this, I'll bring the turkey and we'll do our American duty and stuff ourselves into a stupor."

And as they did just that, Katherine couldn't help but think she had much more to be grateful for than she had imagined when she'd awakened in her empty house just a few hours before.

They were putting the leftovers away when the telephone rang. Katherine and Tammi were transferring turkey and oyster dressing into plastic containers, and paid no attention to Hank's telephone conversation as they plotted all the different ways they could disguise turkey over the next week.

"Maybe we could put it in pizza," Tammi suggested. "I like pizza and..."

Hank was white-faced and stunned-looking as he walked back into the kitchen.

"Hank, what is it?"

Tammi dropped her bowl onto the counter and ran to her father's side. He sank onto a kitchen chair.

"It's my dad. He's had a stroke." He pulled Tammi close and looked up at Katherine with imploring eyes. "I've got to go to McCook. Stay with Tammi for me. Please."

CHAPTER SEVENTEEN

HEATHER STARED at the pale turkey breast rising in a rounded heap over the top of the roasting pan on the kitchen counter, where it had sat for the past two hours.

Thanksgiving dinner was apparently not a priority at Blakely's home. It seemed that Blakely's mother wanted to be properly fortified before tackling the roasting of the bird.

Heather's stomach rumbled in hunger. But during the past week she had learned that Blakely's mother was less concerned with hunger pangs than she was with polishing off a bottle of wine before cooking commenced.

Shrugging, Heather peeked into the refrigerator and snitched another stalk of stuffed celery and glanced at the clock.

By now her dad and Tammi would already be digging into the leftovers. Turkey sandwiches. Maybe a second slice of pumpkin pie. Her mouth watered, and she pretended the celery stalk was a forkful of her dad's oyster dressing.

As usual, she thought bitterly, *that bratty little twerp is getting the long end of the stick.*

And whose fault is that? her conscience asked.

She looked up at the clock again. If she hurried, she might get home before they put all the leftovers away.

And she might even con Tammi into playing dominoes with her. These people never did anything together.

She tossed the last bite of celery into the trash. Seven at night and these yo-yos didn't even have the turkey in the oven. *Who needs this kind of grief?*

As she dashed up the stairs and into Blakely's room to pack up her book bag, she almost smiled as she anticipated how her dad and her sister would react to her holiday surprise.

EIGHT-YEAR-OLDS, Katherine discovered, weren't very interested in curling up in your lap for a bedtime story.

Eight-year-olds wanted to mimic the dance routines on MTV.

"Are you sure your father lets you watch this stuff?" She spoke a little more loudly than usual to capture Tammi's attention. The girl nodded absently but didn't take her eyes off the flickering TV screen.

"What time do you usually go to bed?" Katherine knew there must be routines to follow, she just had no idea what they were. Hank had flown out in such a hurry, ignoring her protests, that she hadn't had the time or the presence of mind to get the rundown on how substitute parent figures were supposed to act.

And now, watching Tammi's rapt absorption with the rock videos, she fought back an unreasonable terror. The life of this eight-year-old was ostensibly in her hands, but Katherine had the sinking feeling that in actuality she was completely at the mercy of this person who barely reached her breastbone.

She looked at the phone. Penny was just a telephone call away. Penny would know what to do. She would know when bedtime arrived and if a bowl of cereal was sufficient breakfast. Or what to do if Tammi had nightmares. After all, her daddy was gone....

She inched forward on the couch. Just a short talk with Penny.

Then she heard the key in the lock at the front door. Expectantly, relieved, she looked over. Had Hank changed his mind? Realized what a mistake he'd made, leaving his little girl with a surrogate-mother washout? She held her breath.

When Heather walked through the door, Katherine's fears of inadequacy escalated right off the meter. If she'd thought an eight-year-old presented problems, what in blue blazes would she do with a troubled teenager who already regarded her as two steps lower than the worst teacher in school?

"Where's Dad?"

From the sound of Heather's voice, it was clear she thought it entirely possible that Katherine had chopped him up and fed him through the garbage disposal.

Before Katherine could answer, Tammi had flung her arms around her sister's waist. "Heather! Daddy said you'd come home. We missed you so much."

"Yeah. Me, too, twerp." Heather smiled reluctantly and gave her sister's head an affectionate scrub with her knuckles before turning back to Katherine. "So, where is he?"

"He's gone. To McCook. I'm sorry, Heather, but your grandfather had a stroke."

"Is he okay?" Heather sat in an armchair, and Tammi perched beside her, unwilling to loosen her hold on her big sister, even though her attention strayed to the TV.

"We're not sure yet."

"Gee." Heather's face was solemn. "When will he be back?"

Katherine would have been grateful for the answer to that one herself. "We don't know. He just left a few hours ago."

"Oh."

Katherine felt the urge to close the gap between herself and the teen with a reassuring hug. But the gulf seemed too wide—much wider than the few feet of living room between them. That feeling was reinforced when Heather looked up, her dazed thoughtfulness replaced by a look of unmistakable mistrust. "So what are you doing here?"

"Taking care of Tammi. Your father asked me to stay. It all happened so quickly. There wasn't time for anything else."

Heather squared her shoulders. "You can go now. I'm home. I'll take care of Tammi."

Tammi's eyes suddenly snapped away from the TV.

Katherine took a deep breath, tried to keep it from shaking in response to the hostility and determination in Heather's voice. "I can't do that, Heather. I'm glad you're back. I know your father will be glad to hear that when he calls. But I can't leave you two alone. Your father asked me—"

"I baby-sit for Tammi all the time. Don't I, kid?"

Tammi nodded, but Katherine could see her uncertainty.

"This is different, I think," Katherine said softly, summoning a smile. She had to do something to keep this from turning into a major confrontation. "He'll be gone all night. Maybe days. I think he'd want an adult here, don't you?"

Heather narrowed her eyes. "Some help you'll be. What do you know about kids? You don't even *like* kids, do you?"

Tammi tugged on Heather's sleeve. "She likes me."

In Heather's unwavering glare, Katherine suddenly saw much more than a teenager looking for trouble. She saw a young girl looking for answers. For reassurance. For some clue that her life might someday be rescued from the turmoil that death and puberty had brought on in the past two years.

Katherine looked from one girl to the other. Even Tammi, she saw, was looking for affirmation. *And the only one to give it to them,* Katherine thought with rising terror, *is a full-grown woman who doesn't know the first thing about playing the role.*

Katherine swallowed hard. *That's what they need: mothering. And who do they get for the job? The only woman in three counties who doesn't know beans about it.* She had a feeling she was about to enroll for some fast on-the-job training.

"Yes, Tammi, I do like you." Sensing, somehow, that the words were too stiff to do the job, she shyly reached out her arms. In a flash they were filled with a tiny warm body. As little arms closed around her neck, Katherine closed her arms around Tammi. Blinking back tears, she looked up at Heather. "I like you, too, Heather. And I owe you an explanation."

Heather grimaced and feigned boredom. "I don't want to hear it. I'm hungry. S'pose I could get a sandwich in this dump?"

"Please." As Tammi snuggled against her on the couch, Katherine knew that this might be her last chance to work things out with Heather. And if she couldn't do that, things might never work out with

Hank, no matter how determined he was. "Just give me a couple of minutes."

Heather shifted in the chair and started to rise.

"Just a couple of minutes," Katherine pleaded. "Then I'll make you the biggest turkey sandwich you've ever seen."

Heather sat back in the chair, clasped her hands behind her head and stared at the ceiling. "Okay. Shoot."

"You're right when you say I don't like children." Katherine could see she'd instantly captured the attention of both girls. "Sort of." Her mouth was dry, her heart fluttering. "At least, that's what I convinced myself of, for years. You see, I was married once before and . . . and I found out . . . it turned out that I couldn't have children."

Katherine paused long enough to compose herself and realized she had looked away from Heather. She forced herself, once again, to look the girl in the eyes. "I had some things wrong with me . . . physically . . . and . . . I wanted children very badly. . . . I'd always planned to have a big family . . . especially daughters . . . but then I had all these tests and they told me I couldn't."

As if sensing Katherine's distress, Tammi huddled even closer and covered one of Katherine's hands with hers.

Heather cocked her head. "You're making this up, right?"

Katherine laughed, a trembling laugh that didn't quite end on a sob. But it was close enough to make her pause again for another deep breath. "I wish I were."

"Then what happened?" Tammi asked, as quietly and intently as if she were listening to the bedtime story Katherine had tried to interest her in earlier.

Katherine caressed the youngster's cheek. The lump in her throat disappeared with the little girl's encouraging smile.

"Then I got real sad. And I tried to cover up my sadness by staying away from children and telling myself I didn't like them." She looked at Heather again, her eyes pleading for understanding. "That's why, when I met your dad, then you two, it reminded me of all the sadness. I was afraid to like you too much. Afraid that... Anyway, that's why I messed things up so badly. That's why I acted so dumb sometimes."

The three sat in silence, exchanging looks. It was Tammi who finally spoke up.

"Daddy says everybody does dumb stuff sometimes."

Heather shrugged. "Sure. We all do. Even me. I've done dumb stuff sometimes. Especially... especially since..."

"Since when, Heather?"

"Since Mom died." She stared at the floor, her shoulders hunched over. "That just didn't seem fair, you know?"

"I know," Katherine said softly, reaching over to put a hand on the teen's knee. "That's how I felt lots of times. Like, 'Why me? What did I do to deserve this?'"

"Did you? Think those things?"

"I sure did."

Heather looked up as if to satisfy herself that Katherine was telling the truth. "Did you ever get mad? I mean, really mad? Mad enough to punch somebody in the nose? Except there's nobody to punch."

Katherine laughed lightly. "Lots of times."

Heather smiled, a rueful smile that was far older than her fourteen years. "No joke? And I always thought I was the only one."

"Me, too." *Is this,* Katherine thought, *what it's like to talk to a daughter?* At the thought, tears misted her eyes. She closed her eyes against them, suspecting they all needed a break from this heavy-duty confession time. *Later,* she thought. *There'll be plenty of time for more later.* "Now, can I interest anybody in a turkey sandwich?"

"Me! I want one!" Tammi sprang up off the couch.

Katherine reached out to goose the youngster. "You already had one tonight."

"I can have another one, can't I?" She turned her big, dark eyes on Katherine. "It's Thanksgiving, isn't it?"

Katherine blotted the moisture at the corner of her eye. "By golly, I think you're right."

UNWILLING TO UPROOT the girls and upset their routine any more than necessary, Katherine packed a few of her clothes and toiletries the next day and brought them to the condo with her. She also brought Baxter, much to Tammi's delight.

When Hank called early the next morning, it was to say that his father's condition was critical and unstable. Katherine could hear the anxiety in his voice, and her heart went out to him.

"Don't worry about anything here, Hank," she said softly, wrapping her arm around Tammi's shoulders and wishing she could do the same for the man on the other end of the telephone line. "The girls are fine and—"

"The girls? Did Heather come home?"

She smiled at the excitement in his voice. "Yes. And, Hank, we had a talk. I tried to explain a lot of things. I think... I hope... everything will work out."

"Thanks, Katie. Thanks so much. For taking care of the girls for me. For caring enough to work things out with Heather. Lord, I worry about her so much."

"You don't have to thank me, Hank. I have to start sometime. Don't I?"

"Yes, love, you do."

He called every day to talk to her and his daughters, and by Sunday night Katherine could tell that the hospital vigil was taking its toll. He sounded exhausted and edgy. When they hung up, she ached with the need to share his burden. She also felt that she would burst if he didn't come home soon so she could take him in her arms and tell him what their separation had taught her. In spite of the physical distance between them, she had grown even closer to him than she had when they'd spent so much time together.

She loved him. And as complicated as that might have seemed a few weeks earlier, it now seemed the simplest thing in the world.

She loved him and he loved her. And the three days she'd spent with his daughters had even convinced her that, given time, she might not be a total washout as a stepmother. Although Heather still kept a wary distance most of the time and Tammi's exuberance sometimes tried her patience, Katherine grew more confident every day that she might be able to handle the demands falling in love with Hank would inevitably put on her. Her few symptoms of anxiety were easily swept away by the challenges of looking after the girls.

Monday morning she managed to get Tammi and Heather off to school uneventfully. She worked in her darkroom all day, then picked up Tammi after school and went back to the condo with her. *Just like a real mother,* she thought as she contemplated the dinner she had planned for them to cook together. *Well, almost like a real mother.*

She was busy peeling onions and Tammi was carefully placing brown-and-serve rolls on a baking sheet when the telephone rang. It wasn't Hank, as she'd expected. It was Penny.

"Listen, is Heather around?"

Katherine tamped the feelings of alarm that had begun to rise within her. "Why, no. Isn't she at work?"

Penny's silence lasted too long. "She didn't show up today."

The next two hours were frenzied. And at the end of that time, nothing Katherine had learned offered any consolation. Heather hadn't shown up for school, either. And none of the friends Katherine had managed to track down had seen her all day.

"What am I going to do?" she asked Penny, who had come over for moral support, bringing a sack of fast-food hamburgers in place of the dinner that had been abandoned in the kitchen. "Oh, lord, I thought I was handling everything so well. And now look what I've done!"

"Hold on. How on earth can you blame yourself for this? This isn't the first time she's pulled a vanishing act, you know. Eat your cheeseburger."

Katherine toyed with the sandwich wrapper. "And I know why she ran off the other times. They were because of me, too."

"HANK WEISBECKER?" The silver-haired woman in the pale pink uniform looked expectantly around the intensive care unit waiting room. "Is Hank Weisbecker here?"

Hank shot out of his seat, certain that something had gone wrong with his dad. It had been less than an hour since he had finally convinced his mother to go home and get some rest. If something happened now, she would never forgive herself.

"What's wrong?"

The volunteer smiled sweetly. "There's a telephone call for you, Mr. Weisbecker. Can you come this way?"

He followed her to one of the telephones near the nurses' station, his stomach quaking with uncertainty. The quaver in Katherine's voice reinforced his fears.

"Hank, I don't know how to say this—I feel so responsible. I just—"

"For heaven's sake, Katherine, what is it?" He snapped the words out, apprehension making him impatient.

"It's Heather. She's gone again."

The sickness in the pit of Hank's stomach, the feeling of doom that had been with him since he'd received his mother's call Thanksgiving Day, intensified. He closed his eyes and gritted his teeth to keep from spewing out the cry of helpless frustration welling up in him.

"Have you called her friends?" He ticked off the names for her, his fear masking itself behind growing irritation each time Katherine indicated she had already checked, with no luck.

"Hank, I don't know what to say. When she left for school, everything seemed fine. She was a little distant, but—"

"Something must've happened. What set her off this time?"

Katherine was silent for a moment. When she spoke, her voice was tight with anger. "I don't know, Hank. Everything seemed fine. Truly."

"Obviously everything wasn't fine. You must've..." He stopped but realized he'd already gone too far.

"You think it's my fault, don't you?"

The hurt in her voice conjured up a picture that aggravated his guilt. He could envision the haunted, beleaguered look in her eyes, the droop at the corners of her usually smiling lips. *Why the hell am I feeling guilty?* he asked himself, clenching a fist to keep from pounding it into the wall. *I'm not the one who's screwing everything up.*

"No, Katherine, I don't think it's your fault." He knew he hadn't mustered much conviction in his voice. He didn't feel capable of it. He was losing his father, and nobody could do anything about that. But surely something could be done to keep him from losing his daughter, too.

"You do. You think I said something. Or did something. You might as well admit it, Hank. I can hear it in your voice."

"Okay. I have to admit, it does seem that I'm having trouble hanging onto my daughter whenever you come around."

"If you'll remember, I didn't ask to get saddled with your problems."

"It didn't seem to be too much to ask. I guess I was wrong about that."

"If you're looking for someone to straighten out the problems you've created with your daughter, Hank, you'll have to look for someone with much better qualifications than me."

"That's obvious."

Hank stewed at the long silence that followed. If Katherine had been taking time to get her temper under control, the sound of her voice told him she hadn't quite succeeded. "Shall I call the police?" she asked icily.

Suddenly, he didn't give a damn about her anger. He was angry, too. Plenty angry. And he felt like making somebody pay for the fear and frustration he was going through. "Do you think you can handle that?"

"Go to hell, Hank Weisbecker. I'll take care of Tammi and I'll call the police. I'll do my best to find Heather. But don't expect me to come along behind you and work some kind of miracle cure after you've botched the job."

Hank was ready to slam the telephone in her ear but she beat him to it.

HEATHER CRAWLED WEARILY out of the van, waving at the college student as he took a left onto a narrow highway heading toward Kansas. He'd been nice. She stuck her thumb out, hoping she'd find someone else who was nice.

She'd learned a lot about how to tell. Sometimes, she could just look at a car as it slowed down beside her and she'd know better than to get in. She avoided noisy, souped-up cars. Slick, fancy vehicles driven by businessmen in shiny suits sometimes gave her the creeps, too.

She hoped the next ride wouldn't be far behind. McCook was still a long way, and she had to get to her dad soon—before he found out she was gone and started to worry again. But she had to see him, be with him. If Grandpa was dying, Dad must be sad and scared. That's how she'd felt when Mom died. And Dad had been there for her, hadn't he?

She had to be there for him, too.

CHAPTER EIGHTEEN

CARL WEISBECKER regained consciousness later that night. Then, within a few hours, he showed signs of movement that gave the doctors hope for his recovery.

As some of the load eased from Hank's mind, it made more room for other worries to crowd in.

Somewhere in the night, his daughter roamed. He refused to give words to the terrors screaming in his skull. That would plunge him headlong into madness.

And somewhere in the night, the woman he loved was blaming herself for his own failures. That gnawed at him almost as insidiously as his fears for Heather.

In the early hours of the morning, when the doctors gave him the news that his father would likely be moved out of intensive care later in the day, Hank went back to his parents' home for a few hours of much-needed sleep.

When he passed the hall telephone on the way to the bedroom where he'd slept for almost twenty years, Hank knew he had one more thing to do before he could rest.

Katherine's voice was so weary and subdued, it pierced his heart. How could he have been so cruel?

"I'm sorry, Katie. All those things I said—it was just my fear. That's no excuse, I know. But . . . can you forgive me?"

"There's nothing to forgive, Hank." The dullness in her voice gave him no relief. "You said what you thought. And maybe you were right."

"I wasn't right. You were right. I've got a teenaged daughter who's out of control and I was trying to find someone else to blame. I've hardly slept since I've been here—I've been sitting up at the hospital because it was the only way to get Mom to go home for some rest. I was worn out—the last thing I needed was one more thing to worry about. And I just...blew up. Lost it. I'm sorry, Katie."

"It's okay, Hank."

He detected some softening in her voice. But not enough.

"Don't worry about me. The police are going out as soon as it's daylight, to ask around the neighborhood, see if anyone saw Heather yesterday morning. We'll let you know as soon as we hear something."

Hank sighed. She wasn't even listening to him. "She'll turn up," he said. "She always has before." He believed it because he had to.

When he hung up and went into the bedroom, throwing his clothes into a heap on the floor and falling onto the bed, he felt no less guilty about Katherine than he had before he called. Knowing her vulnerability, his accusations had been inexcusable.

Somehow, when all the other crises in his life were over, he knew he had to find a way to convince her that she had a place in his daughters' lives—and his.

KATHERINE DIDN'T SEND Tammi to school the next day. The little girl had been so distraught with her father gone and her sister once more disappearing that Katherine decided she needed the comfort of being at home and having some attention showered on her.

No doubt that was a poor decision, too, Katherine decided, castigating herself, but at least Tammi seemed less drawn and pale as she sat on the floor and played with Baxter. She was almost—not quite, but almost—her usual bubbly self. But occasionally she would stop and look up at Katherine, her bright eyes wide with concern.

"Do you think Heather runs away because she hates me?" she asked once, a question that twisted at the pieces of Katherine's already broken heart.

Relying on some instinct that still felt stiff with disuse, Katherine pulled the little girl into her arms and reassured her the best she could.

Another time, Tammi was lying on her back, staring up at the ceiling, with Baxter asleep on her tummy. "I miss Mommy. And I'll bet Daddy does, too."

"Of course he does." *Especially by comparison.*

"But you know what? Since we don't have a mommy and you don't have babies, I don't see why you don't be our mommy. Don't you think that would be way cool?"

Katherine felt her lungs empty of air. She took a few moments to compose herself, aware that her silence had drawn Tammi's solemn gaze.

"I don't know, Tammi. Maybe I just wasn't meant to be a mommy." Hank had certainly come to that conclusion, and the way things had turned out more than justified it.

Tammi shook her head. "Nope. I think you've been a great mommy the past few days. You want me to tell Daddy when he calls?"

Katherine didn't know if the sound coming from her throat was a sob or a chuckle. "No, I don't think so. I think your daddy's already made up his own mind about that.''

HANK AND HIS MOTHER were just about to leave the house to return to the hospital when an unfamiliar car pulled up out front. Hank, who had slept less than two fitful hours after his stilted conversation with Katherine, rubbed his grainy eyes and stifled a yawn.

The yawn died in his throat as Heather, looking at least as weary as he felt, got out of the passenger's side and waved goodbye to the driver.

She eyed Hank warily, no doubt expecting his anger. But when he saw her standing there, with her hair disheveled, her denim jacket crushed and backpack dragging at her heels, all he could feel was relief.

"Go ahead and yell at me," she said, looking even younger and more defenseless in her attempt at toughness. "Let's get it over with."

Hank hadn't cried for two years, but as he rushed to his daughter and swept her into his arms, he had tears in his eyes. She squirmed for a moment, then dropped her bag and returned his hug.

"I won't yell if you won't yell," he said shakily.

"You won't?"

"I promise."

She looked up at him, her stubborn blue eyes a reflection of what she was seeing in his. "What's the catch?"

"No more running away. And no more hitchhiking. Do you have any idea how dangerous that could be? Just thinking about it gives me gray hair."

"Think Katie might like you even if you get gray hair?"

Hank's heart rolled over in his chest. He didn't want the answer to the next question, but he had to ask it. "Is that why you ran away? Because of Katie?"

She shrugged. "Kind of. But not . . . not the way you think. We had a long talk. She told me about how she couldn't have kids and how that made her kind of scared of being around them. And I thought about how scared I was when mom died. I never really thought about grown-ups being scared, too."

"I was scared when your mom died, you know."

"You were?"

"Sure. I had big shoes to fill."

She looked at him thoughtfully. "Anyway, I started wondering if you were scared right now, with Grandpa being so sick. I just . . . I just thought I should be here. With you."

"You think it might have been good to talk this over with someone first? So we wouldn't be scared out of our wits?"

"Sorry. I was afraid someone would try to stop me. I just . . . after acting like such a jerk before, I just wanted to be here." Her voice trembled and her chin started to wobble. "I missed you, dad. I got home and you weren't there and I wanted to be with you."

"I missed you, too." He hugged her again. "Come on, let's go see Grandpa at the hospital. Then we can head home, I think. He's lots better today."

"Dad?" She kept her face muffled in his shirt. "I found out something else, too."

"What's that?"

"You do a pretty good job. Being a dad, I mean." She looked up at him.

TAMMI HAD TAUGHT Katherine about half the words to the new hit song by Dirty Rotten Kidz when the door opened. Pausing in the middle of their duet of the chorus, Katherine felt a sudden and overwhelming sense of loss as Hank and Heather walked into the living room.

Knowing that her short stint as a temporary mother was undoubtedly over, Katherine resisted the urge to hug Tammi close to her one last time.

"Well, this is a surprise." She smiled tightly, feeling just a moment of jealousy as Tammi dashed to her father's side. She wanted to hug them both, but they had each other. They didn't need her.

To Katherine's surprise, in the midst of all the explanations about Hank's father's condition and Heather's appearance in McCook, the teenager suddenly walked over and gave her an awkward hug.

"Thanks for everything," she whispered.

"But . . ." Katherine couldn't imagine what she was being thanked for.

"Come on, twerp," Heather said, giving Tammi's ponytail a yank. "Let's take the mutt for a walk."

As Tammi bundled up and Heather put Baxter on his leash, Katherine started backing slowly out of the room, purposely averting her eyes from Hank's. She had seen the looks he had exchanged with Heather and knew something was up. But the last thing she needed or wanted right now was a showdown with Hank. She wanted to go home. She wanted to watch the gerbil and water her plants and spend an hour doing yoga until she forgot everything around her. She didn't want to be alone with Hank. She didn't want harsh words and more bitter memories to pile onto what she already had.

But the girls were out the door and Hank was walking toward her.

She turned and headed down the hall to his bedroom, where her things were. She would throw everything into her bag and leave.

He caught up with her just inside the bedroom door, grasping a wrist and turning her to face him with one swift movement.

"I love you, Katie. And I'm sorry." He pulled her against him and looked down into her face, his forehead creased with concern. "And you're going to forgive me."

"There's nothing to forgive, Hank." She didn't want to be pressed this closely to him, because it felt too right. It felt too warm, too secure, too much like all her dreams could come true. It wasn't fair to feel that way when it would never be so. She struggled against him. "Just let me go and I'll get out of your way."

"You're going to forgive me," he said, lowering his face to hers, "if I have to kiss you senseless to convince you."

"Hank..."

And he did. He kissed her, his warm lips playing over hers, first tenderly, then teasingly, then insistently. And she had no choice but to respond. Her feelings of defeat wavered and faded from memory as the heat of his lips and the power of his body crushed to hers became the center of her world.

He lifted his lips. "Please forgive me. I was crazy with worry and I took it out on you. Please forgive me."

"Hank..." Her knees trembled. She tried to remember why she had felt so compelled to dash out of his life just moments before.

"Say you forgive me."

"I forgive you."

"And you'll marry me."

Her eyes were suddenly wide open, the quivery weakness washing through her body replaced by a charged anxiety. "Marry you?" She tried to pull away, but his arms merely tightened around her waist.

"You know. In sickness and health. Richer and poorer. All that mushy stuff."

For one crazy moment she was afraid to open her mouth. Afraid the only word she could force out would be a *yes*. "Hank, I can't marry you. That would be a disaster. I'd have a panic attack everytime somebody called me a stepmother."

"Did you have any trouble while I was gone?" His hand brushed a stray curl away from her face.

"No. But that doesn't—"

"If it comes up, we'll deal with it."

"But what about Heather? Heather would run away every other day. You'd never have a moment's peace. I'd—"

"You'd be great. You wouldn't believe what a great talk my daughter and I had on the way home. And it's all because of you."

"Me?"

"That's right." Hank lowered his lips to her face once again, this time dropping tiny, nibbling kisses along the corner of her mouth. "I'll tell you all about it—some other time."

"But Hank..." She couldn't help herself. She let herself melt into him, reveling in the strength of his shoulders under her hands and the swell of his desire against her belly.

"Say you'll marry me so we can get on with the business at hand."

"I'll be a terrible mother," she protested, even as he eased her toward the bed.

"You'll be a great mother," he whispered, slipping a hand lower on her hips to press her closer to him. "And an absolutely sensational wife."

She was breathless as he dropped her onto the bed and started tugging at the zipper on her jeans. "You can't just take a magic wand and wave it over all our problems and make them disappear," she protested weakly. But she hardly paid attention to her own words as his fingers lingered over the rounded softness of her belly.

"Wanna bet?"

As TAMMI WALKED down the aisle tossing petals from her beribboned basket, she was certain that all eyes were on her. She'd never felt as pretty as she felt right now in the yellow dress that was almost just like the one Heather wore.

She was so happy, she felt like skipping. But Grandma Weisbecker and her new grandma from Texas had both told her in no uncertain terms that she had to behave when she walked down the aisle. Then they'd looked at each other with tears in their eyes and hugged like they'd known each other forever.

That had made Tammi want to skip, too.

As she tossed out a handful of the fragrant yellow petals, she caught the eye of the little girl who had also come up from Texas two days ago. Her mother—Aunt Sita, everyone said to call her—and Katie had been crying and hugging a lot, too. Even now, Tammi noticed, Aunt Sita had tears in her eyes.

Somehow, though, all the crying just made Tammi feel more like grinning. But she tried hard to keep a grown-up expression on her face.

She only had two more rows of pews before she reached the front of the church, yet she still had a lot of petals in her basket, so she gave the last two rows a double dose.

She sneaked a quick look at her daddy and Uncle Wes as she stepped to the left, the way they'd told her to. Daddy's smile was kind of nervous, but he gave her a quick thumbs-up before he turned his eyes to the back of the church.

She took a deep, relieved breath. That must mean she'd done okay.

The change in the music electrified her as she too peered toward the back of the small church. Her feet itched to move as she watched Heather coming down the aisle in her yellow dress. Tammi almost dropped her basket, Heather looked so grown up all of a sudden. But then, Heather had been acting pretty grown up in the past few weeks, too. She still wore blue jeans with holes in them and that creepy dragon in her ear—except for today. Heather hadn't even argued when Daddy said no dragon today. She'd just laughed. So Tammi had laughed, too.

Then, just a few steps behind Heather, came Katie, floating along wearing this lacy cloud. Tammi bit her lower lip to keep from giggling right out loud. Katie looked beautiful. Like a fairy princess. Not like a stepmother at all.

But Katie was going to be the best stepmother in the whole, wide world. Tammi could tell that already. Already, everything felt different. Like a family. Like the family she had wished for and prayed for almost every night for the past two years.

And today, it was coming true.

She couldn't stop herself. Right there, in front of everybody in the whole church, she gave a little jump of excitement as Katie stepped into place beside Daddy. "Way cool!"

A wave of quiet chuckles went through the church and Tammi froze, afraid she'd ruined the whole thing. But when she looked up at Katie and her daddy, they both looked down and smiled at her like they loved her no matter what.

Then the preacher started his sermon. "Dearly beloved..."

Daddy had been right all along, Tammi thought. If you just believe hard enough, the magic will work after all.

Harlequin Superromance®

COMING NEXT MONTH

#474 ALL THE RIGHT MOVES • Brenna Todd
New principal Lesley Tyler wanted everything done by the book. Football coach Gil Fielden wanted a winning team. When Lesley enforced the no-pass, no-play rule at Warren High School in West Texas, Gil knew it could cost him the state championship. Which was more important? Winning the title or winning Lesley?

#475 NIGHTSHADES AND ORCHIDS • Kelly Walsh
If only they'd met under different circumstances, Sharon McClure knew she and Steve Nordstrom could have had a future. But Steve's brother had been murdered, and Sharon was the only suspect.

#476 MADE TO ORDER • Risa Kirk
Kay Stockwell wanted no part of Del Rafferty's plan to improve her company's image. She was an engineer who built robots and, as she was fond of saying, she dealt in substance, not style. But Del was a man with a style all his own. It was something Kay was finding hard to resist.

#477 MOON SHADOW • Dawn Stewardson
In 1887, the West was wild—and dangerous. Schoolmarm Emma McCully had to save her brother from being hanged as a horse thief in Tombstone, Arizona. Luckily, her brother's childhood friend, Will Lockhart, showed up to help her. Only one thing about Will had Emma worried. He seemed to believe he was from the future—from the twenty-first century, to be exact....

HARLEQUIN®
OFFICIAL SWEEPSTAKES RULES

NO PURCHASE NECESSARY

1. To enter, complete an Official Entry Form or 3" × 5" index card by hand-printing, in plain block letters, your complete name, address, phone number and age, and mailing it to: Harlequin Fashion A Whole New You Sweepstakes, P.O. Box 9056, Buffalo, NY 14269-9056.

   No responsibility is assumed for lost, late or misdirected mail. Entries must be sent separately with first class postage affixed, and be received no later than December 31, 1991 for eligibility.

2. Winners will be selected by D.L. Blair, Inc., an independent judging organization whose decisions are final, in random drawings to be held on January 30, 1992 in Blair, NE at 10:00 a.m. from among all eligible entries received.

3. The prizes to be awarded and their approximate retail values are as follows: Grand Prize — A brand-new Mercury Sable LS plus a trip for two (2) to Paris, including round-trip air transportation, six (6) nights hotel accommodation, a $1,400 meal/spending money stipend and $2,000 cash toward a new fashion wardrobe (approximate value: $28,000) or $15,000 cash; two (2) Second Prizes — A trip to Paris, including round-trip air transportation, six (6) nights hotel accommodation, a $1,400 meal/spending money stipend and $2,000 cash toward a new fashion wardrobe (approximate value: $11,000) or $5,000 cash; three (3) Third Prizes — $2,000 cash toward a new fashion wardrobe. All prizes are valued in U.S. currency. Travel award air transportation is from the commercial airport nearest winner's home. Travel is subject to space and accommodation availability, and must be completed by June 30, 1993. Sweepstakes offer is open to residents of the U.S. and Canada who are 21 years of age or older as of December 31, 1991, except residents of Puerto Rico, employees and immediate family members of Torstar Corp., its affiliates, subsidiaries, and all agencies, entities and persons connected with the use, marketing, or conduct of this sweepstakes. All federal, state, provincial, municipal and local laws apply. Offer void wherever prohibited by law. Taxes and/or duties, applicable registration and licensing fees, are the sole responsibility of the winners. Any litigation within the province of Quebec respecting the conduct and awarding of a prize may be submitted to the Régie des loteries et courses du Québec. All prizes will be awarded; winners will be notified by mail. No substitution of prizes is permitted.

4. Potential winners must sign and return any required Affidavit of Eligibility/Release of Liability within 30 days of notification. In the event of noncompliance within this time period, the prize may be awarded to an alternate winner. Any prize or prize notification returned as undeliverable may result in the awarding of that prize to an alternate winner. By acceptance of their prize, winners consent to use of their names, photographs or their likenesses for purposes of advertising, trade and promotion on behalf of Torstar Corp. without further compensation. Canadian winners must correctly answer a time-limited arithmetical question in order to be awarded a prize.

5. For a list of winners (available after 3/31/92), send a separate stamped, self-addressed envelope to: Harlequin Fashion A Whole New You Sweepstakes, P.O. Box 4694, Blair, NE 68009.

PREMIUM OFFER TERMS

To receive your gift, complete the Offer Certificate according to directions. Be certain to enclose the required number of "Fashion A Whole New You" proofs of product purchase (which are found on the last page of every specially marked "Fashion A Whole New You" Harlequin or Silhouette romance novel). Requests must be received no later than December 31, 1991. Limit: four (4) gifts per name, family, group, organization or address. Items depicted are for illustrative purposes only and may not be exactly as shown. Please allow 6 to 8 weeks for receipt of order. Offer good while quantities of gifts last. In the event an ordered gift is no longer available, you will receive a free, previously unpublished Harlequin or Silhouette book for every proof of purchase you have submitted with your request, plus a refund of the postage and handling charge you have included. Offer good in the U.S. and Canada only.

HQFW - SWPR

HARLEQUIN® OFFICIAL SWEEPSTAKES ENTRY FORM

4-FWHSS-3

WIN
CARS. TRIPS. CASH!

Complete and return this Entry Form immediately – the more entries you submit, the better your chances of winning!

- Entries must be received by **December 31, 1991**.
- A Random draw will take place on **January 30, 1992**.
- No purchase necessary.

Yes, I want to win a FASHION A WHOLE NEW YOU Classic and Romantic prize from Harlequin:

Name _____ Telephone _____ Age _____

Address _____

City _____ State _____ Zip _____

Return Entries to: **Harlequin FASHION A WHOLE NEW YOU**,
P.O. Box 9056, Buffalo, NY 14269-9056   © 1991 Harlequin Enterprises Limited

PREMIUM OFFER

To receive your free gift, send us the required number of proofs-of-purchase from any specially marked FASHION A WHOLE NEW YOU Harlequin or Silhouette Book with the Offer Certificate properly completed, plus a check or money order (do not send cash) to cover postage and handling payable to Harlequin FASHION A WHOLE NEW YOU Offer. We will send you the specified gift.

OFFER CERTIFICATE

Item	A. ROMANTIC COLLECTOR'S DOLL (Suggested Retail Price $60.00)	B. CLASSIC PICTURE FRAME (Suggested Retail Price $25.00)
# of proofs-of-purchase	18	12
Postage and Handling	$3.50	$2.95
Check one	☐	☐

Name _____

Address _____

City _____ State _____ Zip _____

Mail this certificate, designated number of proofs-of-purchase and check or money order for postage and handling to: **Harlequin FASHION A WHOLE NEW YOU Gift Offer**, P.O. Box 9057, Buffalo, NY 14269-9057. Requests must be received by December 31, 1991.

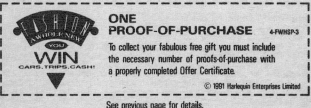

WIN
CARS. TRIPS. CASH!

ONE PROOF-OF-PURCHASE

4-FWHSP-3

To collect your fabulous free gift you must include the necessary number of proofs-of-purchase with a properly completed Offer Certificate.

© 1991 Harlequin Enterprises Limited

See previous page for details.